M000158792

THE MOTHER IN LAW

BOOKS BY KAREN KING

THE MOTHER IN LAW

KAREN KING

bookouture

Published by Bookouture in 2022

An imprint of Storyfire Ltd.
Carmelite House
50 Victoria Embankment
London EC4Y 0DZ

www.bookouture.com

Copyright © Karen King, 2022

Karen King has asserted her right to be identified as the author of this work.

All rights reserved. No part of this publication may be reproduced, stored in any retrieval system, or transmitted, in any form or by any means, electronic, mechanical, photocopying, recording or otherwise, without the prior written permission of the publishers.

ISBN: 978-1-80314-220-3
eBook ISBN: 978-1-80314-219-7

This book is a work of fiction. Names, characters, businesses, organizations, places and events other than those clearly in the public domain, are either the product of the author's imagination or are used fictitiously. Any resemblance to actual persons, living or dead, events or locales is entirely coincidental.

For Isobel, thank you for working your magic on my stories.

16 JULY

My wedding day. I can hardly believe that it's really happening; that we are finally going to be man and wife. After everything that happened, how hard *she* has tried to split us up. I close my eyes at the memory of the lengths she has gone to. Then I shake them from my mind. I'm not going to think about that now. It's over. Today is the happiest day of my life. I open my eyes and smile at my reflection in the mirror. I look so different, with the sides of my shoulder-length light brown hair pulled back off my face like this and fastened at the back with a floral hairpiece, and this gorgeous ivory floaty dress, with its nipped-in waist, plunging neckline and beaded lace bodice, makes me look like a princess. I feel different too. Strong. Loved. I haven't felt loved since my parents died when I was six years old, but I know Sam must love me very much to go ahead with the wedding despite everything *she* has done to stop it. I love him too. We've made it. My smile breaks into a big grin and then suddenly bursts out into a laugh. A joyful laugh of triumph and happiness. Soon I will be Dana Corbett, not Dana Wynters. The start of a brand new, happy life for me.

The door opens and in the mirror I see Lynne walk in

holding two glasses of champagne. 'I was going to say if you've any doubts, now's the time to speak up. Half an hour and you'll be a married woman. But judging by the way you're laughing, you're very pleased that you're marrying Sam.'

'No doubts at all. I can't wait to marry him,' I say as I turn to face my best friend. She looks so pretty in her pale lemon, Grecian-style bridesmaid's dress, but then Lynne would look amazing in a sack. She's been my cheerleader, sounding board and mischief-inspirer since primary school and I'm so pleased that she agreed to be my maid of honour. Otherwise I would have had no one to share my wedding day with. Whereas Sam has an army of people surrounding him.

She looks me up and down admiringly. 'You look stunning, Dana!' Then she holds out one of the glasses. 'Don't spill it over your dress,' she warns.

'As if I would! I'm going to make sure nothing spoils today,' I tell her, holding the stem of my glass carefully and gazing at the crystal clear, light gold liquid sparkling with the tiny bubbles fizzing in it, mirroring the bubbles of happiness sparkling inside me.

Lynne holds up her glass. 'To you and Sam. Happy Wedding Day,' she says.

'To me and Sam.' I clink my glass with hers then we both take a sip of our champagne. Lynne makes short work of hers, but I sip mine, savouring its crispness, so different from the cheap cava or prosecco I used to drink. I know without looking at the label that it's expensive champagne. Nothing less would do for the Corbett family, for Evelyn.

'I could get used to this.' Lynne puts her empty glass down on the coffee table and picks up her bouquet. A beautiful summer assortment of yellow and champagne roses that match her dress perfectly. 'Shall we go?'

I reach for my bouquet – vintage gold, lemon, and cream roses with white peonies – and nod. 'I'm ready.'

I walk slowly out of the room and along the hall, Lynne beside me. I want to savour this day, enjoy every minute of it. As we walk towards the front door to the waiting bridal car, my euphoria starts to fade and a sliver of nervousness coils around my stomach. What if something goes wrong?

I refuse to listen to my doubts. Nothing will go wrong. She has tried and lost. Sam and I are getting married today. Nothing can stop that now.

Unless Sam doesn't turn up.

The only way that would happen would be if he were prevented from turning up.

She wouldn't! Would she?

I shake at the thought that even now, at this last moment, she could spoil things.

The bridal car pulls up outside the church. I pause outside, wondering if Sam has arrived. Two ushers, friends of Sam's family, are waiting by the huge wooden doors. 'Is Sam here?' I whisper.

'He's been here ten minutes,' one of them tells me and I feel faint with relief.

The ushers turn to open the doors for us to walk through. I take a deep breath to still my nerves and hold my head high. This is my moment, and I don't want to ruin my entrance.

I walk slowly in to the sound of 'Here Comes the Bride', Lynne following me, holding her bouquet. Sam, standing at the altar beside Nathan, his best man, has his back to me. I fix my eyes on his dark hair as I make my way up the aisle between the rows of guests, my heart churning. Then my eyes rest on a familiar dark bob, a white fascinator perched jauntily on top of it, sitting next to my future in-laws, Evelyn and Harold, right at the front, as if she is family. Tamara. Her parents are on the other side of her. As I get nearer, I can see that she's wearing a white dress – typical; she always has to try and steal the lime-light. I take a deep breath. It's only a dress. I'm not going to let anything ruin today.

Sam looks over his shoulder, his eyes meet mine and he smiles. My heart melts, as it always does when he smiles at me. Tamara doesn't matter. Nothing matters. Today, I'm marrying Sam, the love of my life, and nothing is going to spoil that. When I reach him and stand by his side, Sam takes my hand in his, his eyes resting on my face. 'You look beautiful. I love you,' he whispers.

'I love you too.' And I do. So very, very much.

It's a wonderful ceremony. When the vicar asks if anyone knows of any lawful impediment why we can't marry, I hold my breath. This is her last chance to spoil things, but there is nothing she can say. I know that. Finally, the vicar says the magic words, 'I now declare you man and wife. You may kiss the bride.' Sam wraps his arms around me and kisses me, and I have to fight back the tears of happiness. We've made it. We are married. Nothing can come between us now.

Evelyn and Harold step forward and both give me a kiss on the cheek, welcoming me into the family. Followed by Tamara. And now I can see that her dress is not only white, it's long, almost reaching the ground. I know she's done it on purpose to upstage me, because I wouldn't agree to her being a bridesmaid, but I don't care. It's just a dress, I tell myself, as I return her kiss on the cheek.

'Look at her, anyone would think she was the one getting married!' Lynne hisses.

'Ignore her,' I whisper back. Tamara has made it clear that she doesn't think I'm good enough for Sam, but I'm not going to let her upset me today. Nothing is going to spoil today.

'Come on, Mrs Corbett, I want to introduce my wife to my colleagues before we have the photos taken,' Sam says, taking my hand and whisking me off.

'My wife.' I repeat his words in my mind and I smile.

After the photos outside the church, we all go back to the manor for the reception. The day goes by so quickly. The photos, wedding speeches – Nathan, the best man, gives a hilarious speech about Sam and some of the things they both got up to at university. I laugh but find it difficult to imagine Sam young and irresponsible; he is always so considerate and sensible. Evelyn purses her lips and frowns in displeasure, but everyone else chuckles. The marquee looks stunning. Lemon table runners on snow-white tablecloths, lemon bows on snow-white chair covers, lemon and white candles in silver holders. And in the middle of the top table is a divine three-tiered white wedding cake, decorated with piped lemon icing around each tier and lemon fondant roses. It's perfect.

'Let's have a photograph of you cutting the cake,' says the photographer. Sam has his arm still linked in mine and leads me over to the table and we stand in front of the cake. He picks up the knife. 'Ready?' he asks.

I nod. With one arm around my waist and the other arm holding the sharp cake knife, Sam places it on the bottom tier. I hold my hand over his as he cuts into the cake. The photographer snaps photo after photo and everyone claps as the knife slides into the icing, cutting through it. Tiny chunks of succulent, rich fruit cake fall out. Sam picks up a few crumbs and puts a bit in my mouth, then in his. The instant it touches my lips, I feel my tongue and lips start to swell and my chest tighten. I cough and my throat closes. Fear seizes me in its grip. I know instantly what has happened. I look around wildly for my bag where I keep my EpiPen, then remember that I left it on my seat. As I struggle to breathe, my hand clutching at my throat, I can hear Sam calling me, see people starting to panic around me. 'Get her some water!' someone shouts.

'Dana, where's your EpiPen?' Sam yells.

'My bag... my seat,' I gasp.

'I've got it!'

I recognise Lynne's voice, but my throat has almost closed and I can't speak, I can't breathe. A vice is tightening around my chest and I know I'm going to die. The wedding cake was supposed to be nut-free, but I now realise that it wasn't. I should have checked. I shouldn't have trusted her. She's done this on purpose. She wanted me out of the way. Dead. So she can have Sam all to herself. I look wildly across the room for her, my eyes seeking her out as my hand clutches my throat. Her eyes meet mine and although her face is a mask of concern, I can see the light of triumph in her eyes. She's won, after all. I underestimated her. My throat is closing up, my lungs are gasping for air, my heart is racing. I'm dying, I realise in horror. I'm dying on my wedding day. I close my eyes as I feel a jab in my thigh. Lynne had found my EpiPen but she's too late, I think, as darkness sweeps over me.

2

JANUARY, SIX MONTHS EARLIER

I pulled my thin jacket closer around me to ward off the biting wind and walked briskly. If I'd realised it was so cold, I'd have worn my navy duffle coat with the fur lining and attached hood rather than this short tweed jacket. I'd chosen it because I wanted to look smart for my job interview, and it looked good with my black trousers and new black ankle boots. First impressions are always important and it had seemed like the interview had gone well. Although I wasn't really looking forward to working in an office with a lot of people, I needed a job now that Premium Windows, the glazing company I'd worked at as a receptionist for the last five years, had closed down just before Christmas. It was a shock when Bill told us he was retiring and the firm wouldn't reopen in the new year. He'd been in ill health for some time but neither Mary, his secretary, nor I had expected it. I'd really enjoyed my job; there'd only been three of us in the office, so it had been a friendly, cosy atmosphere. We'd been like a family. Whereas Corbett and Son, the accounting company I'd just had an interview with, was huge. I would be swallowed up in there and I always feel nervous in crowds. When the agency I'd registered with had sent me details of the job, I'd almost turned down the interview, but I needed a job and couldn't afford to be choosy; my redundancy money wouldn't last long. Thank goodness I had an interview as an admin assistant with a signwriting company the next day as well, which I thought might have suited me better.

A gust of wind whistled around me and I pulled up the collar of my jacket, wishing again that I'd worn my duffle coat. I passed a café and paused to peer through the window. It looked cosy inside and I could see an available table by the window. Perhaps I'd stop for a coffee to warm myself up before taking the train home. As I headed for the door, I saw something out of the corner of my eye, flying through the air towards me. It looked like... it was... a hat. The wind had caught it and was hurtling it down the street, whirling it up in the air, then down again. A dark-haired man was running after it, his open coat billowing behind him, his scarf flapping around his neck. As the wind swirled the hat above my head, I instinctively jumped up and caught it, holding it out triumphantly as the man came to a stop in front of me, his face breaking into a wide smile.

'Yours, I think.' I held out the hat.

'Yes. Thank you,' he said, not showing any sign of being out of breath. Fit, then. As well as handsome, I noted as he took the hat – a brown trilby – and perched it on top of a thick mass of chestnut hair. His chocolate-coloured eyes twinkled as he jested, 'I guess it's always good to start off the day with a bit of exercise!'

He looked a bit young to be wearing a trilby, I thought, but it suited him. As did the three-quarter-length brown overcoat, opened to reveal a white shirt with a beige skinny neck tie underneath a beige waistcoat with a chain running from the middle button across to the left pocket, brown trousers and brogues. His beige and black checked scarf was draped loosely around his neck. Smart but quirky. He was going somewhere important. I was pleased that I'd managed to catch his hat for him.

'You're welcome.' I shivered again as the wind cut through me. I bet he was wondering why I hadn't had the sense to wear a warmer coat.

'You're cold. I noticed that you were about to go into the café, would you allow me to join you and buy you a coffee to thank you for saving my favourite hat? I'm Sam, by the way,' he added.

'I'm Dana,' I told him while my mind raced, wondering whether to accept his offer.

'They do a great line of cakes, too.' He was looking at me, waiting for my answer.

Oh, why not, I thought. I was going to have a coffee anyway and he looked nice. My best friend Lynne was always telling me that I was too trusting, that's why I kept being walked over. 'You always take people at face value, Dana,' she said. 'You need to toughen up a bit, be more selective.' Well, maybe she was right, but something about this man drew me to him. Besides, it was only a coffee in a public café, what harm could it do?

'Really? Well, that's swung it then. Thank you,' I said.

'Great!' His face broke into a huge grin, as if having a coffee with me was the best thing in the world. He pushed open the door and stepped aside for me to go in first.

He was right; there was a delicious selection of cakes. 'Do you have any that are nut-free?' I asked the assistant.

'Yes, we have a wide range here.' She pointed to a selection, and I chose a chocolate fudge cake, with a cappuccino. Sam chose a slice of caramel cheesecake from the same collection, and a white coffee.

'Do you have a nut allergy too?' I asked as Sam picked up the tray containing our cake and coffees and carried it over to a quiet table in the corner.

'No, but I take it you do?' he asked, putting the tray down on the table and pulling out a chair for me.

A gentleman as well as good-looking, I thought as I thanked him and sat down, waiting for him to take the seat opposite me before replying. 'Yes. I had a bad reaction to nuts when I was in my teens. Ended up in hospital. Crazy, as I'd always been okay with them up until then. I've carried an EpiPen with me ever since.' I watched him dig his fork into the cheesecake. 'I'm fine with other people eating nuts around me, I just can't eat them myself.' I shuddered as I remembered that fateful day. I was with Lynne and we'd bought a slice of walnut cake from the bakery, eating it as we walked along the street. I'll never forget the sheer terror of my throat swelling up and not being able to breathe, I really thought I was dying. So did Lynne. She was shouting for help and luckily a doctor was passing by and had an EpiPen on him. His actions saved my life and he stayed with us until the ambulance came. The doctors had no idea why I'd suddenly developed an allergy to nuts but apparently it happens sometimes. I'd avoided them ever since. 'It was very thoughtful of you to choose a nut-free cake too, just in case it triggered me. Most people wouldn't think of that.'

'A woman in our office is allergic to peanuts, and even the smell of them can cause an allergic reaction. I wouldn't want to put you through that,' he told me. 'Not least because you've saved the day for me. It was so lucky for me that you were walking along the street, otherwise I might have lost my hat for good. Do you live around here?'

'No, I've been to a job interview at an accountancy firm near here; that's why I'm dressed in this smart-but-thin jacket instead of something actually suitable for January,' I confessed.

'At Corbett and Son?'

'That's the one.'

Sam stirred sugar into his coffee as I told him how I was a

secretary, but that my current company had recently closed down, so I needed to get another job fast.

'I'm sorry. I hope you get the job,' he said sympathetically.

I wrapped my hands around my cappuccino to warm them. I hadn't thought to bring gloves with me either. 'Thanks, but to be honest I'm not sure it's right for me. It's such a big company! I've got another interview tomorrow at Ace Signage, a small signwriting company, which I actually prefer.'

'Then I hope you get that one instead,' he replied. 'It's important to be happy at work.'

Sam was so easy to talk to and we ended up having two cups of coffee and chatting for ages. So when he asked me to go to the theatre with him on Saturday to see *Les Misérables*, I readily agreed. Sam was good-looking, kind, interesting, perfect. I couldn't wait to see him again. *Don't get too carried away*, I told myself as I sat on the train home, my mind going over the things he'd said and how he'd looked at me, *he might not want to see you again after Saturday*.

Sam had suggested we swap phone numbers so we could let each other know if something came up, so when a text pinged in from him on Saturday morning, I was expecting it to say he couldn't make it. I opened it, disappointment heavy in my stomach then smiled when I read it. *Looking forward to tonight. I'll wait for you in the foyer.*

I shot a message back. *Me too. See you later.*

I wore my favourite outfit – a red and black maxi dress I'd bought from ASOS – for our theatre visit, hoping it would be dressy enough. Sam's eyes widened when he saw me, 'You look stunning,' he said.

'You look pretty good yourself,' I told him. And he did in his blue three-piece suit, this time teamed with a vintage navy bowler, which he took off as soon as we were inside. I loved his quirky dress sense.

I'd been to a couple of plays at the local theatre before, but nothing on this scale. Sam had booked us premium seats in the stalls, which gave us an excellent view of the stage. 'Thank you for a wonderful evening,' I told Sam as we shared a bottle of wine in an intimate bar after the show.

'Thank you for your company. I've really enjoyed this evening, Dana. I'd love to see you again, if you would like that too?' he asked softly.

'I'd love to,' I said eagerly. *Play it cool*, Lynne would tell me, but I didn't want to play games. I liked Sam, he liked me, why not meet again?

His eyes met mine over the rim of his glass. 'Is there any news from either of your job interviews?'

I shook my head. It was thoughtful of him to remember that. 'I'm still waiting to hear from both, but I've got a good feeling about the interview at Ace Signage yesterday, so fingers crossed.' I'd felt at home as soon as I walked in. It was a much smaller office, and the staff had all looked very friendly. Tasha, the boss, said she had a couple of other candidates to see but promised to give me her decision by Tuesday and I was really hoping it would be a positive one. Especially as I had the option to work from home two days a week, with a laptop provided by the company – which would be great as my old laptop took forever to load.

'That's good.' He paused. 'I'm afraid I have a confession to make,' he said slowly, looking a little awkward. A feeling of dread settled at the bottom of my stomach as I waited for him to continue, the spiel going around in my head. He was going to tell me that he was already married or had a girlfriend but he couldn't dump them because he had kids, or some other stupid reason. I should have known that it was too good to be true that a man like Sam was single. Well, there was no way I was going to be the other woman, so he could save his excuses. But what he said next took me by surprise.

'My surname is actually Corbett, and I'm the "Son" in

Corbett and Son, the company you had an interview with on Thursday,' he explained. 'I'm afraid that there's a very strict rule about staff dating, and I feel that as a partner in the firm it wouldn't be professional for me to break that rule.' His big brown eyes met mine. 'So I feel that I must mention it before things go any further. Because I'd very much like to see a lot more of you, Dana, but I know that getting a job is important to you and I wouldn't want you to lose it because of me.'

I was too stunned to reply. Sam was a partner in the firm I went to for a job interview! And he wanted to date me?

'Dana?' He was looking at me, concerned, and I realised that I was staring at him like an idiot.

I swallowed and pulled myself together. I liked Sam. Really liked him. We might have only just met but I had felt an instant connection with him and I definitely wanted to see him again. Not only was he gorgeous and financially comfortable – which made a change from my last couple of boyfriends who were always leeching off me – but he was honest too. All my dreams come true! I nodded eagerly. 'I'd love to see more of you, and don't worry, I doubt if I've got the job at your company anyway, but if they offer it to me, I'll turn it down. It's not really the right job for me.'

'Are you sure?' His hand rested on top of mine, his voice soft, caring.

How could he even think that I would choose a job over going out with him?

'I'm sure. And thank you for telling me.'

'I wanted to be honest from the beginning. I think a woman should always be treated with integrity and consideration,' he told me earnestly.

Wow! I felt like pinching myself. This gorgeous, caring man was really interested in me. I couldn't wait to tell Lynne.

As I was about to go to bed that night, I received a text from him. *Thank you for a wonderful evening. Looking forward to our next date. Sam x*

A kiss! He'd signed with a kiss. I was almost exploding with happiness as I messaged back. *Me too. See you soon x*

I was careful to keep to one kiss, as Sam had done. We hadn't actually made arrangements for our next date; Sam said he had a busy week but promised to meet me as soon as he had a free evening. I was happy with that – I had every evening free.

As it turned out, I didn't get the job at Corbett and Son, but I was offered a position at Ace Signage, so I was delighted. Sam was delighted too when I texted to let him know on Tuesday afternoon. It was the first time I'd sent him a message first, as I usually waited for him to contact me. He'd texted me every day since Saturday, just a quick 'Good morning' and a 'How's your day been?' in the evening. I looked forward to his texts; they made me feel connected to him and reassured me that he was thinking of me even if he was busy.

Congratulations! Let's go out for a meal tomorrow night to celebrate, he messaged.

That would be lovely! was my quick reply. There was nothing I'd have liked better.

I was floating on air all Wednesday evening. Sam was marvellous company. He made me feel so special.

'Here's to a belated but very happy new year to us both,' he said, as we chinked our glasses of champagne. 'One which I hope we spend together.'

'So do I,' I said, warmth flooding through my body as his eyes met mine and held them. It was amazing how well we got on. I adored Sam's easy-going nature. He always had a smile on his face, and when he hugged me, I felt the warmth of his love flow through me. I was falling for him and hoped he felt the same way.

New year, new job, new man, I thought happily. Life was looking good.

3

We'd arranged to meet again on Friday evening, and this time, Sam insisted on picking me up. I tried to be ready for when he arrived so I wouldn't have to invite him in, feeling a little self-conscious about how tiny and cheaply furnished my one-bed flat was, but a button fell off my dress, so I had to change, and Sam was knocking on the door before I even had chance to slip my shoes on. He greeted me with his usual big grin and hug, and stepped in, telling me what a charming flat I had, as if he really meant it. We had a delicious meal at a romantic riverside restaurant, and when he dropped me back, I asked him in for a coffee. He looked so at ease sitting on the patchwork sofa I'd covered myself, drinking his coffee out of one of my sunflower mugs, that my heart melted even further, and I knew in that instant that I wanted to spend the rest of my life with this man. We sat talking for hours, sharing memories, experiences, hopes and dreams. I told Sam about my childhood and he'd looked so sad for me, holding my hand and promising me that from now on, life would be better. I told him not to worry; I'd been fed and clothed and at least I was resilient. 'I'm tougher than I look,'

I assured him. 'And it's made me appreciate the little things in life.'

'That's one of the things I love about you, the way you enjoy everything. It's like you make me see life through fresh eyes.'

My heart stilled at his use of the word 'love'. Don't read too much into it, it's just an expression, I told myself.

Sam's gaze swept around my tiny lounge-kitchen. 'I admire you so much, Dana, how strong you are despite everything, and how you've made yourself such a charming home.'

I knew he was only being kind. I mean, I loved my little, flat but to Sam it must have seemed so small and shabby. I imagined him living in an exclusive apartment in one of those modern city complexes that had gyms and other facilities.

'I bet it's very small compared to your place,' I told him.

He looked at me thoughtfully. 'Okay, please don't let this put you off me but I don't have a place of my own, currently. I have my own rooms in my parents' house,' he told me.

He must have seen how much that surprised me because he quickly explained that his parents had encouraged him to invest in property – student accommodation – as soon as he was eighteen and loaned him the money to buy the first couple of properties, suggesting that he continue to live at home so he could pay the loan quicker and increase his portfolio. 'It made sense. My folks have got a big house with plenty of space, so we're not under each other's feet,' he explained. 'I have several rooms on the second floor.'

'You mean you've never had a place of your own?' I asked. 'What about when you went to university?'

'I commuted and my folks put the money they'd have spent on student accommodation into my property company. I now own five student accommodation lets, have almost paid off the loan my parents gave me and saved enough money for the deposit for a house of my own,' he said.

Wow! That sounded like he was seriously rich to me. My

dream was to buy myself a little house someday and here was Sam owing five houses already. 'Impressive,' I said, suddenly feeling awkward as I realised the difference in our lives, our social status.

He took my hand. 'Not at all. I've had financial help and the backing of loving parents; you've got where you are all by yourself. I'm the one who's impressed.'

His eyes met mine and I could see that he meant it. He could have made me feel so small with the difference in our financial status, but instead he'd made me feel ten feet tall. I loved him even more for that.

We made love that night, and it really felt like making love, not having sex. Later, as we lay in each other's arms in my double bed, Sam told me that he had fallen in love with me the moment he met me.

He loves me, my heart sang.

'I love you too,' I replied. We'd only been on a few dates but I knew that Sam was the one for me.

'Can I see you again tonight?' Sam asked as he sat on the edge of my bed the next morning, drying his hair with a towel.

'Please,' I said, looking over. I leant forward as I noticed a red blemish underneath his hairline at the back of his neck and reached out to touch it. 'Is that a birthmark?' I asked.

He turned to me, his eyes twinkling. 'Yep. Mum says it's a stork bite, from where the stork carried me in its beak.'

I smiled. 'That's cute.'

He raised his hand to caress my cheek. 'Not as cute as your birthmark,' he teased, referring to the port-wine stain under my right breast. I hated it when I was a child but got used to it as I grew older, telling myself that I was lucky it wasn't on my face as these birthmarks so often were.

I felt my cheeks flush as his eyes met mine, recalling just how passionate our love-making had been last night. 'I hope you didn't mind me coming over here, it's so much cosier and more private...'

'I don't mind at all,' I assured him. I would feel awkward staying over at his parents' house, especially so soon after we'd met. Then a thought occurred to me. 'So if you've always lived with your parents, does that mean you've never lived with a girlfriend?'

It was hard to believe. Sam was thirty-five – ten years older than me – good-looking, successful and kind. I would have thought he'd have a queue of women wanting to live with him.

He looked a bit sheepish. 'Obviously I've had girlfriends and they've stopped over a few times, but I've never met anyone I was serious about enough to share my life and home with – until I met you.' He looked at me so adoringly that my heart melted. 'I really can't believe that I've met someone like you, Dana. You're perfect.'

'I can't believe that I've met someone like you either,' I told him. I loved Sam so much and didn't want to spoil things between us, but he was being honest with me and now it was my turn. 'Actually, I have lived with—'

Sam shook his head and put a finger on my lips to shush me. 'The past doesn't matter. Our life starts from now.'

Then he wrapped his arms around me and I snuggled in to him, resting my head on his shoulder. Sam was right; the past didn't matter. All that stuff I'd gone through... I pushed the distressing thoughts away. It was over. I had someone who loved me. Life was good at last.

4

MARCH

I cupped my hands over my mouth, hardly daring to breathe. I couldn't believe this was happening. My eyes brimmed with tears as I gazed at Sam, down on one knee in front of me, holding out the open ring box from which a heart-shaped sapphire surrounded by tiny diamonds was sparkling. An engagement ring. He was actually going to propose.

'I love you, Dana. Will you marry me? Please?' he asked, his eyes resting anxiously on my face, waiting for my answer.

I didn't need to even consider it. This was totally unexpected, but I had no doubt of my answer; this was definitely the thing I wanted most in the world. Sam was perfect. I idolised him, and in the two months that we had been going out, he had often told me that he loved me. But never in my wildest dreams had I thought he would ask me to marry him. Especially so soon. 'Yes! Yes! Please!' I said, clasping my hands together in delight.

I was dimly aware of clapping from the other customers in the restaurant as Sam scooped me up in his arms and kissed me. 'I've been looking all my life for a woman like you, sweetheart,' he whispered tenderly in my ear. 'I can't believe I've found you. You've made me the happiest man alive.'

I am the lucky one, I thought. Sam was fun, caring, sexy, hard-working. He could have any woman he wanted, and yet he had chosen me. And he truly loved me. I could see it in his eyes, feel it in his touch. And I loved him too. So much I thought my heart would burst.

Sam called for champagne, and we toasted our engagement. I was floating in a huge bubble of happiness all evening. After the meal, we went back to my flat and made love. Sam had taken me to lots of wonderful places since we'd met – we'd spent virtually every evening and weekend together – but my favourite times were these, when we were snuggled up in bed.

'When I tell my parents we're engaged, you know they're going to want to meet you at last. I've been talking about you constantly. How do you feel about us all going out for a meal together this weekend?' Sam asked.

It was the first time he'd ever mentioned me meeting his parents, and the thought bothered me. Sam had talked about them a little, and I knew that both his parents were retired now, although his father still kept an eye on the business and was a magistrate, whilst his mother, a former headteacher, now volunteered for the National Trust. They sounded like affluent, middle-class people and I was a little nervous that they might think I wasn't good enough for Sam; that they would want him to marry someone with a much better career – another accountant, or a solicitor, perhaps, with a well-connected family. I could tell by Sam's clothes, the gifts he bought me and the places he took me that he had plenty of money at his disposal. What if his parents thought I was after him for his wealth?

'Relax, they don't bite. And they will love you, just like I do.' Sam squeezed my shoulder reassuringly.

What could I do but agree? 'I hope so. I'd love to meet them.' Actually, I was terrified of meeting them. I'd have preferred to stay in our cosy little bubble, just me and Sam. But I knew I'd have to.

'Good, I'll talk to them about it tomorrow. They will be so happy for me. I can't believe I've met someone as amazing as you and that you've agreed to spend the rest of our lives together,' Sam told me tenderly. 'I love you so much.'

'I love you too,' I told him dreamily. *This is the happiest night of my life*, I thought, as I fell asleep in Sam's arms.

I was plagued by doubts for the rest of the week though, and was dreading meeting Sam's parents. 'What if his parents think I'm a gold digger?' I asked Lynne the next day. I'd messaged her to tell her I was engaged, and she'd immediately replied, begging to meet me for lunch so she could see my new engagement ring, which, of course, I was dying to show off. Lynne had been stunned when she saw it, telling me she thought it must be worth a small fortune.

'Of course they won't. Why should they? Sam's the one who's chased you.' Lynne rested her chin on her palms, elbows on the table, her gaze meeting mine. 'Look, I'm sure that Sam is wonderful, but don't you think it's a bit strange that he still lives with his parents? I mean he's, what, thirty-five, did you say? And he's never had his own place?'

I stirred my coffee thoughtfully. I knew what she was getting at. Lynne, like me, had had her own flat for years, but then she hadn't got on with her parents and I didn't have any. Perhaps it was different if you had a loving home? Plus, it had meant Sam could pay off his business loan quicker. I explained about that to Lynne.

She frowned. 'Well, I still think it's strange. And surely he must have had at least one long-term relationship before? Did they live together at his parents' house?'

'We haven't really talked much about past relationships,' I told her. 'Sam says the past doesn't matter. It's the future that's important.' Not that I'd had many relationships to talk about, apart from a couple of disastrous love affairs, including the six months I lived with two-timing Nick.

'That sounds like he's hiding something to me,' Lynne said suspiciously.

'Of course not. He's had relationships but never been serious enough with anyone to want to live together. Not until he met me.' I was sure that my eyes were sparkling as much as my ring. I was bursting with happiness.

'That's really romantic, Dana. And I can see that you adore him but... well, it's all bit quick, isn't it? You only met each other a couple of months ago. You don't actually know that much about each other, do you?' Lynne pointed out. 'And it seems like he wants to keep you all to himself. I can't believe I haven't even met him yet! I'd have thought you'd be dying to show him off.'

I knew that she was a bit piqued that she'd never met Sam. She'd suggested a double date with her and Spencer a few times, but I'd put her off. My time with Sam was too precious to share with anyone else. Besides, we went to upmarket cocktail bars, restaurants and the theatre, not the local pub and the Chinese restaurant that Lynne and Spencer frequented. As I used to. And I'd never told Lynne this, but I also didn't like Spencer much. He was a bit of a know-it-all and could be quite argumentative. I found him rather overbearing and felt certain that he and Sam wouldn't get on.

'"No point waiting when you know you've found the right one," Sam said to me when he'd proposed, and, anyway, what matters is how we feel about each other, not how long we've known each other,' I told her. 'And, I think it's nice that Sam's so close to his parents. What's wrong with being a loving family?' I had always wanted a close family and really hoped that Sam's parents would like me and welcome me into the fold. It would be so good to feel that I belonged. To have someone who loved and cared for me. 'Besides, his parents live in a big manor in Malvern. Sam's shown me photos of it. There're loads of rooms.

It's not as if they're all squashed up together in a three-bed semi, so why would he be in a rush to move out?'

Lynne narrowed her eyes as she digested this. 'So is he expecting you to live there with him when you get married?'

I wasn't sure I liked the tone of Lynne's voice. She sounded suspicious. As if Sam was tricking me and I should be wary of him, when he was the kindest, most generous person I had ever met.

'Of course not. Sam's saved enough for a deposit on a house now, and we can pay the mortgage between us.' We hadn't actually discussed this yet, but I was more than happy to pay my way.

'That's good. Living with the in-laws never works, no matter how friendly they are,' Lynne warned me as she picked up her barbecue-chicken wrap and took a bite out of it.

'We won't be getting married for ages yet; we've got plenty of time to find a house,' I reassured her.

Lynne was a good friend, and was obviously worried that I'd been swept off my feet by Sam. Well, I had been, but the feeling was mutual. It was marvellous to feel so loved. So wanted. I'd lived on my own ever since moving out of my aunt and uncle's house after leaving college, apart from when Nick had moved in – and that had been a total disaster. None of my past relationships had ever worked out; I seemed to attract the no-hopers, serial cheaters, men who were looking for someone to take care of them. Well, that had all changed. Now I had someone who loved me and was going to take care of me. And hopefully his parents would love me too. I would be wrapped in the warmth of a caring family at last. How perfect was that?

Too perfect to be true, a little voice whispered in my head. I ignored it.

That was my first mistake.

5

'Mum, Dad, this is Dana,' Sam said as we joined his parents at the table on Friday evening. Then he turned and smiled lovingly at me. 'Dana, meet my parents.'

'Pleased to meet you both,' I said, my gaze flitting from the impeccably dressed woman in front of me – not a hair of her short silver coiffure out of place – to the mild-looking, bald, bespectacled man beside her. They were older than I'd expected – in their seventies, I guessed – and looked sophisticated, confident, well-heeled. I had to fight down the urge to curtsy and licked my lips nervously, clutching Sam's hand even tighter.

'How delightful to meet you at last, my dear,' Sam's mother beamed. 'We were beginning to wonder if you were both coming, weren't we, Harold?'

'They're only a little late, dear,' Harold mumbled.

'Sorry, Mrs Corbett, it's my fault...' I stuttered, feeling my cheeks burn. Damn, I was blushing now. Trust me to have made a bad impression already. We were almost ten minutes late, and Sam had said his mother was a stickler for punctuality. And yes, it was my fault because I was so nervous I'd spilt coffee on my dress and had to change at the last minute into a smart top and trousers, and then I'd smudged my make-up and almost burst into tears when I had to redo it. Sam had hugged me. 'Relax, darling. My parents don't bite. I'll message them and let them know we're running a little late,' he'd reassured me, a chuckle lacing his voice. But being late only added to my already almost-out-of-control anxiety. What if they didn't like me and tried to persuade Sam not to marry me? I couldn't bear to lose him, to return to my dull, loveless pre-Sam life.

'Never mind, you're here now. And no formalities, please. We're Evelyn and Harold.' Her smile was friendly, but her eyes were sharp as they fixed on me and I was sure she was taking in my cheap high-street-store outfit. Evelyn was a picture of elegance in a smart navy skirt suit that was most definitely not off-the-peg, whilst Harold wore a brown tweedy sort of jacket over beige trousers and a white shirt with a brown patterned tie. Sam wore his usual style of a slim-legged three-piece suit with a hat – the same trilby I'd caught the day we met, in fact – which he had now taken off.

'Sam has told us so much about you, we feel we know you already,' she continued.

I smiled again as Sam helped me with my coat and handed it, and his hat, to the waiter hovering politely behind us, then I sat down in the seat opposite Harold and tried to relax. Sam's parents seemed to be nice, as, of course, they would be. Horrible people couldn't have raised someone as lovely as Sam. I had to stop thinking that they were going to disapprove of me just because I didn't have much money, when they – judging by the string of pearls around Evelyn's neck and the rings glistening on her fingers – were clearly very well off. I wondered what Sam had told them about me. His mother seemed the sort who would want all the details, which I guess was only natural, as he was their only child. I wished that I had a more impressive life story to tell them.

'Now, is everyone having wine?' Harold asked. 'Or are you driving, Sam?'

'We came in a taxi, so yes, I'd love some wine. How about you, Dana?' Sam asked.

I nodded. 'Please.'

'Excellent. Shall we have a bottle of Merlot?' Harold suggested.

I wasn't a red wine lover, I usually had white, but I didn't want it to look like I was being awkward, so I nodded my agreement. Sam squeezed my hand and gave me a big smile, as if silently thanking me for going along with his dad's choice of wine. I didn't mind; it wouldn't hurt me to drink red for once. I could sip it slowly.

The waiter handed Harold the wine menu and he took his time considering it before ordering. The waiter returned a few minutes later with the wine, four glasses and the food menu.

I watched as the waiter opened the bottle and poured a little in a glass then waited while Harold tasted it. I'd always thought that was so pretentious but Harold obviously took it seriously. He nodded his approval and the waiter half-filled all our glasses with wine then left us with the menus to look at. I nearly fainted when I opened mine and saw the prices. I usually paid less for a three-course meal than they were charging for starters!

'What shall we have to begin?' Harold asked.

'I fancy the butternut squash velouté with toasted almonds,' Evelyn said. Then she looked horrified. 'Goodness, I'm so sorry, I forgot that Sam had warned us you were allergic to nuts, Dana,' she exclaimed.

'It's okay, I'm only allergic if I eat them; it doesn't affect me if anyone else does. Please order what you wish,' I said hastily, grateful to Sam for warning his parents in advance.

'I don't think we'll take the risk, dear – I'm quite happy to have a different starter. And we must make the waiter aware of your allergy when he returns.'

Sam always discreetly warned the waiter about my allergy when we ate out, but Evelyn made it sound as if I would go into severe shock if anyone as much as ate a nut near me and spoke so loudly I was sure the entire restaurant heard her. I felt really awkward, although I knew she was only being considerate. Harold and Evelyn finally choose mussels for a starter, followed by steak, whilst Sam and I both decided on halloumi, carrot and orange salads, but also chose steak for the main course.

'How would you like your steak cooked?' the waiter asked.

'Rare, please,' Harold said. He looked around the table. 'Rare for everyone?'

'Of course,' Evelyn said.

Sam looked at me. 'I think Dana would like it well-done, wouldn't you, darling?'

I nodded, grateful that he'd spoken up because I hadn't wanted to. He knew that I struggled to eat meat if there was any sign of pink in it.

'Three rare and one well-done then,' the waiter said, writing it down on his pad before discreetly moving away.

Harold picked up his glass of wine and held it up. 'To family,' he said.

I'd expected him to toast our engagement but perhaps that would be later. Sam and Evelyn held up their glasses, and I immediately did the same. 'To family,' we all said in unison, and my heart lifted. They had included me in their toast.

I took a sip of the red wine, and as the fruity liquid slipped down my throat, I felt myself relax. It was tasty with a sort of smoky sweetness, not as sharp as I remembered red wine to be. But this was far more expensive than the cheap wine I usually bought from the supermarket.

Then Harold raised his glass for another toast. 'And to Sam and Dana's engagement. Welcome to the family, Dana.'

Evelyn raised her glass. 'To our precious son and his intended bride.'

Sam squeezed my hand, turning to smile at me. I smiled happily back at him. I had wondered if Sam's parents might protest that our engagement was too soon, but they had both accepted it, and me.

It was a delicious meal except that I would have preferred my steak cooked a little more but didn't like to send it back. Sam shot me a look of sympathy when he saw how pink it was inside, then returned to eating his own. I chewed away, fighting down the feeling of nausea that undercooked meat always gives me, and focussed on listening to Sam and his parents chatting. I felt a little out of my depth, so didn't really mind that Evelyn was dominating the conversation and hardly giving me a chance to get a word in.

'How's the fundraising going, Mum?' Sam asked. He turned his head to speak to me. 'Mum and Dad support the National Trust and are both raising funds to renovate a stately home that the Trust has just acquired.'

'Very well, dear. We're having a garden party at Easter and hoping to get a good turn-out. We'll be doing an Easter egg hunt, stalls and a barbecue, and are hoping to persuade a celebrity to come along and open it for us. You'll come along, won't you, Sam? Bring Dana too – she would enjoy it.' Her sharp eyes rested on me. 'Perhaps you could help with one of the stalls, Dana? We're always looking for volunteers.'

The thought of spending an afternoon with Evelyn, Harold and their posh friends made my anxiety go through the roof but how could I refuse? 'Of course, that is, if...' I looked questioningly at Sam, wondering if he wanted to attend the event.

He gave me a loving look. 'We'd be delighted to be there, Mum. I suppose Dad and I will be in charge of the barbecue again.'

Evelyn's face lit up. 'I knew I could rely on you, darling.'

My heart melted when I saw the affectionate look pass between Sam and his mother. It was wonderful that they were so close. Anyone could see that both Evelyn and Harold adored Sam, and that Sam adored them too as I watched the easy way they all chatted. There seemed to be no tension between them, even though they all shared the same house, but I felt a little excluded. It was as if the three of them were their own tight little unit and even though Sam made an effort to draw me into the conversation, I felt self-conscious about every word I said, and how I said it. *It's your paranoia*, I told myself. I was always too self-conscious – a result of living with Aunt Maud, who stamped down hard on everything I said or did wrong. In the end, I'd decided that it was best if I kept as quiet as possible, and was still reluctant to speak much until I got to know people.

It turned out to be a very pleasant meal though, and I liked Sam's parents. I was taken back when Evelyn invited me to join them for Sunday lunch at the manor that weekend and shot a panicky look at Sam, wondering what to do.

'I'm sure you'd be delighted to, wouldn't you, Dana?' he said, smiling at me.

So I nodded and said I was looking forward to it, even though I knew I'd be anxious about it all day tomorrow.

'Mum and Dad really like you,' Sam said as we walked hand in hand to the taxi he'd ordered to take us home. 'I knew they would.'

I glowed at his praise. 'I like them too. You're lucky to have such kind and supportive parents,' I told him.

He squeezed my shoulders. 'They'll be your parents too, soon.'

He had no idea how much it meant to me to be part of a caring family. How I'd envied my friends at school in my teenage years when their parents had turned up to watch the school plays, or they'd gone on shopping trips with their mums at the weekend. Aunt Maud and Uncle Brian had kept me warm and clothed. I'd wanted for nothing but affection. Not that they were unkind, but they weren't the sort of people who kissed and cuddled, and I was always aware that I had messed up their lives. I was pleased when Sam's parents hugged me goodbye, especially when his mother said that she looked forward to seeing me on Sunday. She sounded like she really meant it. I was going to be part of a family at last.

Later, when we were back at my flat, lying in each other's arms, Sam suggested that we get married that summer. He must have seen my surprise – I'd expected a much longer engagement – because he hugged me closer. 'We love each other, we're meant to be together,' he murmured, cuddling me even tighter. 'I can't wait for you to be my wife, to come home to you every night. And you'd make a beautiful summer bride.'

'It's only a few months, though. Will that give us time to arrange everything?' I said.

'I'm sure it will. We only want a small, intimate wedding, don't we?' he asked softly.

'Definitely,' I agreed, relieved. I'd been dreading that Sam might want a big society do, which I'd find completely over-whelming.

'Then what do you say? Shall we get married this summer?'

'Yes, please,' I agreed, nuzzling into him. Summer was a wonderful time to get married, and I didn't want to wait more than a year to be Sam's wife. We were perfect together.

Sam's smile lit up his face. 'Let's start looking for a house of our own, right away,' he said. 'We might even find one we like that we can buy in time to start our married life in it.'

I was so happy, my heart felt fit to burst. A whole new life lay ahead of me. It was all so exciting.

6

Sam picked me up on Sunday and drove me over to his parents' house for lunch. The photos he had shown me didn't do the manor justice. It was seriously impressive– like something out of a *Homes & Gardens* magazine. I gasped in awe when Sam stopped his silver Audi outside a pair of majestic black and gold gates, which opened as soon as he pressed his remote to reveal a long driveway, winding around an immaculate circular lawn. The gates closed behind us as we drove towards a sprawling white detached house, with so many windows I was sure it must have at least twenty rooms, nestled against the backdrop of the Malvern Hills. A sparkling white BMW was parked outside, which Sam told me was Evelyn's car. 'Dad's got a Bentley. It's probably in the garage at the back of the house,' he said casually.

I was overwhelmed by the splendour of it all, glad that Sam had insisted on picking me up this morning rather than arranging for me to drive over myself and meet him there. He was so thoughtful and considerate that he must have guessed that I would feel awkward arriving here by myself, especially in my tatty Ford Fiesta.

'Want a quick look around the back and see where the Easter garden party is being held?' he asked, when we'd both got out of the car and were standing on the drive.

'I'd love to,' I told him.

He reached for my hand and held it as we walked together around the side of the house to the huge gardens at the back. Immaculate lawns, an impressive fountain and colourful flowerbeds greeted me. It was beautiful; the perfect setting for a garden party. There would be plenty of room for stalls, games and anything else Evelyn had planned.

'Look, there's the tree house Dad built me. I used to spend hours up there,' Sam told me. 'And most weekends in the summer I had friends round to play a game of cricket on the lawn.' I imagined Sam playing out here as a little boy and it hit me again how different our childhoods had been. Sam had obviously had everything he wanted and had been very loved. It wasn't my aunt and uncle's fault; they did their best, I reminded myself. It was kind of them to take me in, otherwise I'd have been brought up in care.

'Shall we go in the back way?' I asked, looking over at a large conservatory and what was more than likely the kitchen window. It made sense now we were at the back of the house, but Sam shook his head.

'Mum keeps it locked unless she and my dad are out in the garden.'

So we walked back around to the front of the house again, where Sam took out his keys and opened the polished oak door. I glanced at the gleaming brass letterbox and knocker and thought that Sam's parents must have a cleaner and a gardener; this was too much work for a couple their age. He really did live in a different world to me.

We stepped into a huge mosaic-tiled entrance hall with a stunning chandelier dangling from the ceiling, an antique-looking Chinese vase standing on a small mahogany coffee table, several oil paintings lining the walls and a spectacular tiled staircase with a polished mahogany banister that shouted out to be slid down. Sam must have guessed my thoughts as he grinned and said, 'I used to slide down that when I was a kid. Mum used to go nuts!' Numerous dark wooden doors led off from the hallway and the hall itself was bigger than my entire flat. I was lost for words.

'Mum and Dad will be in the drawing room,' Sam said, taking my hand again and leading me down the hall. I'd worn heels to impress and they tap-tapped along the tiles as we walked, heralding our arrival and making me feel self-conscious. Sam didn't seem to notice, though. He opened the second door on the left to reveal a large room with a fire burning invitingly in the open fireplace and a dark green Chesterfield sofa in the centre, scattered with gold velvet cushions that matched the curtains draped from a pelmet over the large bay window. Evelyn and Harold were sitting in matching chairs either side of the fire, nursing a glass of what looked like sherry each. They both turned to face us as we walked in.

'Ah, here you both are. And perfect timing, as lunch will be served in fifteen minutes,' Evelyn said, taking a sip of her drink. I marvelled that she was sitting down, so relaxed; I would have been in the kitchen, sweating and flustered, if dinner was going to be ready in fifteen minutes. The woman was so composed and efficient she made me feel a little inadequate. 'Do sit down, Dana. Would you both like a glass of sherry – or wine?'

'I'm fine, thank you.' I sat down on the sofa, perching on the end of the cushion, feeling very ill at ease in this spotless room that looked as if it belonged in a magazine advert.

Sam sat down easily beside me and wound his arm around my waist as if to reassure me. I felt myself relax and edged further back on the cushion.

'Yes, we're all right at the moment, thanks, Mum,' he said.

The heat from the flames licked my face. I could see that there were radiators in the room too and wondered if they were on or whether the heat was coming solely from the fire. 'It's lovely and warm in here,' I remarked.

'We always have a fire until March is out,' Harold told me. 'Nothing like a real fire to warm your bones, is there?'

'It's a gorgeous room.' I imagined sitting here on a cold winter's evening, the rich gold velvet curtains drawn, the fire burning. It would be so cosy.

'Warm yourself up for a minute, dear, then come through to the dining room,' Evelyn said. She and Harold put their glasses on the tray and both stood up. 'Harold and I will go and serve up.'

She picked up the tray and walked out, followed by Harold.

When we walked into the dining room a few minutes later, Harold was putting a plate of sliced beef on the large oak table – which was covered with a snow-white tablecloth – and Evelyn was bringing in a pot of vegetables. I bit my lip when I saw the beef; I hoped that she hadn't cooked it rare.

'Sit yourselves down and help yourselves,' Evelyn said, putting the vegetables down in the middle of the table, beside a dish of potatoes. The table was large enough to seat eight people but had only been laid for four, all together at one end rather than spacing the chairs out along the entire table. Sam pulled out a chair for me to sit down, as did Harold for Evelyn. No wonder Sam was so polite and caring when he had Harold as an example, I thought.

I looked apprehensively at the beef. Harold had cut off some slices and I could see that they were pink. I could feel my stomach lurching at the thought of trying to chew it. I automatically scratched the inside of my left palm with the fingernails on my right hand as I tried to stay calm.

Sam must have noticed because he said, 'Mum, remember that Dana likes her meat well-done.'

Evelyn smiled. 'I know. I've cut some slices off for her and put them back in the oven for a few minutes.'

'That's very kind of you,' I said, touched that she had gone to so much bother.

'No trouble at all.' She got up. 'I'll go and fetch your beef now. It should be done.'

She came back holding a plate with a silver cover over it and placed it in front of me. 'I'm sorry, dear, but I left it a little too long. I'm afraid I'm not used to cooking beef this much.'

'Don't worry.' I took the silver cover off and saw that the beef was almost charred. I stared at it in dismay, knowing it was going to be difficult to chew. It was my own fault; why did I have to be so fussy? I had to eat meat cooked rare when I was with Aunt Maud and Uncle Brian, but it had made me feel so ill, the blood reminding me that it used to be a live animal, that I'd resolved never to eat it that way once I left their home. I had tried being vegetarian but my nut allergy made it difficult, so I compensated by buying the best meat I could afford and cooking it well.

'Oh dear, it is cooked too much, isn't it?' Evelyn looked worried, and I felt guilty for putting her to so much trouble.

'It's fine. Thank you for making the effort,' I told her, determined to eat all the beef no matter how tough it was.

And it was tough. I tried to be unobtrusive as I cut the beef into very small slices and chewed it slowly, wondering if I could tuck some into my cheeks, excuse myself and get rid of it down the toilet like I used to do when I was young. No one seemed to notice; they were all chatting away as they tucked into their food, not even giving me a glance or making an effort to include me in the conversation. Or perhaps they had noticed and were being polite, allowing me to struggle with the beef in peace. I wasn't sure. When the meal was finally finished, Sam reached over and took my hand in his. 'Dana and I have decided we are going to get married this summer,' he announced. 'We wanted you both to be the first to know.'

Evelyn looked shocked. 'That's a bit quick, isn't it, dear?' she stammered.

She threw a panicky look at Harold, who quickly added, 'This is a big step, Sam. It isn't like you to act so rashly.'

'It isn't rash. We want a summer wedding. And we know how we feel about each other, so why wait?' Sam replied, turning to smile adoringly at me.

'It doesn't give us much time to organise the wedding,' Evelyn said, having recovered her composure a bit now. 'Next summer would be far more practical.'

'And it will be difficult to find a venue this close to the wedding,' Harold pointed out. 'All the best ones will be booked up months, maybe even a year or more, ahead.'

'I'm sure we'll find somewhere. There are so many places that you can get married in now,' Sam told her. 'We don't want to wait until next year – we love each other. We want to get married as soon as possible, don't we, darling?' His warm brown eyes rested on my face, and I nodded in agreement. 'Then we were intending to jet off to somewhere exotic for our honeymoon,' he continued.

Were we? How exciting! Sam hadn't mentioned this to me; perhaps he'd only just thought of it and would discuss places to go later.

Evelyn and Harold exchanged a look, then Evelyn shrugged her shoulders. 'Well, whatever you want, dear. We'd be happy to help, but it really isn't much notice to organise a big wedding, which is what people would expect you to have.'

'We don't want some big society wedding – we want a small, intimate one, don't we, Dana?'

Evelyn took a sip of her wine, then her eyes lit up. 'I have an idea. We could have the reception here, couldn't we?' she suggested. 'There's plenty of room.'

'That sounds perfect. Would you mind?' Sam asked me.

I shook my head. I was happy to get married anywhere. 'It's a lot for your parents, though.'

'We'd be delighted to help. We can hire a marquee and get caterers in. The garden is always so gorgeous in the summer,' Evelyn said. 'You could have the ceremony in the village church. The vicar is a good friend of ours. I am sure he will fit you in. That's if you want to.' She looked from me to Sam. 'What do you think?'

'It's very kind of you, Mum, isn't it, Dana?' Sam turned to me again. 'It sounds ideal to me. But if you prefer something else, do say, darling.'

It sounded perfect to me, too. It was so kind of his parents and surely meant that they liked and accepted me. At first, I wondered if they were going to try to talk us out of the wedding, but I guess they could see how determined Sam was and didn't want to refuse him. And it sounded marvellous: a beautiful church wedding and a fantastic reception in the grounds of this splendid manor. What bride wouldn't want that? I really was lucky. Plus, this way, I would be saved the stress of organising everything. I could concentrate on the fun things like choosing a dress and flowers.

'Now, we don't want to be pushing Dana into anything. I bet you haven't even had a chance to think about what sort of wedding you want yet, have you, dear?' Harold said, wiping his mouth with his napkin. 'Why not take a little time to mull it over? You don't have to decide now.'

I smiled warmly at him, grateful for his concern for me. 'I think it's a lovely idea and very kind of you both.'

'Don't mention it, dear. It's absolutely no trouble at all. We would be delighted, wouldn't we, Harold?' Evelyn cut in. 'I'll talk to the vicar tomorrow and let you know what dates are available. I presume you're thinking of July or August? We must get planning right away. There isn't much time, you know.'

'Thank you, Mum. We appreciate it, don't we, Dana?' Sam kissed me on the cheek. 'I guess you'd better start looking at wedding and bridesmaids' dresses, darling.'

'I can organise that. I'll get my friend Verity to bring you a selection of dresses – she's a bridal consultant. And I'll get onto the caterers on Monday. Leave it with me,' Evelyn said.

I was a bit taken aback. Was she going to organise the dress and flowers too? I wanted some input. *She's just trying to help,* I told myself. It was going to be an amazing day.

'That's sorted then. Now, when would you like to move in, Dana?' Evelyn asked.

I stared at her, uncomprehendingly. 'Move in?' I repeated.

'Of course. Sam has his own suite upstairs; there's plenty of room for you both. And Harold and I don't have the old-fashioned belief that couples shouldn't live together. In fact, we are all for living together before you get married; that's the only way you can really find out what each other are like.'

'Thank you but, well, I've got my own flat, and we're going to buy a house to move into once we're married, aren't we, Sam?' I turned to Sam for support.

'We are. We'll start looking for one this week.' Sam agreed. 'We really appreciate the offer, Mum, but Dana and I are happy living how we are, until we get our own house.'

Disappointment and something that I couldn't quite put my finger on flashed across Evelyn's face, but she quickly replaced it with a smile. 'Of course, dear. Just trying to help. I thought the money Dana saved on her rent could then go towards your wedding, and that she might like to be on hand here to help sort out the wedding arrangements, but whatever you both prefer. The offer is always there if you change your mind, Dana. And, of course, do stay over whenever you like.' She stood up and started to gather up the plates. Harold rose to assist too. 'Now, help yourselves to another drink while I fetch dessert.'

Later, when dinner was finished, Sam suggested that we went up to his suite to watch a film. I was surprised how spacious and comfortable it was. There were two bedrooms – the larger bedroom with an en suite was obviously where Sam slept, and he used the smaller room as a study – and a spacious lounge with a balcony overlooking the back garden and the Malvern Hills. It was such a spectacular view. No wonder Sam wasn't bothered about moving out. He had everything he wanted here.

Evelyn's offer for me to move in came back to my mind, and I wondered briefly about living here until we got married. It was such a gorgeous house that, for a moment, I was tempted, but then I dismissed the thought. Much as I liked Evelyn and Harold, I agreed with Lynne that it wasn't a good idea to live with 'in-laws'. I wanted Sam and me to have a home of our own. I wanted it to be our home, not theirs. And most of all, I wanted us to have some privacy. Sam's parents obviously adored him and it was a bit difficult for me to get a word in sometimes. I wanted to start off married life just the two of us.

When we were sitting on the sofa later, watching the film, Sam's arm around my shoulder, he kissed me on the forehead and said, 'I know Mum takes over a bit, but she means well. She just wants what's best for me. She had a few miscarriages and was told she'd never have a child. She was devastated, and then I came along. Her "surprise miracle", she always said. She can be a bit over the top sometimes.' He looked apologetic. 'She's just trying to be helpful, suggesting that we live here. We are definitely going to get our own home, I promise.'

I thought of poor Evelyn longing so much for a baby, her distress at her miscarriages and then thinking she would never have a child. No wonder she was a little possessive with Sam, that she adored him so much. It was good that she wanted to help organise the wedding and wanted me to live here, I reminded myself. It proved that she liked me.

'I know, I like your parents,' I reassured him, all resentment now gone.

He smiled and hugged me. 'Good. Now where do you fancy going on honeymoon? How does the Caribbean sound?'

'Perfect!' I told him. I snuggled into him, hardly able to believe how my life had changed in a few short months.

7

Evelyn, as promised, had talked to the vicar, and it seemed he had Saturday, 16 July free, so she had immediately booked it for us. Sam told me that it was all arranged; we were getting married in the village church then coming back to the manor for the reception. He looked delighted. 'I must say, it's very kind of Mum to organise it all and make it so easy for us. She is really happy about the wedding. It's all she talks about.' He hugged me. 'I'm so pleased that Mum likes you. She can be a bit picky when it comes to my girlfriends, but she adores you. And so does Dad.'

It was all very exciting. I couldn't believe that in four months' time I would be married to Sam. A little voice nagged in my mind that Evelyn had chosen the date and the venue for us, but I dismissed it. She was only trying to help. I was relieved that she liked me and that, despite their initial shock, Sam's parents were accepting me so readily into the family. Their back garden with its immaculate lawns, beautiful fountain and colourful flowerbeds would be the perfect place for the reception; it would probably cost us a fortune to hire a venue like that and I was acutely aware that I had no money to contribute to the wedding, so it was all down to Sam and his family. Besides, July was a gorgeous month to get married. And there were still lots of other things for me and Sam to plan. 'I can't wait,' I told him.

Although Lynne had been shocked when I told her we were getting married this summer, she was impressed when I told her about our wedding plans. 'You lucky thing! You've really landed on your feet with Sam. Make sure that his mum doesn't take over the wedding, though – she seems to have sorted out a lot already. Hopefully, you'll only get married once, so make sure it's the wedding day you want.'

'I will. Sam said that Evelyn is really excited about the wedding, which is a good thing, isn't it? I think she's just eager to help,' I said, not sure if I was trying to convince Lynne or myself. 'I'd love you to be my maid of honour. Please say you will.'

'Oh, yes, please!' Lynne practically squealed in delight. 'How many bridesmaids are you having?'

'We haven't discussed it yet. Neither of us have siblings, so I think we'll be keeping things small,' I told her. 'I'll talk about it to Sam this week and let you know.'

'I think it's time I met Sam, don't you?' Lynne said. 'How about coming around this weekend for a bite to eat with me and Spencer?'

It really *was* time she met Sam, and I wanted her to see how wonderful he was, but I wasn't sure about going to their flat. Spencer could be a bit controversial: he liked to start a 'discussion', as he called it, and could be quite obnoxious with his comments. I thought it might be best to meet somewhere neutral. 'That sounds great, but let's go for a pub lunch,' I suggested. I could choose a country pub, keep it casual. I hoped Sam wouldn't mind. I hadn't met any of his friends yet, either. But then our relationship had been such an intense whirlwind, and we were both so busy that when we did have free time, we just wanted to spend it together.

'Next Sunday,' Lynne said. 'At the Coachman, two o'clock.'

'I'll need to check with Sam and get back to you,' I told her.

When Sam came around that evening, I mentioned it to him and to my relief, he thought it was a great idea. 'You've talked about Lynne so much that I feel I know her already,' he said. 'It'd be good to put a face to the name.'

'I've asked her to be my maid of honour,' I said.

'Then I must definitely meet her,' he replied.

'Have you decided who you're going to have as your best man?' I asked, pleased that he'd agreed so readily to meet Lynne and Spencer.

'Nathan, my best friend. He's working in New York at the moment, but I've messaged him and he said he'd be delighted.'

It sounded as if this Nathan had a very glamorous job. 'What kind of work does he do?'

'He's a hedge fund manager. He's working over there until the end of the year, but he'll fly over for the wedding with his partner, Ingrid.'

It hit me once again how different our lives were, and I felt my anxiety rising as I wondered what life would be like when we were married. I would be mixing with a different social circle than I was used to, and I didn't want to let Sam down. Was I doing the right thing, or would it all be too much pressure for me? As if sensing my doubts, Sam reached out and caressed my cheek with the back of his hand. 'Don't look so worried. Nathan and Ingrid are fun – you'll like them.'

My worry was more about whether they would like me. I had led such an isolated childhood with Aunt Maud and Uncle Brian, never allowed friends home to play or to go to friend's houses, so had always felt awkward with people I didn't know, apart from when I was with Sam. He'd put me at ease right away; he accepted me for who I was and didn't put any pressure on me. 'I can't wait to meet them,' I said, trying to sound more confident than I felt.

We met Lynne and Spencer the following Sunday, and to my relief, it all went well. Lynne must have warned Spencer to be on his best behaviour because he didn't bring up any controversial topics. He and Sam got on very well, especially when they discovered that they both supported the same football team. They spent most of the time discussing players and matches, leaving me and Lynne to talk about wedding arrangements.

'Well, what's the verdict?' I asked when we both slipped off to go to the loo, leaving the two men still discussing football. I was anxious to know what she thought of Sam, especially as she'd been concerned that we were rushing things.

'He's lovely. I can totally see why you've fallen for him. And it's obvious that he adores you. You're one lucky lady,' she said.

I grinned with delight. 'I knew you'd like him when you met him.'

'I do. And I understand why you're swept away with it all. Now, when are we going wedding-dress shopping? Have you any idea what style you want?'

'Evelyn said to leave it to her. She's got a friend who's a bridal consultant...'

Lynne looked disappointed. 'You mean that she's going to choose your wedding dress for you as well as the date and venue?'

Now I felt bad. I should go wedding-dress shopping with Lynne; she was my best friend. 'Of course not. We'll go shopping together – we have your dress to get anyway – and can check out some wedding dresses. Then I can see Evelyn's friend's selection and decide which I like best.'

Lynne looked a bit appeased. 'Okay, but remember, this is your wedding. Don't let Sam's mum take over.'

'I won't, but it is kind of her to help. I was scared they wouldn't like me, but they wouldn't be helping with the wedding preparations if they didn't, would they? And they're paying for it all, so I should be grateful,' I explained.

'You're lucky she likes you. Spencer's mum hates me and doesn't even try to hide the fact. Honestly, I can't do anything right as far as she's concerned,' Lynne said, as she reapplied her lipstick. 'You know what a lot of men's mothers are like; no one is good enough for their precious son. At least Evelyn is happy to accept you into the family.' Her eyes met mine in the mirror. 'But you still have a right to have the wedding you want, Dana. Please make sure you speak up for yourself. You're so scared of any conflict you can be a bit of a pushover.'

As we headed back into the pub restaurant, I knew that she was right. I hated speaking up for myself. 'Children should be seen and not heard,' Aunt Maud and Uncle Brian always told me, so I'd learnt to fade into the background, to be unobtrusive and keep my opinions to myself. It was a hard habit to shake off.

'Your friend's nice,' Sam said as he drove me home after the meal.

I was pleased to hear that he liked her. Lynne could be loud and opinionated, but she had a heart of gold. 'She's been like a sister to me,' I told him. 'I was glad to see you getting on so well with Spencer, too. He can be a bit awkward sometimes. Thank goodness you support the same football team – it gave you something to talk about.'

Sam glanced at me and grinned. 'I don't support any football team, actually, but as you said, it gave us something to talk about.'

I stared at him, astonished. 'But you knew all about the players, and the matches...'

'I know a bit, yes. I like to keep abreast of things. Actually, Spencer did most of the talking. I simply went along with what he was saying.'

I hadn't been paying much attention to them, as I'd been too busy talking to Lynne, but when I thought about it, every time I'd tuned into their conversation, it was Spencer who had been talking. Sam really knew how to handle people, I thought in admiration. He was so self-assured, confident and articulate, but he always listened to what I had to say as if it was the most interesting thing in the world and never spoke down to me. He made me feel important.

Or was he simply saying what I wanted to hear, like he did with Spencer? I brushed the doubt from my mind. Of course he wasn't! Sam was kind, thoughtful, loving. When I was with him, I felt like I could cope with anything. And that he would protect me from anything. I felt safe.

In four months' time, I'll be Mrs Corbett, I thought happily. I couldn't wait. A marvellous new life awaited me, and I was eager to seize it with both hands.

8

Sam's parents invited me to dinner the following Sunday to discuss the wedding arrangements. I was pleased to be included, as I'd been worrying that Evelyn would go ahead and organise everything without asking me. I was also pleased to see that she'd served roast chicken this time, so I didn't have to worry about the beef being cooked enough. She was trying to be considerate, I thought thankfully.

'I think it's time we did the guest list,' she said as we tucked into our meal. 'Sam said that you both wanted to keep the wedding quite small, so maybe thirty guests on each side.' She gave me a sympathetic look. 'I understand that both your parents died when you were very young, dear, but an aunt and uncle brought you up. I presume they will be coming? What about other family members and friends?'

I felt my cheeks flush as I tried to formulate my reply. When I'd mentioned to Aunt Maud and Uncle Brian that I was getting married and asked them if they would like to come, they had apologised, saying they were away that week, but wished me all the best and would send us a present. So that was it; there would be no one from my family at the wedding. And the only close friend I had was Lynne – we'd invited Spencer too, of course, and Lynne's parents, as they'd always been good to me. I'd only been at my new job a couple of months and although I got on with the others, I didn't feel I knew them enough to invite them. Which meant four on my side as opposed to good-ness knows how many on Sam's.

Luckily, Sam must have realised how awkward I felt and stepped in. 'Dana doesn't really have any family except her aunt and uncle, Mum, and they can't make it.' He squeezed my hand. 'You're very select with your friends too, aren't you, darling? So it will only be Lynne, her boyfriend and her parents.'

Evelyn raised an eyebrow. 'Really? Well, don't worry, our side will more than make up for it.' She picked up her glass of wine and took a sip before adding, 'And Sam's family is your family now, Dana. Everyone is dying to meet you.'

'Thank you. I'm looking forward to meeting everyone,' I said brightly, which was a lie. I was dreading it, sure that I'd feel out of my depth.

'We'll discuss the wedding a bit more once the garden party is over next week,' Evelyn said. 'I've spoken to Verity and she's more than happy to bring some wedding dresses over for you to look at. She has a splendid selection of designer gowns. I'm sure that you'll find the perfect one amongst them.'

Designer dresses! I could hardly believe it. 'Thank you. I've arranged to go shopping with my friend, Lynne, too, so she can choose her dress. She's my maid of honour.'

'Then Lynne must come over and see the dresses with you – I'll ask Verity to bring a selection of bridesmaid dresses along as well,' she replied. 'What about the other bridesmaids? It would be easier if they could all come over together.'

'Dana is just having a maid of honour,' Sam butted in, once again rescuing me.

Evelyn pouted. 'That's a shame. Tamara would have loved to be a bridesmaid. Julia and Ray are our oldest friends, Sam.'

Tamara? Who was she? Sam had never mentioned her. I darted a questioning look at him as he shrugged. 'Naturally, they will all be invited, but Tamara doesn't even know Dana, so I'm sure she won't expect to be a bridesmaid.'

'But you and she are so close,' Evelyn protested.

'Now, dear, it has to be Sam and Dana's choice,' Harold said gently.

She gave a brief nod. 'As you wish.'

There was a silence as we all finished our meal, and I could see that Evelyn was very put out and not making much of an effort to disguise it. I was dying to ask Sam more about Tamara once we were alone together.

'Are you all ready for the garden party next week, Mum?' Sam asked, finally breaking the silence.

'It's all in hand.' Evelyn looked at me. 'You are still coming to help, aren't you, Dana?'

'Yes, of course. What time would you like me here?' I asked.

'It starts at two, so about twelve thirty, if you can, then we can all get the stalls up ready for people to arrive. And Jojo will be here just before two to open the event.'

'Jojo?' I asked, curious.

'Jojo Daniels, dear. The actor. His parents live in the village and he is a good friend of Sam's.'

I was dumbstruck. Sam was friends with a famous soap star and he was coming to their garden party?

'Jojo and I went to school together,' Sam explained. 'I don't see much of him now, but we usually catch up when he visits his folks.'

'Is he coming to the wedding too?' I asked.

'He's not sure he can make it yet,' Sam replied. 'He'll tell us nearer the time when he knows his filming schedule.'

The discussion then turned to the garden party, which sounded like a spectacular event. I couldn't help feeling nervous at this new world I was entering by marrying Sam. I hoped I didn't show anyone up.

After dinner, Sam suggested that we go for a drive. I readily agreed, pleased to get away on our own. I was desperate to find out who Tamara was, but I managed to wait a whole five minutes after we got in the car before asking the question as casually as I could manage.

He grinned, his eyes still fixed on the road ahead. 'I was expecting you to ask that. Mum did big up our friendship a bit, didn't she? To be honest, Tam and Mum are closer than she and I are these days. Tam's family are long-term friends of ours. Her parents are our nearest neighbours and so Tam and I grew up together. We don't see much of each other now, of course. Tam's a lawyer and works in London most of the time; she's come home for the weekend. I can assure you that she will not expect to be a bridesmaid at our wedding, and will probably rib me terribly about getting married. Tam's a fun-loving singleton who has no intention of settling down.' He paused and glanced quickly at me before returning his attention to the road. 'Do you mind very much if they come to the wedding, though? It will mean such a lot to my parents, especially Mum.'

'Of course not,' I said. How could I when they were such good family friends, and Evelyn was being so helpful with the wedding?

'Thank you. I know this all must be overwhelming for you but I promise you it will be a lovely day.' He carefully negotiated a bend in the road then said, 'You know, we really ought to start looking at houses to buy this week. There's still over three months before the wedding, so if we get a move on and find one we like, we might be able to move in a couple of weeks before we get married, and get the house straight before we go on honeymoon. What do you think?'

'I'd love that,' I said happily. I was marrying a wonderful man, and soon we would be living in our own house. And we were going to Barbados for our honeymoon. I'd never been farther than France and I was really excited about it. Plus, I was getting to choose a gorgeous designer wedding dress. *You've never had it so good, Dana*, I told myself. *Stop fretting. Everything is going to be just fine.*

I couldn't have been more wrong.

9

I arrived at Sam's just after twelve the following Saturday and found the garden already a hive of activity. There were several tables placed around the lawn and people were rushing about, carrying things from the multiple cars parked on the huge driveway at the front around to the back and over to the tables. There was a bouncy castle erected on a square lawn and someone was setting up some skittles on a paved area. A couple with a basket of chocolate eggs each were wandering around and hiding the eggs behind bushes, underneath tables, behind statues and in various other places – obviously for the Easter egg hunt. It really was a beautiful and spacious garden, I thought. It would be the perfect setting for our wedding.

I was so lucky.

Sam spotted me and waved. He and Harold, both dressed in blue-and-white striped aprons, were trying to get the barbecue going. 'Hello, darling,' he greeted me, with a hug and a kiss.

'You all look busy. How can I help?' I asked.

'I think Mum could do with a hand in the kitchen, if you don't mind? Helen, our housekeeper, had to go away last night, unexpected family business, so Mum's coping on her own.'

'Of course.' I hurried over to the kitchen, my mouth watering at the delicious aroma of baking wafting out through the open door. The worktops and table were covered with cakes ranging from simple butterfly cakes to mouth-watering sponges and lavishly decorated meringues. Sam had said all the women from the local WI were baking cakes for today, and looking at this sumptuous array, they'd done Evelyn proud. I felt a bit guilty that I hadn't made a cake myself, but baking wasn't my forté and I decided it was better not to attempt it than risk failure. Evelyn and another woman of a similar age were putting the cakes on trays.

'Ah, Dana. Hello, dear.' Evelyn turned to the other woman. 'Julia, this is Dana, Sam's fiancée. Dana, Julia is our neighbour, Tamara's mum and a very good friend of ours.'

'Pleased to meet you, dear.' Julia nodded at me then grabbed a tray of cakes. 'You'll have to excuse me, these need putting on the cake table.'

'Let me help,' I offered.

'Thank you. Perhaps you could help man the cake stall too?' Evelyn asked. 'We could do with another pair of hands.'

'I'd be glad to,' I agreed, eager to assist in any way I could. 'How about I clear up in here for you first?' The worktop by the kitchen was piled up with baking tins, mixing bowls and other utensils.

'Thank you, dear, that would be very helpful,' Evelyn said. 'I usually clear up as I go but this morning has been so hectic. I do wish Helen hadn't had to leave so suddenly. As soon as the Easter holidays are over, I'm going to have to look for a cleaner to tide us over until she comes back.'

I picked up a tray of cakes and took them over to the cake stall, promising to come back and help serve once I'd cleaned up the kitchen.

I took care with the tidying up, washing the baking utensils carefully in the sink then stacking the dishwasher neatly with the mixing bowls and crockery. I found the dishwasher liquid in the cupboard under the sink so put a capful of that in, selecting a heavy wash programme, then sprayed the worktops with an anti-bacterial liquid. Everywhere was bright and shining when I'd finished. Feeling pleased with myself, I went out into the garden and looked around for the cake stall. Sam waved, so I went over. 'How's it going?' I asked.

'We'll be starting cooking in a minute, but I'm really thirsty. Would you mind bringing us both a can of beer out of the fridge? The low-alcohol one? I don't want to leave Dad to deal with all this by himself.'

'No problem, I'll be back in a jiffy,' I told him.

As I approached the kitchen door, I heard Evelyn cry out and hurried inside, worried that she'd hurt herself. I paused in the doorway when I realised that the floor was covered in a mass of soapy bubbles. I gasped as I realised they were pouring out of the dishwasher. How had that happened? I'd only put one capful in.

Evelyn looked horrified. 'Look at all this mess! If you didn't know how to use the dishwasher, you should have left it alone. I would have done it. Now I'm going to have to wade through all this to turn it off, then clear it all up.'

'I'm so sorry. I'll switch it off and clean up.' I slipped off the white sandals I'd bought especially for today and held up my new maxi dress as I paddled through the suds to switch off the dishwasher, wishing that I'd worn a knee-length dress instead.

'Oh dear, what's happened here?' a haughty-sounding voice asked.

I spun around, to see a beautiful woman standing behind me, a look of amusement on her face. She was effortlessly made-up, her shiny dark hair neatly framing her face in a perfect bob, dressed in a casual white top and coral cropped trousers, that were unmistakably designer, a large Gucci bag dangled from her right shoulder. Who was she? And why was she looking at me like that, as if she was assessing me?

Evelyn's face lit up when she saw her. 'Tamara! You made it!'

So this was Tamara. Trust her to turn up when I'd made all this mess and probably looked a right state myself, ankle-deep in suds, holding up the hem of my dress.

'I told you I would if I could.' Tamara kissed her on the cheek. 'I heard that Helen had to leave suddenly. I see the new cleaner hasn't got used to the dishwasher yet.'

Cleaner! What a cheek! I bristled. Tamara hadn't met me yet, but I failed to see how she could mistake me for a cleaner when I was all dressed and made-up.

Evelyn chuckled. 'Goodness, this isn't my new cleaner, this is Dana, Sam's fiancée. She put the dishwasher on for me but put too much liquid into it.' She turned to me. 'Dana, meet Tamara.'

'Oh, sorry!' Tamara said, although she didn't seem the least bit sorry. She held out her hand. 'Pleased to meet you at last, Dana.'

I paddled back through the suds and, still holding my dress up, shook her hand. 'Likewise,' I mumbled, feeling really awkward.

'Let me help you clean this up. We don't want anyone slipping on it and hurting themselves,' Tamara offered.

'It's fine, I can do it,' I insisted. It was the least I could do after causing all the mess. 'I have to take Sam and Harold a can of beer first, then I'll come back and get to it.' I opened the fridge and took two cans out, checking that they were low-alcohol.

'Don't worry, we'll take the men the beer.' Tamara took the two cans from me and slipped them into her bag.

'You'll find the mop and bucket in the utility room, the door on the left,' Evelyn told me.

'I'm afraid that your dress is going to look rather a mess by the time you've finished,' Tamara said, an amused smile playing on her lips. She reached into her handbag and took out a safety pin. 'Here, use this to pin it up at the front then you'll have both hands free.'

'Thanks,' I mumbled, my cheeks so hot I could have fried an egg on them. How embarrassing! *Tamara must be wondering what Sam sees in me,* I thought miserably as I scooped up the front of my dress, pinning it together.

Evelyn slipped her arm through Tamara's. 'Now come and say hello to everyone. Sam will be so pleased to see you.'

They both walked out and I paddled back through the suds to find the mop and bucket, pausing at the cupboard to take out the dishwashing liquid and check the dosage. One cap it said, which is what I had done, so it should have been fine. *Why can't they use dishwasher tablets like the rest of us?* I thought crossly.

When the suds were finally all mopped up, I dried my feet, put my sandals back on, unpinned my dress and smoothed it down as best I could, then stepped outside. I was astonished to see the garden full of people. I hadn't expected this many to turn up. Suddenly, I had an attack of nerves and stepped back inside. I couldn't face all those people. I was sure that I looked a right state. And I didn't know what to say to them – I am hopeless at small talk.

You can. You can do it for Sam. Just smile and listen, leave them to do the talking, I told myself.

Taking a deep breath, I stepped outside again. Tamara and Evelyn were talking to Sam and Harold, who were now cooking sausages, chicken and beefburgers on the barbecue. I was about to walk over and join them when Sam gave a roar of laughter at something Tamara had said, his head thrown back, his eyes sparkling. I felt a surge of jealousy. I paused, trying to fight my feelings as I watched them. Tamara might be beautiful and confident – and rich by the look of her clothes – but Sam had chosen me, I reminded myself.

Suddenly there was a cry of 'Jojo's here!' A hush fell over the garden as a blond, suntanned man casually walked around the side of the house. Obviously Jojo, he looked at home here, as if he was a regular visitor. He raised his hand in a wave and everyone cheered.

Sam stepped forward to greet Jojo, and they both hugged and slapped each other on the back. I saw Sam gazing around, looking for me. *He wants to introduce me,* I thought in panic. *I can't. I must look such a mess now.* I ducked back inside so they couldn't see me and looked out of the window as Jojo walked over to stand in front of the fountain, took the microphone that Sam handed to him and gave a speech declaring the garden party open and asking people to dig deep into their pockets as all funds were going to the National Trust. The window was open and I could hear his words, clear and articulate. How I envied his confidence. After the speech, Evelyn and Tamara, arms linked once more, went over to chat to him. I watched, feeling more than a bit unsettled by the obvious affection between the two of them. *Anyone would think Tamara was Sam's fiancée rather than me,* I thought a little resentfully. *You're the one hiding in the kitchen,* I reminded myself.

'What are you doing hiding in here? You're missing all the fun,' Julia said as she walked in a little later.

I felt my cheeks flame. 'I came in to go the loo,' I mumbled.

'If you hurry up, you might get to see Jojo – he'll not stay long,' Julia said. 'Come on.'

Meeting Jojo was the last thing I wanted to do, but Julia was looking at me as if she already thought I was strange, so I followed her outside.

Sam came over to me right away. 'You've just missed Jojo, Dana,' he said. 'Where have you been? I was looking for you.'

'Oh, that's a shame. I was tidying up the kitchen for Evelyn,' I told.

Sam wound his arm around my shoulder and pulled me in for a hug. 'That's really kind of you, but I wish I'd known – I'd have come and got you. Jojo was dying to meet you but he couldn't stay long.'

'Maybe another time,' I told him, trying not to think of how relaxed Tamara had looked with Jojo. Maybe she went to school with him too. I had to face it; Tamara fitted in to Sam's world far better than I did. I was an outsider. And looking around at the grand garden party his parents had put on, at Evelyn and Tamara walking around arm in arm, I wondered if I was making a big mistake agreeing to marry Sam.

10

'Could I have a slice of Victoria sponge, please?' a woman asked, pointing to the cake. I'd pulled myself together and gone over to help Julia on the cake stall.

'Of course.' I sliced up the cake and wrapped it in a serviette before handing it to the woman as she gave me one pound fifty.

'It's kind of you to come along and help, Dana.' Julia gave me a warm smile.

'I'm happy to. Evelyn and Harold have been very welcoming,' I said.

'They're a lovely couple. They do such a lot for charity, and Harold is a well-respected magistrate too. But I expect you know that.'

'Sam told me,' I replied. Although Harold was so mild-mannered and quiet it was difficult to imagine him dealing with offenders.

'People can sometimes think that Harold is a pushover, but he can be tough when he has to be,' Julia continued, as if she could read my thoughts. 'I must congratulate you on your engagement. I hear that you and Sam are getting married in July? Evelyn said that you haven't known Sam long, that it's been a bit of a whirlwind romance,' she added.

'We met at the beginning of January,' I said, feeling a little like I was being cross-examined, although Julia's tone was pleasant enough. 'It has been a bit quick, but we're both looking forward to it very much.'

'January? Goodness, it must have been love at first sight!' She looked wistfully over to where Evelyn and Tamara were walking around, still arm in arm. 'Tamara and Sam were inseparable when they were little. Evelyn and I dreamed that they would get married one day, but it wasn't to be.' She glanced back at me, the smile on her lips not quite reaching her eyes. 'I hope you'll both be very happy together.'

'Thank you,' I replied, wondering just how close Tamara and Sam had been. He called her 'Tam' – the only person who did, which indicated a more than casual familiarity and had described her as a 'good friend', not a 'girlfriend' so it seemed there hadn't been a romance between them, although it was clear both mothers had hoped there would be.

People were coming into the garden in droves now, and the cake stall was a major attraction. The stall next to it sold soft drinks as well as cups of coffee and tea, and there were tables and chairs scattered around the garden for people to sit down and enjoy their refreshments. Evelyn really had thought of everything.

'Sorry about that, Dana. We haven't seen Tamara for months – it's been lovely to catch up with her,' Evelyn said when she finally joined us at the stall. 'It's so good of you both to come and support our charity Easter event, Julia.'

'We wouldn't dream of missing it,' Julia replied. 'It really is wonderful to have Tamara home again. The house seemed so empty without her.'

'I know. I'm dreading the day Sam leaves,' Evelyn admitted. She looked at all the gaps on the table. 'I see that you've been busy. That's wonderful.'

'We've been rushed off our feet, thank goodness Dana was here to help,' Julia told her.

'It's very kind of you, Dana. Why don't you take a break and have a look around? I can take over now,' Evelyn suggested.

It would be nice if Evelyn had showed me around and introduced me instead of parading around with Tamara, I thought, then kicked the thought out of my mind. Tamara was an old family friend, and besides, Evelyn was taking my place on the cake stall so I could catch up with Sam.

'Thank you. I will.' I headed over to the barbecue feeling much happier now that Evelyn was in a better mood with me. I'd obviously been forgiven for the dishwasher incident, and I was relieved that Tamara seemed to have left.

There was quite a queue around the barbecue and Sam and Harold were joking around as they served up the food. They make a good team, I thought as I watched them. You could see the bond between them. Sam had the same square jaw and dark brown eyes as Harold, I noticed. It was evident that Sam was close to Evelyn too. They were such a tight family unit. I hoped that once we were married, I'd start to feel part of it rather than on the outside looking in, as I did now.

'I couldn't believe it when Sam said he was getting married.'

I turned to see Tamara behind me. So she hadn't left then. 'What do you mean?' I asked.

Tamara rolled her eyes. 'I thought he'd never let go of his mummy's apron strings.'

Her tone surprised me. She'd acted like she was really fond of Evelyn and yet here she was, speaking almost disparagingly about her. 'I think it's nice that they're so close.'

'Close? That's a bit of an understatement.' Tamara pulled a

face. 'Who do you know that still lives with his mum at the age of thirty-five? I expect you'll be moving in now, too.'

Why was she being so unpleasant? 'No, I'm not. We're buying a house together,' I told her.

'Really?' Tamara folded her arms and looked me up and down. 'Well, don't count your chickens yet. Something might come along and scupper that.' Then her face broke into a false smile. 'I forgot to congratulate you on your engagement.' She leaned forward and kissed me on the cheek. 'Well done for pulling that off.'

She turned and sashayed off across the lawn, leaving me staring after her. What was all that about?

Then Sam caught my eye and waved to me. 'Want to try one of the famous Corbett burgers? I've cooked one especially for you.'

I grinned and nodded, putting Tamara's nasty remarks out of my mind as I joined Sam and Harold on the barbecue stand. The burger, topped with crispy onions, was delicious and I started to relax as I chewed it.

'Here comes the Easter bunny!' Sam said as a round of clapping broke out. I turned to see someone in a furry brown bunny outfit walking along carrying a basket.

'Whoever is wearing that suit will soon be baking hot,' I observed.

'It's Ray, Tam's dad. He loves dressing up and entertaining the children,' Sam said with a grin. 'Apparently he's got a trunk full of fancy dress costumes in the attic.'

'Right, children, are you ready for the Easter egg hunt?' the bunny shouted.

The children cheered and gathered around him. He gave them a small cardboard basket each and they ran off to find the eggs. Every now and again I heard cries of 'I've found one!'

It was a fun afternoon and over a thousand pounds was

raised, which was wonderful. I was so proud to be joining this warm, caring family and decided that I wasn't going to think any more about Tamara's spiteful words.

That was my second mistake.

11

Sam came over on Monday evening and we sat together on my little sofa, looking at estate agent websites on his laptop. It was so exciting. The type of houses Sam was looking at – detached, set in large gardens, four bedrooms – were way above what I had ever imagined living in. 'Are you sure we can afford to buy one of these?' I asked him.

'I've got the deposit already and will have paid off my loan from my parents by June, so the mortgage will be no problem,' he told me. The house was in Sam's name to make things easier, as he was using the same mortgage company he'd bought the student lets with. We'd already agreed my contribution; I could afford it easily once I wasn't paying rent, but Sam would be paying the most – something that he'd assured me he was very happy to do. 'After all, I'll be paying it all when we have a family,' he said. 'I'd like you to be able to stay home and look after the children while they're little, like my mum did with me.' He glanced anxiously at me. 'That is, if you're happy to do that?'

'I'd be delighted to,' I told him. I wanted to give our children a secure, happy childhood; the sort of childhood Sam had.

Sam wrapped his arm around my shoulder. 'We're such a

perfect match,' he said, kissing me tenderly on the forehead. 'I can't wait for us to be married.'

'Neither can I,' I assured him. I sometimes had to pinch myself that this was happening. I'd found the man of my dreams and now was going to have the home of my dreams.

'You deserve it,' Lynne had told me. She'd got over her reservations about Sam since she'd met him and was now behind us all the way.

Sam arranged viewings throughout the week and we viewed a couple of houses every evening. I'd have been happy with any of them, they were so luxurious and spacious compared to my little flat, but Sam wanted a separate dining room and a large garden. Finally, we found a house we both loved. The couple, Mr and Mrs Marsh, were moving to Wales to be nearer Mr Marsh's elderly parents, and wanted a quick move. There was no chain, and we all agreed on completing contracts the first week in June. Which would be perfect.

'That gives us time to move in and get the house straight before we get married and go on our honeymoon,' Sam said.

I was over the moon. I couldn't wait to move into our very own home.

Evelyn and Harold wanted to see the house too, so we took them with us when we went to measure for curtains. As Evelyn looked around, I could see that she wasn't too impressed with it. As soon as we got into the car, she and Harold pointed out a couple of 'flaws'. 'I do think you're rushing this, dear. You know that you can both stay with us as long as you want to,' Evelyn said. 'Why not save a bit longer and buy a house in a nicer area?'

I thought the area was lovely and felt a bit nervous, wondering if Sam would listen to them and call off the sale, but he simply slipped his hand into mine, squeezing it reassuringly as he said, 'Dana and I love it.'

Evelyn pursed her lips but said nothing. She was silent all the way home. Harold started chatting to us, asking how the wedding plans were coming on, as if trying to fill the awkward silence.

'I think your mum is upset with us,' I told Sam when we were alone later.

'She'll come round,' he said, giving me a kiss. 'Now we have our home, we should concentrate on planning our wedding. What colour theme would you like?'

'Something bright and summery... What do you think of lemon?' I suggested. I'd already been looking at some wedding boards on Pinterest and seen some gorgeous pale lemon bridesmaid dresses. It was such a cheerful colour. A happy colour. And my wedding day would be the happiest day of my life. I'd seen some really cute dresses for younger bridesmaids too, and I felt a bit of a pang that I hadn't got any little sisters. Or parents. Family who could come to my wedding and help me celebrate. *I've got Sam and his family now*, I told myself. I'd learned long ago not to hanker after what I didn't have but to appreciate what I did have.

'That sounds good,' Sam nodded. 'Are you expecting me and Nathan to wear yellow suits?'

I cocked my head to one side as I grinned at him. 'I actually think you might like that...' I could imagine Sam wearing a lemon suit with a white tie and waistcoat – and a white top hat. Sam never missed an opportunity to wear a hat.

He grinned back. 'I think we might go for a beige three-piece suit with a lemon-yellow tie, what do you think?'

'I think it sounds perfect,' I told him. 'And a hat, no doubt.'

'Of course.' He pulled me to him and kissed me. 'I can't wait for you to be Mrs Corbett.' He released me, looked questioningly at me. 'Or would you prefer to double-barrel our names? Wynters-Corbett? Corbett-Wynters?'

I shook my head. 'Mrs Corbett sounds good to me.'

'It sounds very good to me,' he murmured, wrapping his arms around me. I sank into them, returning kiss for kiss.

Later, when we'd both dressed again, Sam gave me a credit card. I was surprised to see my name on it. 'I've added you to my card so that you can buy anything you need for the wedding: the dress, flowers, clothes for the honeymoon.'

I was touched that he trusted me like this. 'Do you have a limit you want me to keep to?' I asked.

He shook his head. 'Buy whatever you want,' he said. He passed me a piece of paper. 'Here's the pin number.'

'Thank you.' I was a bit overwhelmed with his generosity. I'd always struggled financially and now I had been given carte blanche with his credit card. Not that I would exploit his good nature.

'Oh, and Mum wants to know if you and Lynne can both come over on Saturday. Verity – the bridal consultant she knows – is bringing some designer wedding and bridesmaid dresses over.'

'I'll check with Lynne. I'm not sure if she's working or if she and Spencer have plans,' I said. I hoped she could make it. I'd appreciate her support and advice.

'Oh no, I'm working this week! I can come over next week?' she said. 'Lucky you, being able to choose a designer dress.'

I messaged Evelyn to let her know that Lynne couldn't make it and asked if could we both come over the next week instead but she replied that it was all organised with Verity so I should come and choose my dress this Saturday and then Lynne's dress the week after.

'I'm so sorry that I'm working, but I'll definitely come with you next week,' Lynne promised. 'Make sure you get the dress you want, though. Don't let Evelyn talk you into anything.'

I knew she would have loved to come along and help me choose, and I'd have loved her input, but Evelyn obviously wasn't going to alter the arrangements. *Never mind, it's kind of her to organise this,* I told myself. At least she was supportive of us getting married.

12

When I arrived at the manor on Saturday morning, I was a bit put out to discover that Tamara was there too, but I tried not to show it. She and Verity were very pally; they'd obviously met before. Not that that surprised me. Tamara seemed to know everyone. The dresses were stunning, definitely not the sort you would get 'off the peg' on the high street. Egged on by Evelyn, Verity and Tamara, I tried several on – using the dressing room off the side of Evelyn's bedroom, which was massive with a maroon velvet chaise lounge that Tamara and Evelyn sat on whilst I paraded about in the dresses. They were all beautiful, but I fell in love with a gorgeous ivory floaty dress with a nipped-in waist, plunging neckline and beaded lace bodice that made me look and feel like a million dollars.

'I must say, darling, that is wonderful,' Evelyn said, clasping her hands in delight as I came out of her dressing room to show them the dress. 'What do you think, Tamara?'

Tamara nodded. 'It's perfect,' she said. 'It makes you look like a fairy-tale princess, and you must feel like you're living a fairy tale, marrying someone like Sam.' She didn't add, 'like

Cinderella marrying the prince' but she might as well have. Her meaning, and the look in her eyes, was clear; she thought I was only marrying Sam for his money. Well, nothing could have been further from the truth. I loved Sam and he loved me.

I guess that, as Tamara and Sam were such good friends, she was simply looking out for him – as Lynne had for me when she warned me not to rush things, I reminded myself.

'I'm very lucky, Sam is wonderful,' I agreed, determined not to retaliate. I wished that Lynne was here with me. I could have done with her support, and opinion. It would have been be good to know if she thought that Tamara was looking down on me and that Evelyn was disappointed that Sam had chosen to marry me, or whether it was just me being sensitive.

Verity walked around me, her finger on her lips, tape measure hanging around her neck. 'I do agree. It's as if this dress was made for you, dear. And it only needs a slight alteration,' she said. 'It won't take long to do that.'

'Wonderful,' Evelyn exclaimed, looking very satisfied. 'Now, Dana isn't having any bridesmaids, but her best friend is being her maid of honour. Can you bring some bridesmaid dresses over next weekend for her to try on?'

'Of course. Do you have a colour in mind?' Verity asked.

'We've decided on pale lemon, so it would be lovely to see any dresses you have in that colour,' I replied.

Evelyn frowned. 'Well, let's not restrict ourselves to a certain colour just yet. I think you should bring a variety of colours and styles, Verity. Give Dana plenty to choose from.'

What could I say? Especially as Evelyn and Sam were paying for everything. I decided not to argue with her, but I'd make sure that I chose a lemon dress. I knew that Lynne would back me up too.

To my relief, Tamara announced that she wouldn't be able to drop by next Saturday, as she was working in London all week. 'It won't matter as I'm not a bridesmaid,' she said with a bright smile – but I knew by the look that she exchanged with Evelyn that it was a dig. I was glad she wouldn't be there; I already hated her being involved with the wedding at all.

Lynne was free next Saturday, and eager to come to the manor with me. She was dying to meet Sam's parents and see where he lived. So we arranged for her to come to my flat and I'd drive us over.

'Wow! This is like something out of a magazine,' she said after I'd pressed the bell on the gate post and the gates opened to reveal the long drive and immaculate lawns.

'I know,' I said with a grin. ' Wait until you see inside!'

I'd half expected Tamara to turn up after all, but to my relief it was just us, Evelyn and Verity, who had brought a selection of bridesmaid dresses with her. Evelyn made it clear she loved a very elegant champagne dress, but I preferred an exquisite lemon Grecian-style design with a halter neck and sequin bodice. It really was stunning. Lynne loved it too and I was glad that she was there to back me up.

'I do think that champagne would be a better theme for your wedding, dear. It's such a sophisticated colour,' Evelyn said, hardly concealing her displeasure, but I wanted lemon; the colour of sunshine and happiness. I wanted our wedding day to be bright, cheerful and happy. So I stood my ground and ordered the lemon dress, telling her that Sam and I had agreed on that colour.

'Lemon is fun and very summery,' Verity said diplomatically. It was a win for her, whatever colour we chose.

'Evelyn's not that bad,' Lynne said when I drove us home later. 'You should meet Spencer's mum. Mind, I think it's a good job that you're not living there. She can be a bit overwhelming, can't she? She was pretty determined to have her choice today. Well done you for sticking to your guns. I know that they're paying for it so you feel a bit obliged to go along with what they like, but remember that it's *your* wedding.'

She was right about Evelyn being determined. I might have won over the colour of the bridesmaid's dress, but over the next couple of weeks, Evelyn ordered the wedding cake and the flowers without even consulting me. 'I know you're busy at work, dear, and I've kept to your colour theme of lemon and white,' she told me when she showed me the photos. The bouquets were beautiful, as was the three-tier wedding cake with its piped lemon icing and lemon fondant roses, so I didn't feel that I could complain. 'You have remembered to tell them about my allergy, so not to make the cake with nuts, haven't you?' I reminded her.

'Of course, dear. The bottom tier is light fruit and the other two tiers are sponge. That was Tamara's suggestion.' She patted my hand reassuringly.

Tamara again. Honestly, that woman was really getting to me. I couldn't wait until me and Sam moved into our own house. Only a couple of weeks to go.

But then, a week before we were due to exchange contracts on the house, Sam phoned me to say that the sale had fallen through. There had been a fire. No one was hurt, thankfully, but the kitchen was badly damaged and the Marshes were pulling out while they got it sorted out with the insurance. 'We couldn't go ahead even if the Marshes wanted to. We'd struggle to get a mortgage on the property until it was fully fixed and assessed after the fire damage,' Sam told me. I was devastated, although relieved that no one had been hurt.

'That's awful. That was our dream home. What are we going to do now? How long until they can fix it?' I'd already imagined Sam building a tree house in the huge oak tree in the garden for our children to play in.

'It could take months. But we'll find somewhere else.' His

voice was soft, soothing. 'It's horrible, but it's not the end of the world.'

Then I remembered that I'd given notice on my flat and was due to leave next Friday, ready to move into our new home. And the landlord already had a new tenant, so there was no way I could persuade him to allow me to stay a little longer. What was I going to do?

13

'Of course you won't be homeless. You can move in with us. Mum and Dad would be delighted to have you stay,' Sam said when, in a total panic, I reminded him of my situation. 'Don't worry, it will all be fine. I'll be over in a couple of hours and we can talk it through.'

Sam was so calm and matter-of-fact about it, but I didn't want to live with his parents. Evelyn was very kind, but she was a little overbearing, and I felt rather anxious around her. I messaged Lynne to tell her what had happened, and she immediately phoned me.

'Come and stay with us. Our sofa's comfy,' she offered. 'Spencer won't mind. It's better than moving in with your future in-laws. That's a recipe for disaster.'

If Lynne had been living alone, I might have been tempted but I'd feel in the way with Spencer there. And I really didn't want to live with anyone except Sam.

I thanked her and told her Sam was coming over in a bit and hopefully we'd work something out. I was so upset about losing the house we had both loved and having to start looking for another home.

Sam arrived with a bottle of wine, a big bunch of flowers and a box of chocolates. 'Mum said I have to tell you that you're very welcome to move in. She's invited you over to dinner tomorrow night to talk about it.'

'It's really kind of her, but I feel like I'd be imposing,' I said, trying to find the words to explain how I felt. I was also a bit worried that if I moved in with Sam, he wouldn't want to leave. Especially as Evelyn had pointed out a few times – with a well-meaning smile – that it seemed such a waste for us to spend all that money on buying a house when there were plenty of empty rooms in the manor. Harold always backed her up, assuring us both that we had a home with them as long as we wanted.

There had to be another option, I told myself. I could book into a B&B, but then I'd be spending money we could use for the wedding and the honeymoon.

Sam was desperate for me to live with him. 'I can't wait to wake up with you every day,' he said, gazing at me adoringly. It was what I wanted too, but in our own home. 'And it would make it so much easier to arrange the house viewings and finalise the wedding arrangements,' he pointed out. 'But only if you want to. I don't want to pressure you.' He gathered me into his arms. 'We could book you into a hotel or a B&B until the wedding, if you prefer.'

That was when it hit me that I would have to move into the manor once we were married, so what was the point of paying for a hotel room for the next few weeks? I felt trapped. If it hadn't been for the fire... *Don't be so selfish,* I scolded myself, *that poor family could have been killed.* It was lucky no one was in and that a neighbour spotted the smoke and called the fire brigade before any more damage was done.

'We'll find another house, I promise you,' Sam said. 'We'll find one we like just as much. I can't wait to have a home of our own.'

I couldn't either. I nestled into him, wishing that this hadn't happened. Wishing that next week we'd be moving into our own house, as we'd planned.

'Let's start looking right away,' Sam said. He reached down and took his laptop out of his briefcase.

We spent an hour or so searching but found nothing suitable. 'We'll keep looking and hopefully we might even find one that's empty with no chain and be able to push the sale through so we move in as soon as we come back from our honeymoon.' Sam pulled me to him and kissed me gently. 'It will be so much easier to organise things if you move in with me, sweetheart.'

He was right, I could see that. I was being churlish and ungrateful. His parents always made me welcome when I went over, and it was kind of them to offer me a home.

So when I went for dinner the next night, and Evelyn and Harold both told me how much they would love me to move in, I thanked them and said I'd be delighted to, if they were sure. They were so pleased that they opened a bottle of champagne to celebrate, which showed how much they really wanted me there. It felt good to be wanted, to feel that I was part of a family.

Now I'd accepted Sam's parents' offer to move in with them, I was actually looking forward to it. I'd be living with Sam, waking up every morning beside him, going home to him every night. And the manor was spectacular. I'd be living in luxury. I'd been silly to worry about it. It was all going to be okay, I told myself. We'd all be one big happy family.

So the next Friday evening, I packed my things, said goodbye to the little flat that had been my sanctuary for the past few years, handed over the keys to my landlord, and drove over to the manor, my new – temporary – home.

And that was my biggest mistake of all.

14

I pulled up behind Sam's Audi, turned off the engine and gazed at the manor, butterflies fluttering in my stomach. This was it. My independence gone, my little flat now someone else's home. I was moving in with Sam and his parents, my life changing forever. I was excited at this new stage in my life, but nervous too. The manor house was such a far cry from my aunt and uncle's semi-detached house in the suburbs, and my own one-bed flat. And I couldn't help remembering how stifled and anxious I'd felt living with my aunt and uncle. Was I doing the right thing moving in with Sam's parents and once again, living in someone else's home?

'If it doesn't work out, promise me you'll just get in your car and come here?' Lynne had said to me. I'd assured her that I would.

I opened the door and got out, my eyes still on the manor. A trickle of apprehension ran through me. I liked Harold and I liked Evelyn too, but there were times when she made me feel a little... inadequate. What if she got fed up with me being there? *It's only for a few weeks*, I reminded myself. *And Evelyn wouldn't invite me to live here if she didn't approve of me, would she? She'd be trying to keep me and Sam apart, not suggesting we live together.*

Sam walked over to join me. He slid his arm around my shoulders and kissed me on the cheek. 'Stop worrying. It'll all be fine,' he said. 'My parents are really looking forward to you moving in.'

I took a deep breath to calm myself down as, hand in hand, we strode over to the front door. Evelyn opened the door before Sam could put his key in it. She must have been looking out of the window, waiting for us to arrive.

'Welcome to your new home, my dear,' she greeted me, her face wreathed in a welcoming smile. 'I'm so pleased that you've decided to join us. I hope you'll be very happy here. Do come in and make yourself comfortable.'

I smiled back at her. 'Thank you. It's very kind of you to invite me to move in.'

'Nonsense, it's no trouble at all. We're delighted to have you here. Delighted.' She stepped aside to let me in. 'Please look on the manor as your home and help yourself to anything you need.'

Sam gave my shoulders a reassuring squeeze, as if to say, *See, I told you so.*

'Now, let me take your coat. Would you like a drink? Tea? Coffee? Or maybe wine?' Evelyn asked as she closed the door behind us.

'Thank you, Mum but I think Dana might want to go straight up, unpack and get settled in, don't you, sweetheart?' Sam's gaze rested on me.

I saw the look of disappointment on Evelyn's face and felt sorry for her. She was trying to make me welcome. It seemed rude not to have a quick cup of coffee with her and Harold when they had given me a roof over my head at such short notice. And the way Sam had worded it had made it seem like it was my choice not to. I didn't want them thinking that I was ungrateful.

'No rush. I'd love a coffee, thank you, Evelyn. Would you like me to make it?' I offered, wanting to let her know that I didn't expect her to wait on me whilst I was living there.

'Certainly not, you're a guest. Make yourselves comfy in the dining room and I'll bring the coffee in to you,' Evelyn said.

'Well, let me carry the cases up while you sit and talk to Mum and Dad. I'll only be a few minutes,' Sam said, heading for the stairs with the two cases that held all the possessions I had in the world.

'Harold will help you, too. Harold, get the rest of Dana's belongings out of the car,' Evelyn said.

I felt my cheeks go hot. 'That's all I've got. I rented my flat furnished, so it's only personal things, clothes and bedding,' I explained, feeling very embarrassed. It wasn't a lot to show for twenty-five years of being on this earth.

'Oh, I see. Well, it won't take you long to settle in, then,' Evelyn said, watching Sam go up the stairs with the cases. When he had reached the top and disappeared along the land-ing, she turned to me and said conspiratorially, 'I'm so pleased that Sam is settling down at last. I thought he would be a bach-elor forever. He's had his fair share of women, of course. There have been plenty who've tried to snare him over the years, as you can imagine – he's so successful and good-looking, as well as kind – but none have ever managed it. Until you.' The look she gave me made me feel like I'd been patted on the back for managing to pull it off. 'Now do go and sit in the drawing room while I make the coffee.'

She turned and headed down the hall to the kitchen, leaving me staring after her, her words repeating in my mind. Was she suggesting that I had gone out of my way to trap Sam? 'Snare him', she'd said. I shook my head. I was being silly, reading too much into her choice of words. Evelyn had never shown me anything other than kindness, even if she was a little bossy. Tamara had said that she'd thought Sam would never get married; maybe his mum had thought the same. I felt honoured that he had chosen me over all the women – women like Tamara – that he came into contact with every day.

'He's lucky to have you too,' Lynne had told me when I mentioned my doubts to her. 'You're gorgeous and clever and loyal. Tamara sounds shallow and spiteful – why would he be interested in her?'

Lynne had always been great at boosting my confidence. Sam loved me and I loved him, I reminded myself. Nothing else mattered.

'There, we can unpack them in a while.' Sam was bounding down the stairs towards me. He put his arm around my shoulder and gave me a big kiss. 'I'm sorry our house fell through, but won't it be lovely to be living under the same roof at last?'

It certainly would. And we were lucky to have our own personal space, I thought, as we went into the drawing room to have a cup of coffee with Sam's parents. Harold was seated in his favourite armchair, the newspaper on his lap, glasses perched on the end of his nose as usual.

'I'm sure you're wanting to get settled in, Dana, so have a quick cuppa to keep Evelyn happy and then you can both get off upstairs. You don't want to be spending all your time with us,' he said as we sat down on the sofa.

He was a quiet, thoughtful man, I thought, wondering not for the first time how two such opposite people managed to sustain an apparently happy marriage. 'It's very kind of you both to let me stay here,' I told him.

'That's what families do. And you're family now,' Harold said.

'Well, not quite, let's not jinx things!' Evelyn came through into the lounge carrying a tray with four cups on it, four small plates and a huge Victoria sponge. 'Help yourselves.'

Evelyn started talking about the wedding arrangements, reminding Sam that he had to go for the fitting for his suit, and that we both had to go to church for the next three Sundays to hear the banns read. There was a month to the wedding, but at last, it was all coming together. Lynne and me had final fittings the next weekend, so she was coming over for that and Evelyn would then keep my wedding dress in her dressing room for me until the day before the wedding, so that Sam wouldn't see it. Evelyn chatted away, and it was an hour later before we managed to escape to Sam's suite.

I was terribly disappointed about our house purchase not going ahead but at least we had these rooms to ourselves, and once inside our lounge, we could access all the other rooms in our suite without going out into the hall and back again, which made it seem like our own little flat. The only thing lacking was a kitchen, although there was a toaster, kettle and a few cups on a tray in a corner of the lounge and a small fridge, so we could make ourselves toast, and a drink when we wanted, which would be especially welcome in the mornings while we were getting ready. And the balcony from the lounge more than made up for not having a garden. I was sure that I'd spend most of my time sitting out there now the weather was warmer. *It'll be okay*, I told myself, *it's spacious and private; no wonder Sam hasn't been in a rush to move out.* I reassured myself that we'd probably hardly ever see Evelyn and Harold. Except that we had to go downstairs for our meals, I remembered. I wondered how that worked; would Evelyn be happy for me to cook for us separately? I mentioned it to Sam.

'Oh, don't worry about that. I always eat with my parents if I'm home, and Mum won't mind dishing up an extra plate for you.'

I wanted to say that I *did* mind, and that I preferred to cook my own food but it sounded petty. *Stop fretting – it will be nice to be waited on for a while*, I told myself.

'I've put your cases in my – our – room,' Sam corrected himself, 'and bought another desk for the study for you to use when you work from home.'

'Thank you.' He really had thought of everything. I walked into the bedroom and saw that he'd laid my case on the bed and opened it up. I looked around, seeing the rooms with fresh eyes now that this was going to be my home too. I'd always been impressed with how spacious and light the room was, and knew that the king-size bed was very comfy, but now my gaze took in the pale oak fitted wardrobes along the left wall and the panoramic window- which gave a marvellous view of the Malvern Hills. I glanced at the door to the en suite on the right wall, along with the full-length mirror and large, pale oak chest of drawers where several photographs of Sam and his parents were placed. I was going to be living in luxury compared to my studio flat.

'Do you want me to help you hang your clothes up?' Sam asked.

'No, I can manage,' I said, turning back and going over to the suitcase on my bed. The doors to one wardrobe were open and I could see that it was completely empty. 'You've cleared the whole wardrobe for me,' I said, surprised. I'd expected him to move some of his clothes over to make space for mine, but not clear a whole wardrobe. 'Thank you. That's very thoughtful of you.'

'Mum did it while I was at work,' Sam confessed. 'I was going to clear it but she got there before me. She's very helpful like that and delighted to have you staying here.'

So his mum came into his rooms while Sam was at work? I didn't feel very comfortable about that. *Stop stressing, she won't do it while you're living here,* I told myself. *It's different when it's just Sam. He's her son. She'll respect your privacy as a couple.*

Wouldn't she?

15

Sam had an appointment with his property consultant the next morning. 'I'll only be a few hours. Have a lie-in, there's no rush. Take your time settling in,' he told me as he kissed me goodbye.

I sat up in bed, sipping the cup of tea he'd made me, my mind going back to the evening before. Evelyn had cooked a lovely roast chicken dinner for us all and I'd helped clear away, although Evelyn insisted on putting the washing liquid in the dishwasher. Then Sam had asked if I wanted to watch a film. I'd agreed, thinking that we would go up to our room and watch it but Evelyn had immediately jumped in and said, 'Oh, Harold and I were going to watch a film too. Let's watch one together. I can open a bottle of wine and we can all have a cosy evening.' What could we do but agree? Although I really wanted a cosy evening snuggled up with Sam in our bed. It had been late by the time we finally managed to escape to our rooms, and Sam took me in his arms as soon as the door was closed behind us. 'Mum means well; she's just trying to make you feel welcome,' he murmured as he snuggled up to me.

I guessed he was right. And it was nice that his parents had accepted me into their home so readily. Besides, Sam and I would have plenty of time to ourselves. He'd be home at lunchtime so we had the rest of the weekend. Tea finished, I hopped out of bed and went for a shower. *I'm going to be happy here*, I thought as I padded barefoot over the carpet to the en suite. *I'm living in luxury in our own private apartment. And it is wonderful to be able to spend every day – and night – with Sam.*

It was a spacious rainfall shower with plenty of room for two, and as I stepped under the cascade of warm water, I couldn't help wishing that Sam was here to join me. We could always have a shower together tomorrow, I thought, and shivered with anticipation at the idea. I took my time, rubbing the shampoo gently into my hair, and then I rinsed it off, leaving the conditioner on for five minutes so that my hair would be soft. Quickly towel-drying it, I slipped on some shorts and a T-shirt, lightly made up my face and brushed my hair, leaving it to dry naturally while I finished my unpacking. I'd already hung up my clothes so they wouldn't get creased, but there were still some odds and ends to put away. Sam had emptied a bedside cabinet for me, and also some drawers in the large chest. He might have been an only child, but I was pleasantly surprised to see that he had no qualms about sharing. I opened the bedroom door to go and get the smaller case I'd left in the lounge last night and looked around in surprise as the lounge door opened. Was Sam back already?

'Morning,' Evelyn stepped inside. 'I've put on a pot of coffee, I thought you might like to join us. Tamara's popped in to catch up on all the news. She's come home for a bit to look after her mum, who's just had an operation.'

'Oh, I'm sorry to hear that about Julia. I hope she recovers quickly.' I didn't like to ask her what the operation was for; it seemed like prying. 'It's kind of you to invite me to join you and Tamara but I'm not really dressed for visitors. I was about to unpack the rest of my things,' I added, trying not to show how put out I felt that Evelyn had just stepped in without even knocking. I could have been undressed.

'Nonsense, you look absolutely fine. It's only a cup of coffee – no one expects you to be dressed up to the nines,' Evelyn had a smile on her lips but her words were firm. She stood in the doorway, waiting expectantly and I felt that I had no choice but to follow her down. Chatting with Tamara was the last thing I felt like doing, so I decided I'd just have a quick coffee, make polite conversation and then come back up.

Tamara was making the drinks, obviously very much at home in the kitchen. She looked stunning in a sleek, strapless floral dress that hugged her body and showed off her tan to perfection. She glanced over her shoulder as we walked in, a big smile on her bright red glossy lips. 'Well, hello again, Dana. I can't believe that you're marrying our Sam next month. Such a whirlwind romance.' Her voice dripped with what sounded like false friendliness to me.

'I know, it's come around very quickly. I can't believe it myself,' I agreed.

'Where did you meet? I've never asked,' Tamara said, bringing over a tray with three coffees – in pretty china cups and matching saucers – on it and placing it on the table. 'I can't imagine you mixing in the same circles, so I'm sure it wasn't at a restaurant or a dinner dance.'

I could feel Evelyn's eyes on me, waiting for the answer, and hoped that my cheeks didn't look as hot as they felt. 'I was... er... going to an interview, and the wind blew off Sam's hat.' I briefly related the story to her.

Tamara looked surprised. 'Goodness, love at first sight! I didn't think Sam was that impulsive. He's always been such a ditherer, takes ages to make up his mind about anything.'

'It was a bit of a shock for me and Harold too,' Evelyn said. 'You know I always hoped you two...'

I gasped at her hurtful words but neither of them noticed.

'Now, you know marriage isn't for me,' Tara said with a smile, as if suggesting that it was her choice she wasn't marrying Sam.

I'm not going to let her get to me, I resolved, but her next words startled me.

'No, much as I love Sam and didn't want to hurt him, and would have loved you as my mother-in-law, Evelyn, I'm far too much of my own person to have agreed to marry him.'

It was almost as if she was saying Sam had proposed to her and she had turned him down; that they had broken up because she was too independent. Why hadn't Sam told me that? When I'd brought up the subject of previous relationships, Sam had closed it down, insisting that the past didn't matter. He was right, of course; it didn't matter. We had both had previous relationships – Sam probably more than me as he was ten years older – yet, whilst I didn't want details of all his exes, when one of them was such a good family friend and had even been invited to our wedding, surely I should have been told?

It doesn't matter, it's me Sam loves, I reminded myself. Tamara was history.

Except that she was still very much part of the family. She and Evelyn were chatting away as if she had never dropped that bombshell statement, as if I wasn't sitting at the table with them, stunned by her revelation... as if she was the one marrying Sam, not me.

Then the back door opened and Harold came in from the garden. 'Boots!' Evelyn ordered, pointing to his feet.

Harold looked meekly down at the wellingtons on his feet. 'They're not muddy,' he said mildly. 'I only came in for a drink.'

'Stay where you are, I'll get you one.' Evelyn got to her feet, walked over to the fridge, took out the filter jug and poured a glass of water, which she handed to Harold. 'Please take your boots off next time.'

'Sorry.' Harold retreated back to the garden, closing the

door behind him. It was obvious who the boss was in that relationship, I thought. Harold was so mild and obliging I doubted if he ever raised his voice.

'Honestly, I don't know why he insists on doing the gardening himself when we pay a gardener to come in three times a week,' Evelyn said, exasperated. She sat back down at the table. 'I was telling Tamara about the wedding before you came down, Dana. She's really looking forward to it.'

'I certainly am. It's an event I never thought I would see. I don't think I'll believe it until I actually witness it.'

I pasted a smile on my face and sipped my coffee, determined not to let her words get to me. I wished that Tamara wasn't coming to our wedding, but as she and her parents were such dear family friends, and it was Sam and his parents who were paying for the wedding, I couldn't really object. I was stunned by her comments, though. The knowledge that I was the first woman Sam had been serious enough to propose to, to live with, made me feel special but Tamara was suggesting that he had proposed to her and she'd turned him down. And Evelyn had openly said she wished that Tamara – the daughter she had always wanted – was going to be marrying Sam instead of me. I was certain now that Evelyn was only making me welcome for Sam's sake. Both women had made me feel very uncomfortable, but I was determined not to show it. I might not be from the same social set as Tamara and the other women Sam had previously gone out with but I was kind and loyal, as Lynne had reminded me. I was resilient too – I'd had to be – and didn't expect everything given to me on a plate, as someone like Tamara might. I appreciated everything Sam and his parents were doing for me, and I vowed that I'd be a good wife to him. We adored each other.

I was suddenly aware that Tamara and Evelyn had both stopped talking and were staring at me. 'Are you feeling all right, Dana? You look a bit pale. You're not getting an attack of pre-wedding nerves, are you?' Tamara asked.

'No, of course not. I'm fine, thank you, but I do have a lot to do. So if you'll excuse me...' I gulped down the coffee and hastily left. I had barely stepped into the hall when I heard Tamara say, 'Well, I never thought our Sam would marry such a meek, compliant little mouse.'

'There's still time for him to change his mind,' Evelyn murmured and they both laughed.

I didn't wait to hear any more. I hurried up the stairs to our rooms, closing the door firmly behind me. Leaning back against it, I took some deep breaths to calm myself down. My heart was racing as if I was under threat. And that was how I felt. An ominous sense of foreboding shivered through me. I wanted to grab my bags and run.

16

Try as I might, I couldn't get Tamara's words out of my mind. Was that really how she saw me? As a meek, compliant little mouse? Was that how they all saw me? Sam too? But I *was* being compliant, wasn't I? Going along with all Evelyn's wedding plans and moving into the manor when we could have rented a place together. Sam had suggested getting *me* a B&B, not us renting somewhere together. Why not?

Was I doing the right thing, marrying Sam? It had all happened so fast; we'd both been swept off our feet by the depth of our feelings.

The questions went round and round in my head. I was so anxious I didn't notice that I'd scratched my wrist so much I'd made it bleed. I looked at the deep scratches in dismay. I didn't want to be starting that again. Whenever I was anxious as a child, I'd scratch myself without realising that I was doing it. My aunt scolded me about it, but the more she scolded, the more anxious I got, and often went to school with my arms covered in plasters. I'd managed to get it under control as I grew up and moved into my own flat. Then it had resurfaced again with all the problems with Nick, but subsided as I got my life together again. I couldn't let it return now. I didn't want my arms covered in scratches on my wedding day. *Calm down for God's sake and stop overreacting*, I told myself as I fetched a plaster to put on the scratch.

Why would Sam move out into a B&B when it made more sense for me to move in here – there was plenty of room? And what does it matter if he once went out with Tamara? I lived with Nick.

When Sam came home, he took one look at my face and gave me a big hug. 'What's the matter, sweetheart? You look upset.' Then his eyes drifted to the plaster on my wrist. 'You've cut yourself?'

'I caught it on the suitcase,' I lied. 'It's only a little scratch.' I lay my head on his shoulder, his concern and embrace consoling me and making my worries seem insignificant. I didn't want him to think that I was jealous and insecure. Even though I was.

'What's troubling you?' he asked again.

'It's nothing really but...'

He put his finger under my chin and tilted it. 'Go on.'

His eyes were full of care and kindness, so I blurted it out. 'Your mum came in to ask me to join her for a cup of coffee, and Tamara was there. And, well, the way she was talking it was...' I lowered my gaze, feeling like an immature, jealous child. 'Like you two went out together and you wanted to marry her, but she refused.'

'I think you might have misinterpreted her words, Dana,' Sam said gently. 'Yes, our families are close friends and our mothers – as mothers who are friends often do – hoped Tam and I would get married, but that was their little fantasy. Tam and I are friends, and have never been anything more.'

I lifted my eyes to look at him and could see that he was sincere. 'Sorry, it's just that I feel a little out of place here. Your mum is so... refined... and Tamara is beautiful and clever and...' I swallowed, wondering whether to tell him about the nasty way

Tamara had described me and how Evelyn had said there was still time for him to change his mind, but I worried that it would make me sound petty and immature. And I didn't want to cause any trouble; it was awkward enough living here already.

Sam pulled me into his arms and kissed me soundly. 'You are beautiful too, and kind, and gentle. You're perfect and I love you exactly the way you are.'

Did he really think that? *Of course he does, he's marrying you.*

'I know it's a bit awkward for you living here, darling, but you'll soon settle in, and it's not for long. Let me have a quick shower, then how about we browse the local estate agents' websites for houses for sale? If we see any we like, we might be able to organise a couple of viewings for tomorrow. That will cheer you up, right?'

'Yes, please,' I donned a smile. 'I'll make us a coffee.'

Sam's eyes twinkled. 'Or you could join me in the shower?'

I grinned. 'Now that sounds like a great idea.' How could I doubt that Sam loved me when he made it so obvious that he found me irresistible?

He took my hand and pulled me to my feet, wrapping his arms around me, tracing a trail of kisses from my lips down my neck.

We both sprang apart as the door opened and Evelyn stepped in. 'Lunch is almost ready,' she said.

Sam looked at me apologetically. 'Give me five minutes to take a shower,' he said.

'Of course,' she nodded. 'Why don't you come down now, Dana? We're eating in the garden today. You can help me carry everything out.'

Bang went our shared shower.

Sam squeezed my hand. 'If you don't mind, darling.'

'Glad to help,' I said, and followed Evelyn down the stairs. I was going to have to talk to Sam about putting a lock on the door. We couldn't have Evelyn walking in on us like that; we needed privacy as a couple.

Evelyn had made ham and cheese wheatmeal rolls and a summer salad, followed by strawberries and cream. She opened a bottle of prosecco too, and we all sat out in the garden for a couple of hours, chatting and enjoying the sunshine. It was very pleasant, and I felt foolish for my earlier resentment and turmoil. It was only natural Evelyn would have become fond of Tamara, given she was the daughter of their close friends and nearest neighbours, and that Tamara and Sam had become good friends too and then retained that friendship as they grew up. Yes, their remarks had been spiteful, but they weren't to know that I would overhear them.

Enjoyable as the afternoon was, I was anxious to get started on the property search we'd planned though and was trying to think of a polite way to broach the subject when Sam got to his feet.

'Thank you for a delicious lunch, Mum, but Dana and I have some things to do now. We want to try to organise some house viewings for tomorrow.'

I got up too. 'Let me help you clear away first.'

'Don't worry about that. Ruby is in today – she'll sort it out.' Ruby was the new cleaner. She'd been with the family a month or so now, coming three times a week – including Saturdays – for several hours at a time, an amazing luxury to me. 'Don't forget that we all have to go to church tomorrow to hear the banns read,' Evelyn reminded us.

'We'll be there,' Sam promised.

Then we went upstairs and worked our way through some estate agents' websites, compiling a list of houses we were interested in, and securing a viewing for that evening and two for the next day. I felt excited, sure that one of them would be right for us.

'We'll go and see this house now, then have a bite to eat.

And we'll have lunch out tomorrow before the other viewings,' Sam suggested, and I readily agreed, happy to spend some time together.

'Ah, there you both are,' Evelyn was walking up the stairs as we came down. 'I was on my way up to let you know that I've invited the vicar for lunch at one tomorrow, after the church service. You will be there, won't you?' It was more of an order than a question.

'It's a bit awkward, Mum. We have a couple of houses to view tomorrow so were going to eat out,' Sam told her.

'Surely you can change the appointments for another time? It will seem so rude if you aren't there when the vicar has agreed to marry you at such short notice, and is reading out your banns in church.' She gave Sam a disappointed look. 'And I don't know why you're bothering to look for another house when you have this whole suite to yourselves. It's just throwing money away. Or are your father and I so difficult to live with that you can't wait to get away?' Her voice broke a bit, and she blinked as if she was fighting back tears.

Sam immediately stepped towards her and put his arms around her. 'Of course not, Mum. You and Dad are great. We're very grateful for you putting us up, aren't we, Dana?'

'Yes, it's very kind of you,' I quickly agreed, feeling guilty as I saw the tears glistening in the older woman's eyes, but hoping that Sam wouldn't agree to us living here just to make her happy.

'You know what it's like when you get married, Mum. You want your own home. To be independent.' He gave her shoulders a comforting squeeze. 'Look, we'll stay for lunch with the vicar tomorrow and move the house viewings to a bit later. Don't be upset. I won't be moving very far away and you'll be welcome anytime.'

Evelyn dabbed her eyes with a tissue. 'Sorry, darling. I'm being silly. It's only natural that you young people want your own place. Take no notice of me. It's just that I'll miss you so much.' She patted his hand.

'Poor Mum, she's going to be lost without me,' Sam said when Evelyn had finally gone back downstairs. 'You don't mind if we move the viewings back until later, do you, sweetheart? I think we really should have lunch with the vicar.'

I shook my head. 'Not at all.' I felt a bit panicky though, sure that Evelyn was going to try to persuade us to continue living with them. *I can't and I don't want to. Not with how she walks in anytime she feels like it, and Tamara always popping in now she's moved back home for a bit.* We'd never have a moment to ourselves. I didn't say anything about my fears to Sam, though, not wanting him to think that I was ungrateful and being disrespectful to his mum.

I loved the house as soon as I set eyes on it. Victorian, with a walled garden and ivy growing up around the door, it looked enchanting. Inside, there was a lovely big lounge with a conservatory, a kitchen-diner, a utility room, a large garden, three decent-sized bedrooms, two with en suites and best of all, it was empty, so would be a quick sale but Sam shook his head. 'It's a bit too close to the neighbours, and I'd prefer a separate dining room to a diner-kitchen,' he said. 'Like the Marshes' house.'

If he thought that house was near to the neighbours, he should try living in a flat! I thought. I could understand his reservations, though. He was used to a separate dining room, and the 'neighbours' living a few minutes away. Even so, I liked it. I could imagine us living there.

Sam squeezed my hand. 'I know that you're anxious for us to get our own home, and so am I, but it's too important a decision to rush. We can get one so much better. Let's see what the houses we're viewing tomorrow are like,' he said.

For a moment, I wondered if I should stand my ground;

Tamara's words that I was meek and compliant were still ringing in my ears.

I'm not meek and compliant; I'm easy-going and considerate, I reminded myself. *And it's important that we both like the house.* Besides, we had chosen one we both liked before – even if the sale had fallen through at the last minute – and would do again. I had to stop panicking. We would soon be in our new home and away from Evelyn.

17

After lunch with the vicar the next day, which was actually very pleasant and made me feel even more excited about the forthcoming wedding, we prepared to go on our other two house viewings.

'Harold and I would really love to come with you, if we're not in the way, of course?' Evelyn said.

My heart sank as Sam turned to me. 'Would you mind?'

Yes, I did mind. I wanted this to be just me and Sam, but how could I say that without sounding rude and petulant? I remembered how Evelyn had pointed out a few things she didn't like about the Marshes' house and how I'd been worried that Sam would pull out of the purchase. I didn't want her to do that again. Then the perfect answer came to me.

'I think we should do the initial viewings ourselves, like we did before; it seems a bit much if four of us turn up, especially on a Sunday. But if we decide we like one of them, your parents can come with us to the next viewing.' I said.

'Yes, you're right,' Sam nodded.

I could see the sparks of annoyance in Evelyn's eyes, but she pasted a smile on her face. 'Of course. We wouldn't want to intrude. We just thought it would be helpful to have someone else's opinion. We might notice things that you don't. Buying a house is a big commitment; you need to be sure that you get the right one for you.'

'Don't worry, Mum. As Dana said, if one of these houses is suitable, we will definitely take you both to see it, just as we did before,' Sam promised.

'I'm pleased to hear it. But do you have to dash off right now? We've bought a new bench for the garden and Harold could do with a hand putting it into place. It will only take a minute. Why don't you go out with them, Dana? You can help them decide where to put it,' Evelyn said, without giving us the chance to object.

I was sure they could decide that without my help but agreed anyway. Leaving my handbag on the chair, I went outside with Sam and Harold.

The bench wasn't that heavy, but clearly was too much for Harold by himself. After a bit of debate, we decided it looked best by the hedge, facing down towards the fountain and flowerbeds.

That done, we all went back inside, and I grabbed my bag ready to go to the house viewings. Luckily, it hadn't taken long to put the bench into place and we still had plenty of time.

Evelyn sidled up to me. 'You could do with a quick brush of your hair and retouch of your lipstick, if you don't mind me saying so, dear,' she whispered.

Gosh, I must look a mess for her to mention it! 'Thanks.' I opened my handbag and reached inside for my brush then cried out in pain as something cut into my hand.

'Owww!' I shrieked, pulling my hand out of the bag, my eyes widening in horror when I saw that my hand was dripping in blood. What had happened? How had I cut my hand?

'What the hell?' Sam was beside me in a flash, looking at my bleeding hand, then grabbing my handbag and tipping the contents out onto the coffee table. Out tumbled my purse, phone, lipstick, tissues, screwed up receipts – and compact mirror, which was cracked with a jagged edge sticking out. I gaped at it in disbelief. How had that happened? I'd used it earlier and it was completely fine. At no point had I dropped my bag. I'd put it carefully onto the chair when we went out into the garden. I hadn't even knocked it against anything. How could the mirror crack just like that?

Harold shot a look at Evelyn, who was horrified. 'Oh my goodness!' she gasped, her hand flying to cover her mouth, her eyes wide. She grabbed the newspaper from the coffee table and a handful of tissues from the box, dashed over to me and placed the newspaper under my hand, which was dripping blood onto the carpet, then handed me some tissues. 'Wrap these around your hand to stem the blood while I go and get something to clean you up with,' she said.

I couldn't move. I was frozen to the spot, my eyes glued to my gashed hand and dripping blood. Then I started shaking as I realised how much more serious this could have been. What if the broken glass had cut an artery in my wrist? How had this happened?

Sam put his arm around my shoulder. 'It'll be okay. Mum will sort it, don't worry.'

Evelyn was soon back with the first aid kit and a bowl of water. It stung like mad as she wiped the blood from my hand and I bit my lip trying not to cry out. Not only was I worried how this had happened, I was also concerned that if we didn't hurry up, we'd be late for our first house viewing.

A look of concern crossed Evelyn's face as she peered at the cut. 'It's a very nasty gash. You need to be more careful, Dana. It's a wonder you didn't slice your hand open.'

' I don't understand how it happened...' I protested.

Sam was wrapping the broken mirror with a sheet of newspaper. 'You must have dropped your bag and the impact broke
the mirror.' His eyes were full of concern.

'I didn't drop my bag!' I protested. 'And the mirror was fine
this morning. You saw me use it when I touched up my lipstick.'
I couldn't understand it. I had used the mirror just before we
came downstairs.

'It can't just break by itself, Dana,' Sam pointed out.

Evelyn was still peering at the cut. 'I think this needs
stitches – it's very deep. You should take her to the hospital,
Sam.' She picked up a bandage and started to wrap it around
my hand.

'I don't think I need to go to the hospital right now. This
bandage will keep it clean,' I said, even though deep down I
knew that Evelyn was right and I probably did need a couple of
stitches. I tried not to wince as she finished wrapping the
bandage. My hand felt really sore. 'It'll be fine until tomorrow
and I'll go to the doctor's. The nurse will stitch it,' I protested.
'We've got the house viewings to go to.'

Sam shook his head. 'I think you need to get this checked
out, darling. Come on, let's get you to the hospital. I can
rearrange the house viewings.'

I felt like crying, and not just because my hand was hurting
like hell. I didn't want Sam to rearrange the viewings. Someone
else might see the houses and put in an offer first. It was too late,
though. Sam was already on the phone to the estate agents,
apologising and telling them that he would phone later to
rebook. I bit back tears of pain and frustration.

Harold suddenly appeared by my side, holding out my bag.
'I've cleaned it all out for you. There's no glass inside, I promise.
I've taken the liberty of wiping all your things down, to make
sure they're okay, and putting them back inside too.'

'Thank you,' I said gratefully, thinking how unobtrusively he'd done that for me.

'Come on, darling. Let's get you to hospital; that must be very painful,' Sam told me. As he placed his hand around my shoulder and led me out, I glanced over at Evelyn and was sure I caught a smirk on her face, which was quickly replaced with a look of concern. 'I hope you won't need many stitches, dear.'

She's pleased that I've hurt my hand and we can't go to the viewings, I suddenly realised. *She doesn't want Sam to move out. She wants to keep him here.* I bet Evelyn had only wanted to go with us so she could point out faults with the houses and talk Sam out of buying one. Well, I was going to make sure that Sam rebooked those viewings as soon as possible. I didn't want to stay here any longer than I had to. Evelyn might have been friendly and welcoming on the surface, but she was too controlling, too possessive with Sam. She never gave us any time alone and wanted to be involved in everything we did. Perhaps it was because he was her only child and she'd had him late in life, but even so, she had to learn to let go of Sam and she wouldn't do that until we moved out. And, whether she likes it or not, we are not staying here.

It wasn't until much later, when we'd returned from the hospital with my hand now stitched and bandaged, that I remembered the look that Harold had shot at Evelyn when he saw my cut hand. And how Evelyn had insisted that I go out and help Sam and Harold with the bench. It was almost as if she had wanted us all out of the house.

And when I came in, she had insisted that I tidied my hair and touched up my make-up. Which meant I had to open my bag to get my lipstick and mirror.

A sinister thought wormed its way into my mind. Had Evelyn smashed the mirror and put it back in my bag in the hope that I would cut my hand and not be able to go to the house viewings?

I batted it away instantly. That sounded crazy.

But it was the only thing that made sense. I knew that Evelyn desperately wanted to keep Sam at home with her. Would she do anything to stop us moving out into our own house?

18

The estate agent had managed to move the viewings to Monday afternoon. I was working from home that day, but when I explained to Tasha, my boss, about my injured hand, she said I could take the afternoon off if I could just finish doing some emails for her. Sam managed to reschedule his afternoon appointments but had to go into work early in the morning to get some paperwork done, so I went straight into the bedroom we used as an office to work. It proved a bit difficult with my sore right hand – which had indeed required three stitches and now had a dressing on it – but fortunately, I had audio software on my laptop so could keep the typing to a minimum. I was lucky the cut wasn't worse, and was still puzzled about how it had happened. In the light of the day, I guessed that I must have knocked the bag against the arm of the chair when I put it down. It was ridiculous to believe that Evelyn would deliberately break my mirror then put it back in my bag.

Work finally finished, I shut down my laptop and went into the lounge to make myself a cup of tea before I showered and changed. I was excited about the viewings we had today; we'd both been really impressed with the properties when we viewed them online and I was sure one of them would be suitable for us. I hoped so. I was desperate for us to have our own place.

Taking my tea with me, I headed for the en suite, undressed and put a plastic glove on my hand to protect the dressing, then stepped into the shower and turned it on. Lathering myself with shower cream, I daydreamed about living in our own house, where we could lock the door and shut everyone out. I was sick of Evelyn walking in whenever she wanted.

I'd showered and was struggling to zip up my dress when Sam came back. 'Let me help you,' he said, hurrying over to do it up for me.

'Thanks,' I said, turning around to kiss him.

'Is your hand painful?' Sam searched my face. 'You look a little pale. I could postpone the viewings.'

I shook my head vehemently. 'No, I'm fine. I'm looking forward to going.'

There was no way I was going to postpone the viewings. I couldn't wait to move into our own home.

Evelyn was placing a beautifully arranged vase of flowers in the hall when we came down the stairs.

'How's your hand today, Dana?' she asked.

'It's okay, thank you,' I replied.

'Thank goodness for that. Those handbag mirrors are dangerous. I'd get one in a case if I were you, dear. We don't want anything like that to happen again.'

'I will,' I told her.

'I expect you're both off to your house viewings soon. Do let me know how you get on. I hope one of them is suitable for you. Although why you want to throw money away on buying a house when this one is plenty big enough for all of us, I'll never know.' She shook her head in mock despair.

'Thanks, Mum. We're feeling hopeful, aren't we, darling?' Sam turned to me and I nodded.

I fell in love with the first house as soon as we walked in. It was even better than the Marshes' house. It was a large, detached house with a double garage, electric gates (hooray, Evelyn and Harold couldn't just pop in!), three bedrooms and a secure back garden. I could just imagine our children playing there. The second house was nice too, but I felt that it didn't have as much character as the previous one. Sam really liked it though, and I could understand why. It was more modern and spacious.

'There's a few people interested in this one, so I wouldn't dally about too much if you want it,' the estate agent said as we left. 'Phone me if you want another viewing tomorrow to help you make up your mind.'

'Thank you. We'll talk about it tonight and let you know,' Sam told him.

'Oh, Tam's here,' Sam said, when we got back to the manor and saw a car parked in the driveway. I suppressed a groan. I hoped that she wasn't going to be a regular visitor while she was at home, looking after Julia.

As we opened the door and stepped inside, Evelyn popped her head out from the kitchen. 'Do come and join us in the garden. Tamara is here,' she added unnecessarily.

I really, really wanted to go straight upstairs, but Sam had already taken my hand and was heading down the hall.

Harold, Evelyn and Tamara were all sitting around the wicker table, where a bottle of cava stood in a bucket of ice next to three glasses containing various amounts of the bubbly drink. There was also a bowl of crisps and some strawberries. Tamara turned as we came out and flashed a big smile at Sam. 'Hi, how did the house-hunting go?'

'We've seen two that we like, so we're going to discuss them this evening, and maybe take another look tomorrow,' Sam told her.

'Do sit down, Dana, you look a bit pale.' Tamara indicated

the chair next to her. She glanced at my bandaged hand. 'I heard you had a nasty accident yesterday.'

'It could have been so much worse,' Sam said as I reluctantly sat down in the chair. 'Thank goodness she didn't cut an artery.' He perched on the end of the wall so that he was slightly behind, and between me and Tamara.

'So lucky. Now tell us about the houses. Which one is your favourite?' Tamara said, changing the subject from my cut hand.

'We have a slight difference in opinion on that.' Sam smiled. 'We're going to sit down and do a list of pros and cons tonight.'

'Really? Tell us more.' Tamara looked really interested, as did Evelyn and Harold. 'Do you have photos of them?'

Sam got up the estate agent's website on his phone and showed them photos of both houses. Evelyn and Tamara immediately cooed over the one Sam liked, saying how modern it was. 'Such a fantastic layout, and it seems you'll get plenty of light,' Tamara said. 'And the kitchen and dining room look perfect for hosting dinner parties.' She turned to smile at me. 'Someone in Sam's position will be expected to entertain clients now and again. You'll have to hone your cooking skills.'

I hadn't thought what married life would be like with Sam; I'd been too caught up with the wonder of being his wife. Yes, he was an accountant, and a successful one, but it hadn't occurred to me how that might mean he'd be holding dinner parties, entertaining clients and business colleagues. He hadn't done any of that while we were dating. I shot Sam a questioning look, but he was too busy showing Tamara the photos on his phone to notice me. I tried to douse the flames of jealousy and insecurity that were rising in me as I watched them huddled over the screen, their heads close together. We'd never discussed what he expected of me as a wife, I realised.

What about what you expect of him as a husband? I could almost hear Lynne's voice in my head, telling me to stick up for myself and not be a pushover.

'And this is Dana's favourite,' he said, switching to the listing.

There was a silence. I felt the blood rush to my cheeks. None of them liked it.

'I can see why. It's got a lot of character and the garden is beautiful,' Harold said. I could have hugged him. He was smiling reassuringly at me now and I found the courage to speak up.

'Yes, it has. The photos don't really do it justice.'

'I'd love to see it. Can you get another appointment, perhaps tomorrow or Wednesday evening so we can come and view them both with you?' Evelyn asked.

'I'll give the estate agent a call now and find out,' Sam said, dialling the number. 'Answerphone,' he mouthed as he left a message.

'The banns are being read again in church on Sunday. Will you be attending? You could join us for lunch afterwards?' Evelyn asked Tamara.

'Thanks, but I've got plans for the weekend,' she replied, to my relief.

Just then Sam's phone rang. It was the estate agent confirming that we could see both houses tomorrow evening after work.

'Excellent. Harold and I are both free. We can come with you,' Evelyn said to my dismay.

19

'It is charming, but it's a bit higgledy-piggledy, dear.' Evelyn managed to make the word 'charming' sound like an insult. 'And it needs compete renovation. Do you really want the bother of all that?'

As I'd expected, Evelyn was making it clear that she didn't like 'my' choice. As soon as she walked in, she wrinkled her nose with distaste.

I bit my lip. Seeing the house through Evelyn's eyes, I had to agree that it was a bit dated, but it had such a homely feel. I could imagine me and Sam having a family there. Children playing in the garden, meals around the table in the kitchen. We would be happy here, I knew we would. 'I think it's homely and cosy,' I said defensively.

Evelyn nodded. 'I see what you mean, dear, but is "homely" the look you're going for, Sam? Someone in your position needs to have a home suitable for inviting people to, holding the occasional dinner party in. Quaint as this house is, I don't think it's really suitable for your entertaining needs, do you?'

Entertaining? That was what Tamara had said yesterday, and I hadn't had a conversation about this with Sam yet. I was only a basic cook. To my relief, he noticed my panic this time and gave me a reassuring smile. 'Don't worry, we won't be entertaining a lot, and when we do, I'll get caterers in.'

Evelyn pursed her lips disapprovingly but said nothing.

As I had guessed, Evelyn preferred the next house, Sam's favourite. 'Oh, this is perfect,' she said, admiring the spacious lounge with its white walls that led into a big dining room. 'This is more like the sort of house a successful accountant like you should live in. You have to think of your position, Sam.' She frowned. 'The kitchen is a little on the small side though, and the garden could do with being a bit bigger. What if you want to hold a garden party?'

She was looking for faults, I was sure of it. The kitchen, with its fitted cupboards and island in the middle, was plenty big enough, and the garden was huge.

'Honestly, dear, I think you should take your time,' she continued. 'Look at a few more properties. There is absolutely no rush. You've got that spacious suite of rooms to live in for as long as you like.'

'I know, Mum, and we're very grateful, but we really do want to start off married life in our own house,' Sam told her gently.

'As I said yesterday, there is a lot of interest in this house. It's empty and all the paperwork is in order, so it would be a very quick sale,' the estate agent said. 'I would urge you not to take too long to make up your mind because I think it will be snapped up soon. We already have a couple interested; they're just sorting out their mortgage.'

I made a snap decision. Although I loved the other house, I would prefer to live in this one than stay any longer than necessary with Evelyn and Harold and if I agreed to this house Sam would probably put in an offer right away.

'I think you're right and this house is more suitable for us, Sam,' I said, touching his arm. 'I'm happy to go for it if you are.'

'You don't have to decide now...' Evelyn started to say but Sam nodded.

'Yes, I am.' He turned to the estate agent. 'We'll offer the full asking price. And we are chain-free, and have got a mortgage agreed in principle already, as our last place fell through.'

'I do think you're being a bit hasty, dear. Isn't he, Harold?' Evelyn looked to her husband for support. 'You need to look around a house a few times before you put an offer. It's such a big decision.'

'They're old enough to make that decision, dear,' Harold mumbled.

'We're both delighted with it,' Sam assured her. 'It's the perfect home for us and we'll be able to move in when we come back from our honeymoon.'

I caught a strange expression on Evelyn's face before she turned away as if to compose herself. Was she angry? It unnerved me for a moment as I realised how much she didn't want Sam to leave home. Was that why Sam had never moved out before?

The estate agent phoned the buyers, ending the call with a big smile. 'They've accepted your offer,' he said. 'Congratulations.'

I hugged Sam gleefully. We'd done it. We'd got our own house. And, as it was empty and ready to go, hopefully nothing would go wrong this time.

Evelyn had regained her composure now and congratulated us both as if she really meant it. I was puzzled, had I imagined that she was angry?

I had the impression that Evelyn wasn't very pleasant when she didn't get her own way and there was no way I wanted to get on the wrong side of her. I wanted us all to be one big happy family. So the sooner Sam and I were in our own house, the better. And what did it matter if it wasn't my first choice? Both houses were a big step up from the one-bedroomed flat I'd been living in. Being part of a couple meant sharing and compromising sometimes. It was a small price to pay for a loving husband and a gorgeous home.

'Let's go and get changed, then we'll go out for a meal to celebrate,' Sam told me when we got home. 'How about the Chinese restaurant? I can book us a table for about nine?'

'Perfect!' I said, beaming.

Evelyn looked disappointed. 'I've already got dinner organised – I prepared it earlier. Salmon en croute and summer salad, followed by strawberry pavlova, your favourite. I thought we could all celebrate together. Unless you prefer not to, of course. It's just that you're not going to be with us much longer, so your father and I want to spend as much time as we can with you.'

'I guess we could go for a Chinese tomorrow...' Sam looked at me and I nodded. Much as I had been looking forward to having a meal out together, I didn't want to upset Evelyn any further. Although I didn't want to live with my in-laws, I did want a good relationship with them, if possible. After all, we were only with them for a little while longer, we'd be moving in to our own home in a few weeks.

I helped Evelyn lay the table, putting out four place mats, napkins and cutlery sets. 'Would you set another one please, dear? Tamara has just messaged to say she's bringing back a book she borrowed, so I've invited her to dinner too.'

It's a wonder she hadn't invite her to come and see the house with us, I thought, annoyed.

'I'll finish laying the table while you freshen up and get changed,' Evelyn offered.

Get changed? I was wearing a perfectly respectable summer skirt and top, why did I have to get changed for dinner at home? Sam had already gone upstairs, saying he needed to send a couple of emails so I couldn't turn to him for support. Before I could reply, the kitchen door opened.

'Yoohoo!' Tamara stepped in, looking drop-dead gorgeous in

a vintage, floral, off-the-shoulder maxi dress that revealed an expanse of flawless golden skin, immaculate make-up and her shining dark bob.

She held out a bottle of champagne. 'I've brought this with me so we can celebrate properly.' She walked over to Evelyn and kissed her, then Harold, then me. 'Congratulations! I hear you've made an offer on the house. I'm so pleased for you both. I hope it all goes through this time.' She put the bottle of champagne down on the table. 'You're going to miss Sam though, aren't you, Evelyn?'

'We will, and it seems such a waste of money when they have their own suite upstairs. Still,' she lowered her voice to a whisper, obviously not intending me to hear, 'what Dana wants, Dana gets.'

Her cutting words made me jerk my head around to see if she was serious but Evelyn had turned her back on me and was talking to Tamara, who was looking over her shoulder at me in amusement, obviously realising that I'd heard Evelyn's spiteful words. I swallowed. That was so unfair. It was only natural that I would want to start off married life in my own house. It was what Sam wanted too. And I had given in and let him have his choice of house. One minute they were accusing me of being a pushover, and now they were insinuating I was demanding. I just couldn't win with them.

'Sorry to take so long...' Sam came in, pausing as he noticed Tamara. 'Hello, Tam, what brings you here?'

'Evelyn invited me to join in your celebrations. I hear you've put in an offer on the house.' Tamara sashayed over and gave Sam a kiss on the cheek. 'I expect you and Dana are very excited.'

'We are,' Sam said, his face breaking into a smile. He walked over to me and put his arm around my shoulders. 'We can't wait to be in our own home, can we, darling?'

'It certainly will be a new experience for you, Sam. I look forward to seeing it,' Tamara teased.

'As soon as we get settled in our new house, we'll invite you around for dinner, won't we, darling?' Sam said, turning to me.

That was the last thing I wanted, but I forced a bright smile on my face as I nodded. Of course, Sam would want to entertain his parents and friends in their new home.

I felt awkward all through the meal. Tamara dominated the conversation, bringing up things from their childhood, laughing at shared jokes that I wasn't party to. It was as if I was invisible as they all chatted and laughed around her.

'Would you get the pavlova and cream for us, please, Dana?' Evelyn asked when the main course was finished.

'Of course.' I got to my feet and went to fetch it, glad to be away from the conversation for a bit. When I returned, I placed the pavlova on the table and was about to put the jug of cream down between Tamara and Evelyn when I felt someone jolt my elbow. The jug tipped up and cream poured out over the table.

'You *are* clumsy, aren't you?' Tamara said, her eyes dancing with amusement. Had she deliberately nudged me?

Evelyn tutted and immediately jumped up, grabbing a pile of serviettes to soak up the cream. Tamara got up too. 'I'll go and get a cloth.'

'I'm sorry,' I stammered.

'Accidents happen,' Harold said, giving me a reassuring smile.

I was sure that Tamara had deliberately made me spill the cream to make me look bad in front of Sam. To show him that I wasn't a suitable wife for him. That I'd show him up. I gritted my teeth and said nothing as Tamara cleaned up the spilt cream. *If only the damn woman would go home!*

Finally, Tamara got to her feet, ready to go. 'I'll see you out,' Sam said, walking to the door with her, leaving me feeling like a spare part.

'Those two get on so well. It's a shame they didn't go ahead and get married,' Evelyn whispered to Harold, her voice laced with disappointment. His forehead creased into a frown. 'Evelyn!' he reprimanded her sharply.

I stared at her, taken aback by her remark. 'What do you mean? Sam said he and Tamara were never together...'

'Did he?' Evelyn looked at me cagily. 'Well, it's in the past now.' She stood up and started to clear the table. 'I expect it would never have worked out. Tamara is far too independent.'

Meaning that I wasn't? That I was a pushover.

They were right though, weren't they? I'd given in about moving into his parents' home, the wedding plans and about the house we bought. But then they had all pressured me too. They all made me feel as if I was naïve, inadequate. The only thing I had put my foot down about was moving into our own home, and then Evelyn had twisted that to make it look like I was demanding.

They'd tried to make me look incompetent right from the beginning, I thought, remembering the incident with the dishwasher. I'd measured the detergent carefully and was now beginning to think that someone else had added more to make me look useless so that Sam would think twice about marrying me, then he wouldn't move out.

Well, they hadn't succeeded. I loved Sam and he loved me and I wasn't going to let anyone drive us apart.

20

I lay in bed that night, listening to Sam snoring softly beside me, my mind in too much turmoil to sleep. The day had started off so well; if only we had stuck to our original plan of going out for a meal to celebrate instead of allowing Evelyn to guilt us into eating with them. Then the dreadful row, our first ever, would never have happened.

Fighting back the tears that threatened to burst out into loud sobs, I thought back to a few hours ago when, after Evelyn's cutting remarks, I had gone on up to our apartment, leaving Sam talking to his dad. He had walked in half an hour later, his mouth set in a grim line. 'What's going on, Dana?' he'd demanded. 'Mum is really upset. She said that you've been questioning her about my relationship with Tam. I told you that we were never an item. If you had further questions about it you should have asked me, not my mum.' He strode over to where I was seated on the sofa, browsing Pinterest for soft furnishings for our new home.

I looked up nervously, not liking the angry edge to his voice. I'd never seen Sam angry. 'I didn't question her at all. Evelyn said that it was a shame that you two hadn't gone ahead and got married, and all I said was that you'd told me that Tamara was never your girlfriend.'

A dark frown creased his forehead and anger flashed in his eyes. 'That doesn't sound like Mum. And it's not what she told me. She is really upset that she might have caused trouble between us. Are you saying she's lying?'

I swallowed, knowing I had to choose my words carefully. I didn't want to cause a rift between Sam and his mum. 'No, of course not...'

Eventually, I managed to convince Sam that it was all a misunderstanding and promised that I would apologise to Evelyn for upsetting her tomorrow, and he'd calmed down.

I closed my eyes tight, the memory of our row still deeply upsetting me. Why had Evelyn twisted my words like that? From what Sam said, she had made it sound like I didn't believe Sam and was jealous of Tamara. It was as if she and Tamara were ganging up, trying to stir things between me and Sam. I'd got Tamara's number; she was a troublemaker. She didn't want Sam for herself but didn't think I was good enough for him. But why was Evelyn doing it? Actually she was worse than Tamara, who made it clear she didn't like me. Evelyn was welcoming to my face but lying behind my back to turn Sam against me.

'You don't really know much about Sam, do you?' Lynne had said when I'd told her we were getting married.

I was realising now that she was right; I knew very little about him.

Sam murmured in his sleep, turned over and put his arm around me and I relaxed as I nestled into his embrace. *I know he loves me and I love him,* I thought happily. *That's all that matters.*

Sam was already up when I woke the next morning. I lay in bed, my mind in turmoil. Things had got a bit heated last night and we had both said things we hadn't meant. It had been an awful argument. Thankfully, we'd made up before we went to sleep but I was still shocked and hurt by how bad the row had got.

The bedroom door opened and Sam came in with a cup of tea, looking very contrite. 'I'm so sorry, sweetheart. I overreacted and I'm sure you did too. It's just I know Mum would never try and cause trouble between us, but I understand that you don't know her as well as I do. And that all this,' he waved his arm around, 'probably makes you feel a little... ill at ease.'

'It does,' I told him. 'And I'm sorry too.'

He hugged me, and I sank into the warmth of his embrace, glad that things were right between us again.

'I couldn't bear to lose you,' he whispered.

'I couldn't bear to lose you either,' I said, tears springing to my eyes.

'Let's make a promise never to row like that again,' he murmured, his breath warm on my neck.

I nodded. More arguments were the last thing I wanted.

'I'm in the study doing some paperwork for an important meeting tomorrow,' he said, kissing me. 'You have the morning off, don't you? Why don't you take it easy for a bit? No rush to get up.'

'I will,' I said – I was feeling quite exhausted.

I drank my tea and had a leisurely bath, then sorted out my clothes for work, carefully selecting a long-sleeved cotton top to hide the deep scratch on my arm.

'How are you doing?' I asked, taking Sam a coffee when I was dressed.

Papers were strewn all over his desk and folders piled up on the floor beside it. 'I've got to head off in a few minutes so will have to finish tonight,' he said, swivelling around on his chair and taking the mug of coffee from me. 'Thanks, I need this.'

'Is it all right if I work in here?' I asked. I wanted to do a bit of admin before I went into work that afternoon, keep in Tasha's good books, as she'd been so good about me having two weeks' holiday for our honeymoon.

He took a swig of his coffee and nodded. 'Sure, that's fine. But please don't move any of those papers. My desk might look a mess but I need the papers in that order.'

'I won't, I promise.' I never touched anything on Sam's desk. I had my own desk to work at.

Sam took another swig of coffee and stood up. 'I must go to work now.' He kissed me warmly on the lips. 'Have a good day, darling. See you tonight.'

'You too,' I replied, relieved that everything was back to normal between us. I hated us falling out.

I put the laptop on my desk and started work. It got really hot and stuffy so I put the floor fan on, making sure the cool air was blowing just over me and away from Sam's desk. Admin finished, I switched off the fan and shut down my laptop. I was meeting Lynne for lunch before going into work, and was looking forward to having a catch-up. I guessed that I'd better try and sort things out with Evelyn before I went to work, I thought, going down to find her. She was in the kitchen, loading the dishwasher.

'Morning, Evelyn.'

She turned around. 'Morning, dear.'

Well, she seemed pleasant enough today. I plunged in. 'Sam said you were a bit upset because you felt I was questioning you about Tamara yesterday. I'm sorry you felt that way. I didn't mean to upset you.'

Evelyn stood up and wiped her hands on her apron. 'Bless you, dear, you didn't upset me. I was merely concerned that Sam wasn't being truthful with you. But as he said, it's all in the past now.' She walked over to the kettle. 'Do you have time for a cup of tea before you go to work?'

So she was still insinuating that Sam wasn't telling me everything about his relationship with Tamara. That he was keeping secrets. 'Thank you but I'm afraid that I don't have time.'

'Dana.'

I turned around and threw her a questioning look.

'You need to stand up for yourself, dear. Don't let Sam walk over you. He can be a bit... controlling.'

Her eyes met mine across the kitchen. Then she turned back to loading the dishwasher. I felt another seed of doubt plant in my mind as I remembered the row last night. And Sam's anger. Had Evelyn deliberately set me up to cause that row with Sam? Was she telling me to stick up for myself so that we would argue and maybe split up?

Or was she genuinely warning me?

'You look shattered,' Lynne said when I sat down beside her. 'And how's your hand?' She pointed to my bandage.

'Still painful, but healing okay,' I told her.

She leaned forward. 'Is everything all right, Dana? You look so wiped out.'

I could hear the concern in her voice. 'It's fine, honestly. It's just a bit stressful living with Sam's parents. I feel in the way and that I don't quite live up to their standards – well, Evelyn's standards. Harold's okay.'

'I thought it might be like that. Don't let them get you down – you're amazing. Sam thinks so too, that's why he wants to marry you.'

'I know he does.' I didn't want to tell her about the row we'd had. All couples row and Sam had said he was sorry.

'How's the house-hunting going?' she asked.

'Oh my God! I haven't told you! It's going great. In fact... we've seen one we both love and we've had an offer accepted on it! It's perfect and it's empty, so we can move in as soon as we come back from our honeymoon. Here, let me show you.' I got out my phone, tapped into the estate agent's website and got up the particulars.

Lynne peered at the screen, scrolling through the images. 'Oh wow! That is literally gorgeous. I'm really pleased for you. You lucky thing! When's the house-warming?'

I laughed. 'Well, we need to have the wedding first! Just think – only a few more weeks and Sam and me will be married and in our own home,' I said, happily. Then everything would be perfect. I knew it would.

21

It was a busy afternoon at work, and I was glad because it meant I was too preoccupied to think about Evelyn and Tamara. By the time I arrived home, I had convinced myself that I had been oversensitive because of my own lack of confidence. I smiled when I saw Sam's car in the drive, glad that he was home early too.

I went straight upstairs, pausing at the door of our lounge, as I heard Sam shouting. What had happened? I hurried inside and saw the study door was wide open. I walked over, then gasped in dismay at the pile of papers blowing all over the floor. What had happened? Then I noticed that the fan was now switched on and facing Sam's desk. What was going on? Sam hit the off switch and glared at me, his eyes dark, his jaw clenched. 'Why the hell did you leave the fan on and blowing over my desk? I told you I needed to keep the papers in this order. It's going to take me ages to sort them out now for the meeting tomorrow.'

'I turned it off!' I protested. 'And it was facing my desk, not yours!'

I stooped down to pick up some papers, then put them on Sam's desk. I could understand him being annoyed – I would be too – but this wasn't my fault.

Sam scooped the rest of the papers up and slammed them down on the desk. He looked so tired and stressed. I knew he'd been working hard on this project and having the paperwork messed like this was the last thing he needed. I wanted to give him a hug but he looked so angry I wasn't sure he would welcome that.

'I'm so sorry this has happened, Sam, and I get why you're so annoyed but I did turn off the fan. I promise I did.'

He ran his hand through his hair and shot me a look of exasperation. 'So how did this happen, then?'

I bit my lip anxiously. 'I have no idea. Someone else must have...'

He glared at me. 'Who, Dana? Who do you think came up to our rooms while we were both at work, moved the fan over to my desk, switched it on and walked back out again?'

It sounded stupid. Far-fetched. But that was the only explanation.

'It wasn't me so it had to be someone else. Maybe Ruby came in to clean, and it was hot so she put the fan on and forgot to turn it off again?' I was clutching at straws, trying to find a reasonable answer, trying not to point the finger at Evelyn again.

'Ruby has strict instructions not to come into my study. And even if she did, are you seriously suggesting that she deliberately turned the fan towards my desk and left it blowing the papers off?'

'It wasn't me. Truly it wasn't.'

Sam's lips tightened and he turned away. 'I don't have time for this – I need to sort out these papers. I have an appointment with the client tomorrow. Let's put it down to you being under stress because of the wedding. Mum said lots of brides-to-be feel the pressure as the wedding gets nearer. She thinks that's why you're so—'

'So what?' I demanded, stung that Sam had been discussing me with his mother. How dare he?

'You're not your normal self, Dana. You know you're not. You're so touchy, and clumsy and, well... everyone's walking on eggshells around you.'

I folded my arms. 'Really? Is that what your mother said?'

'She's just worried about you. You seem so stressed.'

Evelyn had really been stirring it, hadn't she? I swallowed, remembering Tamara saying that I was meek and compliant. Was Evelyn doing this because she was confident that I wouldn't speak up for myself? Anger rose up in me.

'I'm stressed because I feel undermined here. Your mother makes it clear that she would prefer you to marry Tamara. And things are happening... the broken mirror in my handbag, this...'

'For God's sake, are you implying my mum broke your handbag mirror? And is responsible for this mess today?' Sam asked incredulously.

'Well, someone did it and it wasn't me.'

'I haven't got time for this, Dana. I accept that you didn't mean to do this. Let's just forget it. I don't have time to argue. Now will you please leave this study so I can sort out this mess?'

I wanted to stand and argue my case but Sam's jaw was clenched, his eyes dark. I could see that he was at the end of his tether.

I turned and walked out into our bedroom, where I sat on the bed, tears stinging my eyes. Sam might not believe me but I knew that someone was trying to cause trouble between us and I was pretty sure it was Evelyn. She was so two-faced; sweet to my face but dripping poison in Sam's ear.

Unless Sam was right and I was so stressed I didn't know

what I was doing? I was sure I'd turned the fan off, but maybe I hadn't. Maybe I had knocked the other switch instead, the one that made the fan swivel around, and it had spun around to face Sam's desk and somehow got locked.

I put my hand on my arm where the plaster covered the big scratch. Was I being paranoid? Was it all starting up again?

22

Sam came into the bedroom a couple of hours later, wrapped his arms around me and hugged me close. I shut my eyes, trying not to wince as his arm pressed down on the scratch, glad that the argument was over. He kissed me on the neck and I rested my head on his shoulder. 'I'm sorry I lost my rag a bit last night and just now. I guess you're not the only one who's stressed. Please forgive me, sweetheart. I love you.'

I swallowed, not wanting another argument to start. 'I love you too,' I whispered.

He held me close and I could feel his love. I loved him so much and I knew he loved me. It would be all right. I had to try and relax, stop worrying, then maybe I would stop doing things wrong. When I got nervous I often became confused and panicky. That's what must be happening now. And, like Sam said, he was stressed too, which was why he was snappy.

'Everything's going to be all right. I totally understand that this is a very stressful time, and that it must be difficult for you living here with me and my parents, but it's only for a little longer. The house sale is going through, the wedding is all arranged, and Mum is doing most of the wedding preparations. All you have to do is relax,' Sam said softly.

I nodded. 'I know. I'm sorry.' How could I tell him that it was his mum and Tamara's attitude to me that was making me so stressed?

'So am I. Now, let's go out for a meal tomorrow night. Put all this behind us, shall we? I'll tell Mum not to cook us any dinner. And I won't let her invite herself,' he said with a smile. 'I do know that she can be a bit much. Her heart is in the right place though, I promise. And she does like you. So does Dad. They have never once tried to talk me out of marrying you.'

No, because she's being clever and planting doubt in my mind instead. But how could I tell Sam that?

'That sounds wonderful,' I said, with a smile. I was so glad we were back on track. I couldn't bear it when we argued. I was determined not to allow Evelyn or Tamara to cause trouble between us again. I couldn't face going down for dinner though, when Evelyn called to say that it was ready, so was relieved when Sam suggested that he bring our meals up on a tray so we could eat them in our apartment while we watched a film.

We both left for work at the same time the next morning and didn't bump into either Evelyn or Harold, much to my relief. I didn't think I could deal with her right now. When I arrived home, I tried to rush straight upstairs but Evelyn came out of the lounge, almost as if she was waiting for me. 'Ah, Dana. I hope you're feeling better now?' she asked.

I managed to summon up a smile as I replied. 'Yes, I am, thank you. Excuse me but I have to go straight up and get changed. Sam and I are going out for dinner.'

'Yes, he told me. I'm glad to see that you're over your little argument. I must say, you're very forgiving. I'm sure that's why Sam loves you so much.'

I stared at Evelyn's retreating back, as she walked back into the lounge. What did she know about our argument? How much had Sam told her? And what did she mean by saying that I was very forgiving? Was she saying that she thought Sam was in the wrong?

She's playing games, trying to get into my head, I thought. *Well, it's not going to work, I'm on to her now.* I quickly made my way upstairs, had a shower and got changed. I was putting my make-up on when I was surprised to hear a knock on the door. Lipstick poised, I frowned and looked over at the door. Was Evelyn actually knocking?

'Come in!' I shouted, continuing to apply my lipstick. The door opened and Evelyn came in, holding out a small plate with a couple of chocolate cookies.

'I wanted to apologise again for inadvertently upsetting you,' she said sweetly. 'All I want is for us all to get on. I know you and Sam are going out for a meal but I've baked your favourite biscuits. Will you at least have one before you go? A peace offering?' She put the chocolate biscuits down beside me and stood waiting, twisting her hands together anxiously.

'Thank you. That's very kind of you.' They did look tempting. 'I think I should save them until after our meal, though.'

'Go on, have one now. Just one won't hurt,' Evelyn coaxed.

It looked like she was making an effort, the least I could do was meet her halfway, I thought. 'Okay, just the one,' I agreed. I picked up one of the biscuits and took a nibble. It was very tasty, so soft and moist with a rich chocolate flavour.

'They're delicious,' I told her.

Evelyn's face lit up. 'Enjoy.' She put the plate down beside me and went back downstairs.

I picked up another biscuit and ate that, then couldn't resist finishing off the last one. It would be a while before we were eating, so three biscuits shouldn't spoil my appetite.

Sam came home a little later. 'You look gorgeous,' he said, wrapping his arms around me and nuzzling my neck.

'Your mum came up to say sorry that she'd upset me and

brought me a couple of biscuits she'd made,' I told him. 'They were really tasty.'

Sam looked pleased. 'That's very kind of her,' he said. 'I did have a word with her yesterday, so hopefully she'll be a bit more thoughtful.'

I hoped so too. I felt as if a weight had been lifted from me. 'Perhaps I am being a bit oversensitive. I am stressed about the wedding and the house move,' I admitted, not wanting to put all the blame on Evelyn. I wanted us all to get along.

'It's only natural, but honestly, darling, try to relax. It will all be fine. I promise.' He kissed me and I snuggled up in his embrace, enjoying the warmth and the closeness. I was so lucky to have Sam in my life. He was right; I need to relax. Everything would be okay.

We left for the meal, chatting happily. I was really looking forward to the evening.

But as soon as I'd ordered my meal, I started getting terrible stomach cramps and a few minutes later had to dash to the loo in agony. By the time I came back, the meal was on the table, going cold. Sam looked at me in concern. 'Are you all right, Dana?'

'It's my stomach, but I think it's settled down now,' I told him.

It hadn't. I had to run to the loo several times that evening and was hardly able to eat a thing. Sam apologised to the restaurant manager and we left early. Then, after asking if I was sure I didn't need a doctor, Sam retreated to the spare room for the night, saying he needed to be up early the next morning, and that he didn't want to risk catching my stomach bug. I felt ill, lonely and embarrassed, but of course I understood his decision. He couldn't afford to get the bug and have to take time off. After crawling back into bed after yet another trip to the loo in the night, I thought miserably that I was glad Sam was sleeping in the other room. I felt so yucky and just wanted to be alone. I'd been looking forward to our evening and now it had been ruined and I was going to have to take tomorrow off work. I hated doing that, especially as I'd only been in my job a few months. Where on earth could I have picked up such an awful bug? I wondered. I was just grateful I didn't have sickness too; that would have been terrible. Exhausted, I closed my eyes, and started to drift off to sleep. Then an image of Evelyn smiling and handing me the plate with just three biscuits on it popped into my head.

I snapped my eyes open. Had Evelyn put something in the biscuits to upset my stomach in order to ruin our evening?

The idea wormed its way around my mind. It seemed strange that Evelyn had brought up only three biscuits on a plate; why not bring some for Sam to share when he came home? And she had been desperate for me to eat them, I remembered, as an image of her apologising and beseeching me to eat her biscuits flashed across my mind.

I thought back to all the things that had happened since I'd been here; the dishwasher overflowing, the broken mirror in my handbag, the fan being turned on, the things Evelyn said, twisting events to Sam to make it look as if I was questioning him, and now this stomach upset just when Sam and me were going out for a meal together. Was it that far-fetched that Evelyn was waging a secret war against me, determined to make sure that me and Sam didn't get married?

23

The next morning, I woke up to find a note from Sam propped up against my clock.

Hope you're feeling better. Didn't want to wake you, you looked so peaceful. See you later xx

I glanced at the clock. Ten thirty. It was a good job I'd emailed Tasha last night to tell her that I was too ill to come into work. I decided I should phone her though and see if there was any work I could do from home. I didn't want my boss to think that I wasn't pulling my weight, especially when I'd be having a couple of weeks off next month to go on our honeymoon. Thank goodness I wasn't working tomorrow, I thought; I'd be recovered for Monday.

'I'm so sorry. It's some sort of tummy bug, it only came on late last night,' I apologised down the phone. 'I am feeling a little better now though so is there anything I can do from home?'

Tasha sounded pleased that I'd offered and gave me several tasks to do. 'If you're sure you feel well enough,' she added.

'I am,' I told her. 'I just didn't want to come into work and have the whole office coming down with the bug.'

I had a shower and changed the bedding, made myself a peppermint tea to settle my stomach and went into the study to work. I didn't know if Evelyn knew that I was home ill but I was determined to stay out of her way. Last night's thoughts were still fresh in my mind and I felt uneasy around her.

After working for a couple of hours, I heard raised voices downstairs. Were Evelyn and Harold arguing? Harold was always so quiet – although I could easily imagine Evelyn shouting.

I opened the door a little and listened. It was definitely Evelyn's voice I could hear. I ventured out onto the landing and looked down. Evelyn and Ruby were standing in the hall and Evelyn was pointing to the floor where I could see the huge Chinese vase that usually rested on a small table was lying broken. Ruby looked upset.

'That vase was a family heirloom. I can't believe that you've been so careless,' Evelyn shouted.

'I'm sorry, Mrs Corbett. It was an accident. I'll pay for a replacement.'

'You certainly will! I'll be docking twenty pounds a week out of your wages until it's paid for,' Evelyn told her. 'Now please clean up this mess and try not to break anything else before you finish the cleaning.'

Evelyn turned and walked out of the front door. Ruby watched her go, such a look of pure hate on her face that a chill ran through me.

Why did Ruby hate Evelyn so much?

As if sensing that I was there, Ruby glanced up at me. Our eyes met for a few seconds, then she dropped her gaze and walked off, coming back a few minutes later with the vacuum.

I retreated back to my room, wondering why Ruby continued with her cleaning job when she obviously didn't like it. She was employed by an agency, so surely she could get alternative work? She'd only been working at the manor for a couple of months, so it couldn't be family loyalty that was keeping her here.

I felt restless and after half an hour or so I went downstairs, knowing that Evelyn wouldn't be back for a while, wanting to put the sheets in for a wash. The lounge was deserted so, guessing that Harold would be in the back garden, I went into the kitchen and then through into the utility room. Putting the sheets in the washing machine, I went back through to the kitchen to get some iced tea. Looking out of the kitchen window, I could see Harold pruning the hedge, so thought I'd take a jug out to him, thinking he might be grateful for a drink. I took the biscuit tin out of the cupboard and opened it, expecting to see the chocolate cookies, but instead it contained fruit ones. Had all the chocolate cookies been eaten? Or had only a few been made especially for me? Puzzled, I put the biscuit tin onto the tray too. Harold might be glad of a snack, too.

I was about to pick up the tray when I noticed some petals on the table; they'd fallen from the vase of flowers. Knowing how Evelyn hated mess of any kind, and not wanting Ruby to get into any more trouble, I picked them up and carried them over to the bin, pressing the pedal with my foot to open it. As the lid popped open, I saw a familiar blue wrapper. Ex-Lax. My aunt always kept some in as she often had trouble 'doing a number two' as she called it. I stared at it. Could Evelyn have put some of that in the chocolate cookies she gave me? Was that why I had such an upset stomach? But surely it wouldn't have worked that quickly? *It might do if you put a lot in, and used artificial sweetener too*, I reasoned. Evelyn always used artificial sweetener instead of sugar in her drinks.

'Hello, Dana, are you feeling any better?'

I spun around as I heard Harold's voice behind me, the lid

slamming shut as my foot released the pedal. The sudden change of subject and attitude surprised me.

'Much better, thank you,' I told him, walking over to the tray on the table. 'I was just bringing out a jug of iced tea. I thought you might appreciate a drink.'

He nodded. 'Thank you, that would be very welcome.'

'Shall we sit outside?' I asked him.

He nodded and picked up the tray, taking it out to the table.

'So, how are you settling in? Are you comfortable here?' he asked as I poured out the iced tea.

I thought about my answer. It was kind of Evelyn and Harold to invite me into their home, and sitting here, out in the sun, chatting to Harold, it seemed a ridiculous idea that Evelyn had tried to harm me. I'd simply picked up a tummy bug. It happened. And what if there was an Ex-Lax wrapper in the kitchen bin? Lots of people took Ex-Lax. It was perfectly normal. I nodded. 'Yes, I am. The rooms are lovely, and you and Evelyn are very kind. It will be nice to have our own house, though. I hope that doesn't sound ungrateful.'

'Of course not. It's perfectly natural for a young couple like you two to want your own home. I keep telling Evelyn that.' He opened the tin of biscuits, took out a fruit cookie and bit into it, then leaned forward and said conspiratorially, 'Between me and you, Evelyn is dreading the day Sam leaves home. She's built her whole life around him. And I must admit, we will both miss him terribly.'

'I did get that impression.' I chose my words carefully as I sipped my refreshing drink. 'I'm sure you'll both soon adjust. Perhaps you might want to move to a smaller house, then?' I suggested. 'Lots of couple do when their children have left home. You could downsize and treat yourselves to holiday abroad, a cruise maybe.'

'This is our family home and we will never sell it.'

I almost dropped my glass at the sound of Evelyn's voice.

She was standing behind me, an angry look on her face. Did she think I wanted her to sell the house so Sam could have some of the money? Was she so against me because she believed I was marrying Sam because he was rich?

'I didn't mean any harm. I was just thinking of what was best for you and Harold. This house is so big for the two of you.'

'Which is exactly why it makes sense for you and Sam to live here instead of making him waste money on buying a house.'

'Now, Evelyn, we must respect their decisions,' Harold said.

'It's a foolish waste of money,' Evelyn said briskly. She pulled out a chair and sat down beside me. 'Is your stomach better now, Dana? Sam said that you've been ill all night.'

'Much better, thank you,' I told her. 'I think it was something I ate.' I watched her expression, wondering if she'd give herself away, but she merely nodded.

'I wouldn't be surprised.' She reached out to take a cookie out of the tin. 'The trouble is, you never know what they put in things nowadays. That's why I always prefer homemade food, if possible.' Her eyes met mine as she took a large bite out of the cookie and chewed it.

The way she looked at me made me shiver. Had she put something in the chocolate cookies she gave me, or was I reading too much into what she was saying?

I got up. 'Well, I'll leave you both to it. I need to go back up and finish some work off. I promised to email it over to my boss today.'

As I walked away, I could feel her eyes boring into my back but I didn't turn around. Why would Evelyn want to make me ill? A stomach upset wouldn't stop me moving out or marrying Sam, would it? It didn't make sense.

24

Sam was working from home on Monday, so I left him to it and set off for my office. There was only a month until our wedding, and I was counting the days until we could move into our own new house. When I returned, I was put out to find Tamara sitting in the garden with Sam and his parents. She was back again, then. Sam stood up to greet me with a big hug, and I reminded myself that I was the one Sam loved and was marrying, and I had no reason to be jealous of Tamara. I plastered a smile on my face and sat down in the chair Sam pulled out for me. 'Hello again, Tamara.'

'Hello, Dana. We were just discussing the wedding arrangements, weren't we, Sam?' She smiled at Sam who had now sat down next to me and was holding my hand. 'We thought it would be good to have lots of photos over by the fountain. The Malvern Hills make such a lovely backdrop.'

What was she doing discussing our wedding? That was up to us to sort out, I thought crossly, but I bit back the retort. 'Sounds good,' I said pleasantly, wishing that Sam had waited for me to come home to have the discussion.

'We've ordered the marquee for the reception to arrive the

day before,' Evelyn said. 'That way we'll have time to get it all laid out.'

'Yes, that sounds perfect,' I agreed. I loved the idea of laying out the tables in the marquee. At least if it rained – and fingers crossed, it wouldn't – it wouldn't ruin the reception.

'We're so lucky to be having a summer wedding. Dad and the gardener, are pulling out all the stops to make sure the garden is at its best.' Sam squeezed my hand as if he could sense my unspoken resentment.

'It will all look beautiful,' I said. 'Thank you both.' I flashed a smile at Evelyn and Harold. 'It's very generous of you.'

'You're welcome. We must give our only child a good send-off,' Evelyn smiled. 'And Tamara has offered to help on the day, haven't you, dear?'

'Of course. Anything for my friends.' Tamara smiled at me.

I suppressed a groan; she was the last person I wanted there, but I forced a smile and replied as calmly as I could, 'How kind.'

The next day, when I came home, I saw Tamara's car in the drive again. Couldn't that woman keep away for a day? The lounge and kitchen were empty and I could hear laughter coming from the back garden. I walked out of the patio doors to find rows of tables and chairs laid out on the lawn. Sam, Tamara, Evelyn and Howard were all sitting on the patio having a drink.

'Are you having a party?' I asked, looking at the tables and chairs, although I had a feeling I knew the answer.

'We've done a rehearsal, just to check the layout for the reception,' Sam said, getting up. 'What do you think?'

They'd all been doing wedding preparations without me again! I swallowed down the anger as I surveyed the setting. I imagined the tables and chairs with their covers and bows. They would look gorgeous. I was so glad that I'd chosen lemon now; it was such a pretty, summery colour. We were so lucky that Evelyn and Harold were allowing us to have the reception here;

it was a gorgeous setting, and was saving us such a lot of money, I reminded myself. But I really wished that they had waited until I came home so I could help with setting everything up too.

'It's amazing,' I said. 'I'd have liked to have been involved too, though.'

'Honestly, all we've done is laid out the tables and chairs and I was happy to help,' Tamara said. 'Oh, and we've been going through the menu options,' she added.

'Could I take a look, please?' I asked, sitting down next to Sam.

'Of course.' Evelyn picked up a folder off the table and handed it to me. A wedding folder. This was the first time I'd seen it. I opened it up and saw photos of the cake, the chair covers, the bows, the bouquet and candle decorations. I stared at it in disbelief. I half expected to see a photo of the wedding dress there too. 'I had no idea you had done this,' I stammered.

'Tamara did it,' Evelyn said. 'She wanted to help.'

'I only printed out what we all decided, to make sure everything was covered,' Tamara said. 'We don't want to find that we've missed something out on the day, do we?'

'It's all what you'd expected, isn't it?' Sam asked, looking a bit worried. I obviously wasn't hiding my feelings very well.

I nodded, not trusting myself to speak. Why had no one shown me this folder until now? It was almost as if it wasn't my wedding. As if it was all happening around me.

'Are you upset about Tam helping with the wedding plans?' Sam asked when we went back to our suite later that evening.

Yes, it's my wedding, I wanted to shout. 'I just feel that everyone is more involved in the preparations than I am,' I told him.

'You've been out at work, Dana, while I've been working

from home, so was around to check things with Mum. And Tam is trying to help Mum out while she's living at home, looking after Julia. I guess I should have asked them to wait until you came home before they did a practice run of the garden arrangements, but I never for a moment thought you would object.'

'I don't.' I was starting to feel petty.

'Then what's the problem?'

'There isn't one... It's just that I want to be involved with everything too. It's *our* wedding, after all, and I feel like it's being planned around me.'

Sam kissed me on the forehead. 'I'll make sure I check everything with you in future, I promise.'

25

I had Thursday morning off, as it was my turn to do the Saturday morning shift this week, and I was determined to spend it finalising the wedding preparations. I should have taken a more active interest in the wedding from the start, instead of standing by and letting everyone else have their say. Well, it was only three weeks away and I was going to make sure that I personally checked over everything, starting with deciding on the locations for the wedding photos. Sam had a meeting with a client that morning but we were going to visit our house that afternoon, after I'd finished work. The survey had been done, everything was in order, and we wanted to measure up for curtains. I showered and dressed, intending to go out into the garden.

As I stepped out into the hall, I heard a door open and glanced along the hallway to see Ruby coming out of Evelyn's bedroom. She turned to close the door, then stiffened when she noticed me. 'Good morning, Dana. Mrs Corbett asked me to open her bedroom window for her to let in some fresh air. I'll be cleaning up here in a few minutes. Would you like me to clean your rooms today?' she asked politely.

'No, thank you. We'd prefer to clean our own rooms,' I told her. I had been really put out when I'd come home the other day to find the apartment had been vacuumed, the bed changed and the clothes I'd left on the chair put away. Sam had explained that their cleaner always did his rooms as well as the rest of the house and I'd resolved then to have a word with Ruby when I got chance. I hated the thought of someone in our rooms, mooching around – it was bad enough with Evelyn dropping in unannounced when we were curled up on the sofa watching a film. 'There's no need to tell Evelyn that, though, I don't want you to have your wages docked.'

'That's kind of you. Very well, I'll make a start with the main bathroom. Her Highness will be home soon and will read me the Riot Act if I haven't cleaned up properly,' Ruby said. She opened the cupboard where the upstairs cleaning equipment was kept and took out a cleaning caddy and vacuum cleaner, then set off along the hall with them.

I was surprised at her referring to Evelyn as 'Her Highness'. Did she sense that I didn't get on too well with Evelyn either? Or did she think she could be a bit freer with me as I'd told her I wouldn't let Evelyn know that she wasn't cleaning our rooms? I watched Ruby go into the main bathroom, wondering again why she worked for Evelyn when she clearly hated the job.

I thought no more about it until the next evening. Evelyn was in her room, getting ready to go out, and Sam and I were in the garden talking to Harold when she came outside, looking very upset. 'Harold, have you seen my ruby drop earrings?'

Harold looked at her, puzzled. 'I presume they're where you always leave them, in your jewellery box.'

Evelyn shook her head. 'They're not there. They've gone.'

'Are you sure you put them away, Mum? Dana sometimes takes out her earrings and slips them in her purse or handbag. Could you have done that?'

Evelyn looked shocked. 'What! An expensive pair of ruby

and gold earrings! As if I would. Dana wears mainly costume jewellery, so of course, she might do that. I always put my jewellery away safely when I return home. Always.'

I resented her remark that I always wore costume jewellery, even though it was true – apart from the gorgeous sapphire and diamond engagement ring Sam had given me.

'I think someone has taken them,' Evelyn suddenly announced.

As soon as she said that I thought of Ruby, looking so suspicious as she came out of Evelyn and Harold's bedroom. She said she'd gone in to open the bedroom window but then why had she looked so awkward? And she clearly disliked Evelyn. Had Ruby taken the earrings? Surely not, when she must know that she would come under suspicion. I wondered whether to mention that I'd seen Ruby come out of Evelyn's room but then decided not to. It didn't make her a thief, did it? She was the cleaner so had a perfectly plausible excuse to go into any room. And how did I know that the earrings had been stolen? Evelyn could have simply misplaced them. I lost things all the time.

'Now, dear, let's not jump to conclusions. I'll help you look, I'm sure we'll find them,' Harold said, getting to his feet.

'I don't need you to help me. I'm perfectly capable of looking myself, and I can assure you that I have searched everywhere and my earrings are definitely missing. Which means someone has taken them.' Evelyn looked upset.

'Come on, Mum, there are only us four here. We wouldn't take your earrings,' Sam told her.

Evelyn pursed her lips. 'Well, they can't just have disappeared. I'll talk to Ruby tomorrow; she might have seen them. Right now, I need to get ready or we'll be late.'

She went back upstairs, coming down a few minutes later wearing a pair of delicate pearl drops with a matching necklace. As she and Harold left, my mind went back to Ruby. Had she taken the earrings? I didn't want to suggest that she was a thief and get her into trouble but if the earrings really had been stolen, then I had to admit that Ruby could be the culprit.

When I came home from work at Saturday lunchtime, I found both Evelyn and Sam waiting in our lounge for me. I could see right away that they were both furious.

'Is there something wrong?' I asked, trying to fathom out why Evelyn was sitting in our lounge.

'There certainly is!' Evelyn stood up indignantly. 'Explain this if you can!' She pointed to the coffee table where I could see her ruby and gold earrings on a coaster on the coffee table. Beside them lay my floral jacket.

'Oh, you found them. That's great.' I was relieved that Ruby hadn't taken them. I liked her.

'Is that all you can say?' Evelyn had her eyes fixed on my face. I felt my heart beat faster. What was she suggesting?

Then Sam butted in. 'How could you, Dana? After everything Mum has done for you. If you liked the earrings that much, you could have asked Mum for them. She would have given them to you.'

I was stunned. 'You think I took them?' I shook my head. 'That's ridiculous. Why would I?'

'You tell me.' Evelyn glared at me.

'There's no point denying it, Dana. Mum found them in your jacket pocket.' Sam's face looked like thunder and his voice was cold, accusing.

I couldn't believe it. How could this happen? 'I didn't take them. I promise.'

'Then how did they get there?' Sam demanded.

'I don't know.' I shook my head, my legs buckling under me. Fearing that I was going to faint, I sat down on the sofa, staring at the ruby earrings winking accusingly at me from the table. Then a thought occurred to me. What made Evelyn suspect me?

'What made you come into our rooms and search my jacket pockets, anyway? Why did you think I had them?' I asked her.

'You were wearing that jacket yesterday and Tamara pointed out how much you loved the earrings when you saw me wearing them the other day. So I decided to look in your pocket and there they were.'

I had admired the earrings, but I was just trying to be friendly. 'I didn't put them there. Why would I steal from you? Me and Sam are getting married soon; you're going to be my family,' I protested in disbelief.

'Maybe you thought that you wouldn't be found out until after the wedding?' Evelyn said.

I turned to Sam, who had remained silent whilst his mum threw these accusations at me. He looked angry, betrayed, hurt. How could he suspect me of doing something so horrible?

'I promise you that I didn't take the earrings. Someone must have planted them in my pocket.' I looked pleadingly from Evelyn to Sam. 'I would never steal anything. Never.'

'Really, Dana. It would be far better if you just admitted it and apologised than lie. That makes you both a thief and a liar. Thank goodness you've been found out before you married my son.' She threw me a contemptuous look, picked up her earrings and walked out.

Leaving me to face Sam.

26

Sam was furious, I could see that. I was furious too. I hadn't stolen those earrings. The only explanation for them being in my pocket was that someone had planted them on me to make me look like the thief. I was really hurt and upset at how willing Sam was to believe this of me, and resented that Evelyn had come into our private space to look through my things. It was like some sort of nightmare.

Sam was glaring at me now, his arms folded, a muscle tightening in his jaw, his eyes cold. 'Well, I'm waiting for an explanation, Dana.'

Suddenly, I couldn't take any more. How dared they treat me like this? How could Sam even think this of me? I glared back at him. 'And I'm waiting for an apology.'

'What?' His eyes darkened. 'An apology for what?'

His expression made me nervous, but I wasn't going to let this go. If we were over, we were over. I would rather finish with Sam and go and sleep on Lynne's sofa than be branded a thief. I was sick of it all. Sick of how Evelyn looked down on me; sick of how she treated Tamara like she was Sam's girlfriend rather than me; sick of how Tamara looked down on me, sick of how

Sam expected me to tiptoe around everyone; sick of the fact that everyone's feelings were apparently far more important than mine. And now, how they were all so quick to brand me a thief. Okay, the earrings being in my coat pocket looked bad, but I didn't put them there. In fact, I wouldn't have put it past Evelyn to plant them there.

'I'm not a thief,' I said firmly. 'I did not steal your mum's earrings and have no idea how they got in my pocket. Obviously, you all consider me a thief, so you won't want me in the family. That's fine. I don't want to marry someone who thinks I'm a thief. The wedding is off, and if you give me half an hour to pack my bags, I'll be out of your house, and your life for good.'

Sam's jaw dropped open. I had never stood up to him like this before – never stood up to anyone actually – but whoever was trying to cause trouble for me had gone too far. They were obviously determined to split up me and Sam; well, they'd succeeded. There was no way I was going to be thrown out like a thief, though; I would walk out with my head held high and let them all know what I thought of them. They were not pinning this on me.

I strode past Sam into the bedroom and started taking my clothes out of the wardrobe. My suitcase was in the hall cupboard and I could have kicked myself for not stopping to get it out. Now I would have to walk past Sam again to get it, or maybe he would bring it into me if he was so anxious for me to go. *Evelyn and Tamara have won,* I thought, fighting back the tears as I piled my clothes onto the bed, then opened the drawer of the dressing table and started taking out my underwear.

'What the hell are you doing, Dana?'

I looked over my shoulder in surprise at Sam's question. He was staring at me in complete bewilderment.

'I told you I'm leaving. If you could please get me my suitcase, I'll pack my stuff and be gone.'

'But we're getting married in three weeks' time.'

Was he for real? He still expected me to marry him when he thought I was a thief? I could just about tolerate Evelyn thinking that of me – I knew that she didn't think I was good enough for her son – but for Sam to think it was unbearable. I just wanted to get out of this awful house as soon as I could. I should never have agreed to move in. Evelyn and Tamara had done their best to split us up right from the beginning.

'The wedding is off! And I'm sure your mum and Tamara will both very delighted to hear that. Why don't you go downstairs and tell her the wonderful news?'

'Are you serious? You're actually calling off the wedding?'

His question floored me. I spun around, furious, my eyes fixed on his face. 'Sam, you and your family think I'm a thief. That I sneaked into your mum's bedroom, stole her earrings and hid them in my coat pocket. Why on earth would you want to marry me? And more to the point, why would I want to marry you when you think so little of me?'

'So you're saying you didn't steal the earrings?' he demanded.

'Of course I didn't. Why would I?'

'Then how did they get in your pocket?'

'How the heck do I know? All I know is that I didn't put them there!' I snapped.

Sam frowned, his anger subsiding a little. 'Are you suggesting that someone planted the earrings in your pocket?'

'Well, I most definitely didn't put them there, so you draw your own conclusions!' I shot back.

'Who would do that? And why?' He looked genuinely confused now, as if he was mulling over the idea. I had to admit that it did sound implausible, but what other answer could there be?

I sighed, my anger deflating like the air out of a balloon. 'I don't know, Sam. Someone who wants to make me look like a thief, who doesn't want us to get married. Lots of things have been happening since I've been here. It's as if someone is trying their best to make me look unsuitable, to make sure that our wedding doesn't go ahead. Well, they've won.'

Seeing as he'd made no move to get my suitcase, I marched past him, went to the hall cupboard and grabbed it myself, wheeling it behind me as I walked back into the bedroom, past Sam who was still standing by the doorway looking at the pile of clothes on the bed as if in a daze. I lay the case on the bed, unzipped it and started stuffing my clothes into it. I hadn't messaged Lynne yet but I knew that she would let me stay there until I sorted myself out. Putting up with Spencer was better than living here.

'I don't want you to go. I love you. I want us to get married,' Sam said. He walked over to me and reached out for my hand but I snatched it away. 'Let's forget about this – it's all been a misunderstanding. Maybe you found the earrings on the floor, picked them up and put them in your pocket without thinking.'

I met his gaze and said slowly and clearly, 'No, Sam, I did not. I did not put those earrings in my pocket. Someone else did. And if you think it was me, then you don't know me at all.'

He licked his lips. 'But Dana. There's only you, me, Mum and Dad here. None of us would do that to you.'

I stared him out. 'All I know is that I didn't put them there. I would never, ever, steal from anyone. And certainly not from your mother.'

My eyes held his, refusing to blink, and I could almost hear the cogs in his brain working, assessing everything I'd said. He nodded slowly. 'Okay, I believe you. I don't know what's happened here, but I believe that you didn't take Mum's earrings.'

I let out my breath. 'Thank you.'

He pulled me towards him and held me close. 'Please don't

go. You're the best thing that's ever happened to me. Please stay and marry me.'

I was angry and hurt that he'd thought I was a thief, but I really believed that he loved me. And, I reminded myself, the earrings had been found in my jacket pocket. Besides, if someone really was trying to split us up they'd have won if I walked out.

Did that matter? I asked myself. I was sick of playing second fiddle to Evelyn, of Tamara's gloats, of the constant battle to be heard. I couldn't take any more.

Soon we'd be married though, off on honeymoon and then moving into our own house. I was fighting a battle between my feelings of outrage and my love for Sam.

Sam placed his finger under my chin and tilted it up, his eyes looking adoringly into mine. 'Please don't call off the wedding, sweetheart. I love you. We can get past this.'

I was lost when I saw the love in his eyes. This wasn't his fault. The evidence was pretty damning and his mum had been pouring poison in his ears. I nodded. 'I love you, too. And yes, I will still marry you but I think it's best if I go and stay with Lynne until the wedding. I can't stay here when your family think I'm a thief.'

'Please don't go. I'll talk to Mum and Dad.'

Finally, I gave in to his pleading and he left me to unpack again while he went down to talk to Evelyn and Harold.

When he came back, Evelyn was with him.

'Sam seems to think there's been some misunderstanding, so I'm prepared to give you the benefit of the doubt,' she said, her eyes glinting. 'I've got my earrings back so let's say no more about the matter.'

I wanted to make her admit that she didn't think I was a thief but Sam was looking at me imploringly, so I merely nodded. 'I would never steal anything from you. Never.'

'Very well. Then let's forget all about it. I'll go back down to Harold and leave you two in peace.'

Neither of us said anything until Evelyn had walked out and closed the door behind her. Then Sam held me in his arms. 'Thank you,' he said.

I returned his hug but inside I was shaking. Who had planted those earrings on me and why?

27

I couldn't stop thinking about it all weekend though, and despite Sam's best efforts to make it up to me, I could see that it was on his mind, too. Whilst I was pleased that he had finally believed me, or at least given me the benefit of the doubt, I had to face it; someone was out to cause trouble for me. Someone had deliberately planted those earrings in my pocket to make me look like a thief. My first suspect was Evelyn. She'd made it clear that she didn't want me to marry Sam. I was pretty sure she was behind the other things too; the broken mirror, the dreadful stomach upset I'd had. She was probably doing it to make sure that the wedding didn't go ahead.

Or was it Ruby? I couldn't think of a reason for her to do such a thing. I barely knew her; why would she try to get me into trouble? Unless she'd taken the earrings for herself but Evelyn had noticed they were missing, so had slipped them in my pocket in panic? I'd asked her not to clean our rooms though, so was it likely she'd sneak in there and risk getting into more trouble?

Or maybe it was Tamara? Evelyn said that Tamara had pointed out I'd liked the earrings; she was obviously the one who'd planted the seed of doubt in Evelyn's mind. Could she have taken them from Evelyn's bedroom and slipped them in my pocket to make me look like a thief, so that Sam and his parents would think that I was unsuitable for him? Anyone could walk into our room – we had no lock on the door, despite me asking for one (Sam wouldn't agree as it would upset his mum). And although Sam often worked from home, and I occasionally did, there were many times when we were both out, so wouldn't know if someone had come in or not. I could imagine Tamara sneaking upstairs when Evelyn and Harold were out in the garden. It would only take her a few minutes to slip the earrings in my pocket to frame me then go back out again. *I wouldn't put it past her*. It was obvious that she didn't consider me to be good enough for Sam, and she was very close to Evelyn – maybe they were in cahoots? They'd tried to drive me away but it hadn't worked, so now they wanted to blacken my name and turn Sam against me. And they had almost succeeded, I remembered angrily.

I hadn't told Lynne about the earrings, knowing that she would be outraged on my behalf and tell me to leave; that I couldn't marry someone who had been so ready to believe I was a thief. *There's nothing but trouble ahead, Dana*, she'd say. I didn't want to listen to it. I knew that me and Sam were solid. He'd proved that by believing me even when I had to admit that everything pointed to me. We would be fine once we were living in our own house. Besides, Lynne had enough going on in her own life. She and Spencer were going through a bad time and she'd recently said she thought he might be having an affair. 'If I find out he is, it's over,' she told me. She didn't need my problems on top of all that.

Three more weeks and then we'll be out of here and in our own place, I told myself, but I couldn't afford to relax. I had to stay alert because if either Evelyn and Tamara – or both – were really intent on splitting me and Sam up, they wouldn't give up;

they'd be increasing their efforts now the wedding was so near. I had wondered briefly if I should move out just to get away from them but then changed my mind. I'd be playing into their hands. I needed to stay with Sam, where I could keep an eye on what was going on, not give them the chance to pour more poison into his ear. After all, it wasn't as if I was in danger.

Was it?

I thought back to the broken mirror. That could have cut my hand badly. If it have been an artery, I could have been killed. I shook my head. I didn't think that whoever was behind this wanted to harm me, but to frighten me and drive me away. Well, I wasn't going anywhere, I thought determinedly. All my life I'd avoided conflict, turned away from trouble. Not any more. I loved Sam and he loved me. I was going to stand my ground, fight for our relationship. Once we were married, everyone would have to accept it.

I felt much stronger once I'd made the decision and put all thoughts of Tamara and Evelyn out of my head as when I went to work on Monday. It was a busy day in the office and I was glad of the distraction.

Tasha let me go an hour early, as she wanted me to come in at eight the next day, so I was home before Sam. As I pulled into the drive, I saw that Evelyn's car was there and took a deep breath to compose myself. I really didn't want to have to deal with her right now. I'd go straight up to our rooms, I told myself. She wouldn't be expecting me home yet. I let myself in and was about to go upstairs when I heard raised voices coming from the kitchen. Evelyn and Harold. Whilst I had often heard Evelyn berating Harold, I had never heard him shouting before.

'Sam is a grown man, he's entitled to make his own decisions. Just keep out of it.'

Was he talking about me? Did he suspect Evelyn of meddling too? I had to hear more, so I crept along the hall towards the lounge, glad that I was wearing my sneakers, which wouldn't make any noise on the tiles.

'I'm just looking out for my son! You might not care who he marries but I do.'

'*Your* son? He's my flesh and blood.'

'How dare you? How dare your bring that up!' Her voice rose to a screech. 'I forgave you for your sordid affair, kept your shameful secret all these years, and brought Sam up as my own. How dare you rub that in my face now?'

I gasped and immediately put my hand over my mouth. Sam was Harold's child by another woman?

'Because you won't let go of him! You're obsessive! It's time he left and got a home of his own,' Harold retorted.

'You just want him out of the way because—' Her words were cut off as there a crash. Then silence.

28

It was deathly quiet. Had Evelyn hurt Harold? I was so worried that I was wondering whether to go into the kitchen and make sure that everything was all right when the door opened and Sam walked in. 'Hello, Dana. This is a nice surprise. I wasn't expecting you home yet,' he said.

I turned, quickly walking towards him in case Evelyn and Harold had heard him. I didn't want them to come out and find me right outside the kitchen where they'd been rowing. It was best if they didn't realise what I'd overheard until I'd had time to work out what I was going to do about what I'd just learnt. 'I finished early because I have to go in an hour earlier tomorrow,' I explained.

'Ah, you're both home.'

I jumped with a start as Harold's voice came from behind us. He was uninjured then. What about Evelyn? Her sentence had been cut short by that loud crash. What had happened? Why hadn't she come out of the kitchen to greet us too?

'Hello, Dad. Is Mum about?' Sam asked.

'She's in the garden,' Harold told him. 'Good afternoon,

Dana. I didn't expect you home so early. Did you both come in together?'

He was lying! Why? I didn't want to turn around and face him, worried that my face would give away what I had just heard and that I knew he was lying. My mind was racing. Had Harold hurt Evelyn? Was she lying on the floor unconscious? Should I go into the kitchen and check? Maybe she was too upset to face us, I thought. It was a terrible row, and for Harold to throw back at her that she wasn't Sam's real mother when she idolised him and had brought him up as her own was cruel.

Perhaps it had made her lose her temper completely. I had to admit that I thought that it was more likely it had been Evelyn who had thrown something rather than Harold. He was so mild it was hard to imagine it being him.

Hard to imagine him having an affair either, though. But then it would have been years ago, when he was in his early forties. I'd seen some photos of Harold and Evelyn when they were younger and they were a good-looking couple. Both would have had their fair share of admirers.

I took a deep breath and tried to compose myself before glancing over my shoulder.

'Hello, Harold. Excuse me, I need to use the bathroom,' I replied, deliberately not answering his question. 'Why don't you go and say hello to your mum?' I suggested as I gave Sam a quick kiss on the cheek. Then I hurried upstairs, my heart pounding, the heated conversation I'd just heard going round and round in my head, and the possible consequences. Harold had had an affair and Sam was the son of that. Evelyn wasn't his biological mother. It was mind-blowing.

And they'd kept it a secret. Never even told Sam.

I had to tell him. I couldn't keep this from him.

Once in the safety of our suite, I sat down on the sofa, my mind racing. Sam had told me that Evelyn was so overprotective of him because she had had several miscarriages and been told that she would never have a child, then he had come along. Her surprise baby. Was that why she'd taken him on as her own, and never told him the truth about his birth? It explained why she was so overbearing with Harold, and why he meekly went along with everything she said – because he felt guilty, and Sam was a constant reminder of that guilt.

I felt sorry for Evelyn. It must have been devastating to keep having miscarriages, constantly grieving for the baby that could have been, then being told that you would never have a baby, only for your husband to have a love child with his mistress. That would have destroyed me. Yet, Evelyn took on that child and brought him up as her own, so she obviously was a kind, loving person. Who was Sam's birth mother and what had happened to her? I wondered. Why had she given him up and never tried to make contact with him?

Different possibilities played out in my mind. She was young. Or she didn't want to be a single mum, so had dumped the child on Harold's doorstep. Or had Harold and Evelyn paid her off, made her sign a contract never to get in touch with her son again? I'd heard of both scenarios happening.

Or maybe she was dead.

Whatever the story, I thought that Sam had a right to know the truth but how could I tell him what I'd overheard? It would devastate him. *I'll wait until after the wedding*, I decided. Maybe I could find out a bit more before telling Sam.

Unless he did know but never mentioned it, looking on Evelyn as his mother? After all, his mum would have registered his birth and the information would be on his birth certificate, so surely he had seen that? Maybe he didn't want to talk about it and who could blame him?

'You look stunning!' Sam said when he returned a little later. He walked over and wrapped his arms around me, kissing me on the neck. 'And I need to apologise to you. We all do. Ruby has just come to do the cleaning and she said that she found the earrings on the floor and slipped them in your jacket, which was on the back of the chair in the lounge, because she thought it was Mum's. We should never have blamed you. I'm sorry, sweetheart. I hope you will forgive us.'

I was stunned. I remembered looking for my jacket the other morning and realising when I was at work that I'd left it in the downstairs lounge. So Ruby must have put them in my pocket, then. Although how could she have mistaken my floral jacket for one that Evelyn wore? It didn't make sense. When I got back home, the jacket had been placed on the back of the sofa in our room, so I presumed that Evelyn had taken it up. I was relieved that my innocence had finally been proven, though. Sam had his arms around my waist now, and gently turned me around to face him. 'Am I forgiven?'

I smiled, pleased that the mystery was solved and no one thought I was a thief, and that it had proved to be an innocent explanation, not a conspiracy. 'Of course. I'm glad that we all know how those earrings got in my pocket. I thought someone had planted them there to make me look bad.'

His eyes widened. 'Of course not. Who would do that? It was just an awful misunderstanding. Mum and Dad want to apologise to you too – they feel terrible. Do you mind having a drink with them in the garden for a bit so that we can clear the air?'

'I'd love to,' I agreed, relieved. Thank goodness Ruby had spoken up. Now, perhaps we could put it all behind us and all get on. Soon Evelyn and Harold would be my family. I didn't want there to be bad feeling between us and, now I knew a little about Sam's real origins, I realised how kind Evelyn must be to take on her husband's illegitimate baby and bring him up so lovingly. As for who his real mum was; that was nothing to do with me and it wouldn't be fair to tell Sam, I decided. Evelyn had been hurt enough. I'd keep her secret for her.

29

When we joined them in the garden, both Evelyn and Harold looked very at ease, with no evidence of their earlier row. And no visible bruises on Evelyn, I noticed with relief. They were full of apologies. 'I hope you will forgive us, Dana. It was wrong of us to accuse you of stealing my earrings but you have to admit that the evidence did point towards you,' Evelyn said, sounding very contrite.

She was right; it had. I decided to let bygones be bygones even though it still narked me that she'd let herself into our rooms and gone through my stuff. 'It was horrible that you all thought I was a thief,' I admitted. 'But I'm so pleased that you all know the truth now. Thank goodness Ruby admitted that she'd found the earrings and put them in the jacket pocket.'

'Yes, she was beside herself when she heard that you'd been accused of stealing them. Especially when it was her fault. She should have told myself or Harold personally, or if she couldn't find us then leave a note with the earrings on the coffee table, not put them in a jacket pocket. She's lucky to keep her job.'

'Oh no, please don't blame Ruby. I'm sure she didn't mean any harm,' I said. The last thing I wanted to do was get Ruby into trouble. It was all just an awful misunderstanding and she had spoken up as soon as she realised what had happened.

'Well, I have given her a stern talking to. I don't want anything like that to happen again,' Evelyn said firmly. 'Now, let's forget all about it and focus on the wedding. It's almost upon us.'

'Good idea,' Harold agreed. 'How is the house purchase going?'

'The survey has been done, and we've all agreed a completion date. We'll be able to move in as soon as we come back from honeymoon,' Sam said.

At last. And there was no danger of this house sale falling through, as the house was empty. The sellers had been renting it out for the last couple of years and when the last tenant moved out, they'd decided to sell it. It was all coming together. I couldn't wait to go on our honeymoon. Two glorious weeks in Barbados then home to our very own house. Life was looking good.

Harold brought out an ice bucket with two bottles of prosecco in it, and Evelyn fetched a bowl of strawberries and jug of cream from the kitchen. As we all sat chatting in the sun, I relaxed. The past few days had been difficult, but I was glad things were sorted out now.

A couple of days later, when Ruby came to clean, I made a point of going and thanking her. I found her cleaning the windows in the conservatory.

'Thank you, Ruby, for clearing my name. I really appreciate it,' I told her.

She turned around, her brown eyes puzzled. 'Sorry, Dana, I don't know what you mean.'

'Evelyn's ruby earrings,' I explained. 'Everyone thought I'd stolen them until you told Evelyn that you'd found them and slipped them into the jacket pocket on the chair, thinking it was Evelyn's.' I gave her a big smile. 'I can't tell you how grateful I am. It was my jacket on the chair, not Evelyn's, so everyone thought I had stolen the earrings and hidden them there.'

I could see the confusion clear in Ruby's eyes, and she nodded. 'That's okay, think nothing of it.'

For a moment, we both looked at each other. Then she shrugged. 'I'm glad it's all sorted but I'd better get on now.'

'Yes, of course,' I said, sensing that Ruby felt awkward but not sure why. Perhaps she felt bad about me getting into trouble because she hadn't told Evelyn straight away about finding the earrings. Ruby had turned back to the window now to commence her cleaning, so I left her to her work.

Lynne came over on Friday evening for a final fitting for the wedding and bridesmaid's dresses as Verity was busy at the weekend. Sam left us to it and went for a round of golf with his dad.

'How's it all going? Are you still having trouble from the PM and the NFH?' Lynne asked as we sat on the balcony sipping smoothies. She had come a little earlier so we could have a catch-up. She had christened Evelyn 'Possessive Mum', and Tamara 'Neighbour From Hell', and the nicknames, combined with the nonchalant way she spoke about the situation, always brought things into perspective for me and made me realise how much I'd hyped up things. It was because I wasn't used to living in a family unit, I reminded myself, and had never had many friends around me.

'It's all smoothed out now,' I told her. Lynne and Spencer had made up but I still hadn't told her about the latest developments at the manor; the missing earrings and finding out that Evelyn wasn't Sam's birth mother. It would have felt disloyal. I knew that Sam would hate me gossiping about his family. 'Tamara hasn't been around for a few days; she's working in London this week.'

'Good. I half expected her to be here for the dress fittings.' Lynne slurped the last of her smoothie and put the empty glass down on the coffee table.

'So had I,' I admitted.

We both turned as there was a knock on the door. 'Dana, dear, Verity's here,' Evelyn called.

Evelyn knocking was a nice change – usually she just marched in. I guessed that she was still feeling guilty about calling me a thief. 'Come in!' I called.

The door opened and in came Evelyn and Verity, each carrying a dress zipped up in a white protective cover.

'Two weeks to the big day!' Verity said, with a smile. 'Are you feeling nervous?'

'A little,' I admitted. 'Not about marrying Sam,' I added hastily in case Evelyn thought I was having second thoughts, 'but I'm nervous about the day itself. I hope I don't mess up.'

'Of course you won't. It's not a trial, you know. It's your wedding day,' Verity said. 'No one will be judging you. Just enjoy the day, and if something does go wrong, then laugh it off. No one will probably notice. Not that anything will go wrong, I'm sure,' she added reassuringly. She handed the dress she was carrying to me and Evelyn handed the other to Lynne. 'Now go and put these on and make sure they fit.'

Lynne and I retired to the bedroom to try the dresses on. They fitted perfectly.

'You look beautiful,' Verity told me when I came out of the bedroom and did a twirl. 'Doesn't she, Evelyn?'

'She certainly does,' Evelyn said with an approving nod.

I felt myself glowing with her praise.

Lynne came out next, looking stunning in the lemon gown.

'I love that colour; it's so summery,' Verity said.

I glanced at Evelyn, knowing that she had wanted me to choose a champagne colour scheme but she merely smiled. 'We've carried the colour over for the chairs sashes and bows, and the cake icing,' she told Verity. 'I've ordered some sunflowers to be put in crystal vases on the tables, too.'

Had she? My eyes shot to her face. No one had told me.

'Sorry, did I forget to mention it? It was Tamara's idea but we can alter it if you wish.' Evelyn's dark eyes met mine.

I didn't dare look at Lynne, knowing she would tell me that I should stand up for myself; this was my wedding. What did it matter? I told myself sunflowers would look stunning.

'You didn't mention it, but it doesn't matter, I adore sunflowers,' I told her. 'No need to alter it but perhaps you could keep me in the loop with any other details I don't know about,' I replied in what I hoped was a cool but friendly manner.

Evelyn raised an eyebrow. 'Of course. Sam told us to go ahead and do what we saw fit, knowing how experienced Tamara and I are at organising events.'

I was saved from replying by Verity examining my dress, checking that it fitted snugly around the waist, across the chest and under the arms. She did the same with Lynne's dress. 'Perfect. These can be hung up and put away now.'

'I'll take them. We don't want Sam seeing them before the day – it's bad luck,' Evelyn said.

As soon as we'd changed out of the dresses, she whisked them away to her room.

Verity packed up her things then put her arm on mine. 'I hope it all goes well on the day. I'm sure it will. You'll be a beautiful bride.' Then she said quietly. 'And remember, it's your day. Do it your way.' She stepped back as Evelyn returned.

Did Verity think Evelyn was being overbearing too? I wondered.

Lynne stopped for a little longer, and we enjoyed having a chat, catching up with what was going on in each other's lives.

'It's been great to spend some time together – I hope we can still do this when you're married,' Lynne said as I walked her to her car.

'Of course we will. Why wouldn't we?' I asked, puzzled at her remark.

'Dana, you're going to be married to an accountant, the son of a super-posh local family. You'll be busy hosting dinners and garden parties, and going to charitable events. I don't think you'll have much time for meeting up with me. And did you see the look Evelyn gave me? She obviously doesn't think I'm a suitable friend for you. She'll be introducing you to more "worthy" women.'

'Rubbish! You're my best friend and always will be,' I said, giving her a hug. 'Getting married won't change that. And Sam and me will be living in our own house; it will be up to us who we see.'

Lynne gave me a pensive smile. 'I hope so. Anyway, see you on the big day!' she waved cheerfully and got into her car.

I stood for a while, waving her off, her words resounding in my mind. Was that what Sam would expect of me when I became his wife? To be like Evelyn? Tamara had suggested that too. I shook my head. Of course he wouldn't.

30

Sam had to meet a client the next morning, so he was out early. I sat in bed, browsing for home furnishings on my laptop. I was so excited about moving into our house; our 'forever home' as Sam and I had taken to calling it. He wanted us to live there for the rest of our lives, have children and bring them up there, giving them the childhood he'd had. I wanted that too. I was determined to furnish the house elegantly – no more patchwork cushions and throws; I wanted to impress his parents, show them that I had taste and could be the sort of wife they expected Sam to have. I researched designer furnishings, bookmarking several to discuss with Sam, then went for a shower. I wanted to be ready for when Sam came home, and was looking forward to spending a leisurely weekend together. Today, we were going out for a drive to explore the area around our new house.

I chose a bright summer dress and slipped on my white Skechers then picked up the cup to take into the lounge, intending to refill the kettle so we could have a coffee before we went out. I was surprised to find the lounge still dark, as Sam usually opened the curtains when he went in. I switched on the light, put the cup down, shook the kettle to make sure there was enough water in it and switched it on. Suddenly, a tingle shot up my arm, I was thrown across the other side of the room and everything went dark. I landed on the floor feeling dazed and confused.

'Dana! What the hell!' Sam was standing by the open doorway, the light from the hall shining in. He sprinted over and knelt down beside me. 'Are you okay?'

'What happened?' I asked groggily. 'I switched on the kettle and...'

Horrified, I realised I'd had an electric shock. Sam helped me up onto the sofa. 'Sit still for a few minutes while I check it out,' he ordered. Still in a daze, I watched as he went over and opened the curtains. Sunshine flooded in. Then he went to the kettle, pulled out the plug and examined the lead. I heard him swear under his breath. 'The flex is almost broken in half, Dana! It's a wonder you weren't killed!' He looked over at me, his eyes going to my feet. 'Thank goodness you were wearing trainers.'

I shuddered as I remembered how I usually padded about with bare feet but had thankfully stopped to put on my Skechers this morning because we were going out. Their rubber soles had probably saved my life.

'Everyone all right?' Harold peered around the open door. 'The electricity has tripped and we can't find anything wrong downstairs.'

'It's the kettle, Dad. The flex is frayed by the plug. Dana got a bad shock from it.'

'What!' Harold went pale as he looked at me. 'Are you all right, love?'

I nodded. 'A little shook up, that's all.'

'I'm not surprised.' He went over to check the wire Sam was holding. 'That really is in a state. I'm surprised you haven't noticed it before.'

'I didn't stop for a drink this morning, I was in a rush,' Sam replied. 'But it was fine last night. There again, we wouldn't notice it right by the plug, would we? We always keep the kettle plugged in.'

Harold nodded. 'Well, I'll take that away and your mum will get another one today. Thank goodness it wasn't more serious.'

I got to my feet and walked over, wanting to see the lead myself. The outer covering of the flex was severely frayed with the wires exposed. I shivered. I could have been killed.

Sam put his arm around me. 'I'm so sorry, sweetheart. I had no idea the lead was in this state. I dread to think what could have happened.'

He looked so worried that my heart went out to him. 'It's not your fault. These things happen,' I said.

'I'll go and switch the electricity back on now I know what's caused it to trip,' Harold said, picking up the kettle and lead and going out with them.

I was literally trembling. I couldn't believe what had happened. I could have died.

'Do you want to postpone the drive?' Sam asked. 'You must be really shaken up. I know I am. I could have lost you.' He pulled me closer. 'I couldn't bear that.'

'I am a bit but a drive would do me good,' I told him. 'Please let's still go.'

He kissed me gently on the forehead. 'If you're sure.'

I nodded. 'I am.'

The drive did make me feel better. The house was situated on the outskirts of a village, with plenty of countryside around it, and we had a lovely stroll around. I was so looking forward to living there.

Harold gave us a new kettle when we returned to the manor and made us both promise to regularly check the flex to make sure it wasn't worn out.

'It's very unusual for a kettle flex to wear like that,' Evelyn remarked. 'I wonder if you perhaps tugged at the wire a bit, or twisted it around? You must be more careful, dear, you do seem a little accident-prone. You could have been badly hurt.'

Her coal-black eyes rested on my face and I felt a shiver run down my spine. The way she looked at me, it was almost as if she was warning me. Could she have sneaked in and cut into the cord while I was in the shower? I shook the thought from my head. As if she would do that! And Sam could have been home at any time, so he might have been the one to put the kettle on. Evelyn would never risk hurting him.

31

'Hurry up, Dana, we'll be late!' Sam shouted up the stairs the next afternoon. We were going for Sunday lunch with Sam's colleague, Daniel, and his wife, Stella. I was so nervous about making the right impression, I'd changed half a dozen times and the bed was piled up with clothes. I was practically in tears as I realised that I had nothing suitable to wear. Sam moved in classier circles than me, and my chain-store clothes just wouldn't do. A couple of times I'd been tempted to buy a new outfit with the credit card Sam had given me so that I had something decent to go out in, then thought better of it as the card was meant to be for wedding things. Even so, I would have bought an outfit if I'd known about lunch today but Sam had only sprung it on me yesterday, so I hadn't had time to go shopping even if I'd wanted to. He said it was a last-minute invitation from Daniel, and not to stress over it; it was just lunch at a country pub. But how could I not stress? I was sure that Stella would be dressed in expensive clothes.

Sam came into the bedroom, surveyed the mess and frowned. 'What's all this?'

'I've got nothing decent to wear,' I told him, my eyes filling with tears. 'I wish you'd given me more notice. I could have bought something.'

'It's Sunday lunch at a country pub, Dana. Jeans or shorts and a T-shirt will do. I'm sure that's what Stella will be wearing.'

'If she is, I bet it'll be a designer T-shirt and jeans,' I told him, images of Tamara in her designer clothes flashing across my mind.

He rolled his eyes in exasperation and started looking through the clothes piled up on my bed. 'How about this? You always look lovely in this,' he said holding up a pale blue pin-striped jumpsuit with thin straps and a tie front that I'd bought online. It was one of my favourite outfits, but I'd thought it was too casual to wear today.

'Are you sure?' I asked.

'Positive.' He gave me a cuddle and gazed down at me. 'Stop stressing, you always look gorgeous. But if you're so worried about your clothes, buy some more. Use the credit card I gave you and buy a whole new wardrobe if you want.'

'Thank you.' I wrapped my arms around his neck and kissed him. 'I won't be long, I promise.'

'I'll carry on down, then. I wanted to talk to Dad. I'll meet you out the front.' He glanced at his watch. 'Fifteen minutes, max. Can you do that?'

'Definitely,' I nodded.

I pulled myself together, blaming my meltdown on pre-wedding stress. Honestly, my nerves felt so taut that I was sure any moment now they would snap.

It wasn't just pre-wedding stress though, was it? I reminded myself as I stepped into my jumpsuit; it was everything that had happened since I'd moved in. The electric shock, cutting my hand, my sudden tummy bug that no one else had, and then being accused of being a thief. On top of that was the secret that was gnawing away at me; that Evelyn wasn't really Sam's mum, but the result of his dad's affair. I felt terrible keeping it from Sam, even though it was mainly because I didn't want to spoil his relationship with Evelyn. Although if I was honest, part of the reason I had kept the secret was that I couldn't cope with the fallout that would inevitably occur if I revealed it to Sam. The more I thought about it, the more I realised that he had a right to know. I decided I wouldn't tell him until we'd been on honeymoon and were settled in our own place, though. Or maybe I'd tell Harold that I'd overheard and make it clear that he had to tell Sam or I would. That way I wouldn't have to deal with Evelyn or talk to Sam about it myself. Harold was bound to be shocked and upset that I knew, but I wouldn't be judgemental; it was a long time ago and he was a good man who'd clearly made a mistake. I'd just gently point out that Sam had a right to know his true heritage. My mind eased now I'd sorted that out, I quickly tidied up my hair and make-up then went to get my sneakers from the bottom of my wardrobe. There was no sign of them. Where on earth had I left them? There wasn't time to search for them now; my white sandals would have to do. I slipped the sandals on, grabbed my white bag and hurried out.

'Are you ready, Dana?' Sam shouted up the stairs.

'Coming!' I pulled the door behind me and ran along the hall to the staircase. As I cleared the top step my sandal twisted, I lost my footing and, screaming, plunged down the first set of stairs.

'Dana!' I heard Sam shout then it all went blank.

When I came to, I was lying on the sofa in our lounge and Sam was sitting beside me, holding my hand.

'Sam?'

He bent over and kissed my forehead. 'Are you okay, darling? You gave us such a scare tumbling down the stairs like that. You hit your head and knocked yourself out. I was worried that you might have concussion.'

'My right side hurts,' I told him. I gathered that I must have fallen on it.

'I'm not surprised. I had a check and it's very bruised, but nothing's broken, thank goodness. Luckily you only fell down the first lot of steps, so it wasn't a high fall. If you'd have fallen down the second flight, you could have been killed.'

I could feel my eyes widen with shock. Killed. The first flight of stairs only had six steps to a landing, then there was a long flight down to the hallway. A tiled floor. I felt sick. Sam was right; if I had fallen down those, I probably would have broken my neck.

'It was my fault, shouting at you to hurry up,' Sam said. 'That's what made you run down the stairs. I'd never have forgiven myself if anything had happened to you.' His face clouded over, and I reached out and held his hand.

'It wasn't your fault. I was hurrying, yes, but I wasn't running. It was my sandal.' I remembered feeling the sandal give way under me.

'The fall broke the strap. I've brought your Skechers for you to wear instead,' Sam told me. 'And I've cancelled lunch. You're going to find it painful to walk for a while. All your right side is badly bruised. And we don't know if you're concussed yet.'

I remembered that we were meant to be going out for lunch with Daniel and Stella. 'I'm so sorry we've had to let them down.'

'That's the least of my worries! I thought you might have broken your back or your neck...' He swallowed and I could see that he was terribly upset. It must have been such a shock for him to see me plunging down the stairs.

'Daniel and Stella both send their love and best wishes and said they look forward to meeting you at the wedding,' Sam was saying. 'Now, you concentrate on recovering. That's the important thing.' He raked his hand through his hair. 'Honestly, darling, at this rate, I'll be pushing you down the aisle in a wheelchair.'

'I'm sorry.' He was right: it was one thing after another.

But were they all accidents? This had to be; no one pushed me.

'Don't apologise, I'm just so relieved that you are relatively unharmed.' He squeezed my hand tight and looked at me lovingly.

'So am I.'

There was a knock on the door and then it opened.

'The doctor's here.' Evelyn came in followed by a tall, friendly looking man. 'Ah, good, you're conscious now, Dana.'

'I don't think I need a doctor,' I told Sam, feeling bad for calling out a doctor who must have patients who were properly ill to see, not someone who'd taken a tumble down half a dozen stairs.

'Joe is our family doctor. He's always happy to come out if we don't feel up to going to the surgery, and we are very worried about you.'

Of course the Corbetts would have their own private doctor, I thought, as the man walked over to me, a reassuring smile on his face. 'I hear you've had a bad tumble, Dana. Evelyn wanted me to check you over, just to make sure everything is okay.'

'Thank you.' It was kind of Evelyn to be so concerned, I had to admit.

'I'll go and make coffee,' Evelyn said. 'Would you like one, Joe?'

'I'd love one, thank you,' the doctor said.

Sam could have made the doctor a coffee with our kettle but I guessed that Evelyn was going downstairs to give us some privacy. When she had gone out, the doctor carefully examined me. 'You've got a few bruises on your arms and legs; you might find it painful to walk for a couple of days,' he said.

'But otherwise she's okay?' Sam asked anxiously. He was sitting by me, holding my hand.

'Nothing broken, but do keep an eye out for any signs of concussion. She's had a nasty blow to the head,' the doctor said. 'You're going to need a couple of days off work, Dana.'

I didn't want to take time off this close to our honeymoon. 'I'm working at home tomorrow, and I should be fine to go into the office on Tuesday,' I said.

After making me promise that I wouldn't move off the sofa, Sam and the doctor went downstairs. I must have dozed off again because I woke to find Evelyn standing over me.

'How are you, dear?' she asked.

'I'm all right, really,' I said weakly, thinking it was nice that she was concerned about me but her next words sent a chill through me.

'You need to be careful, Dana, you could have been killed.' Her dark, pebble-like eyes were boring into me and I sensed a hint of a threat in her voice. Almost as if she was warning me.

Then I remembered the sandal twisting, causing me to slip. Sam had said that the fall had broken the strap but what if the strap had been broken before? Was that why I slipped and fell?

She bent over and patted my hand. 'Now, you rest and take it easy a bit.' She leaned a bit closer. 'Goodness me, the way you're going, you'll be lucky to make your wedding day.'

32

Evelyn's words kept repeating over and over in my mind. *The way you're going, you'll be lucky to make your wedding day.* I wrapped my arms around myself and shivered. Was I in danger?

When Sam had come back after speaking to the doctor, I'd asked him where my sandals were and it turned out that his mum had thrown them out. 'The heel strap was completely broken, Dana. You couldn't have worn them again,' he said. So there went my evidence. And I hadn't been able to find my Skechers but they had mysteriously appeared again. They were under the bed, Sam told me when I asked him where he found them.

Was it all just a coincidence? Was I imagining the threat in Evelyn's voice?

I really needed someone to talk to and the only person I could think of was Lynne. So I sent her a text telling her what had happened and asking if she could phone me when she was free.

I tried to think back to the moment before I fell. I distinctly remembered my sandal twisting on my foot and was sure that was what had made me lose my balance. I was convinced it had been tampered with and that I hadn't noticed because I was in such a hurry but I couldn't prove that. Especially now that my sandals had conveniently been thrown away. I really wanted to talk to Sam about it, but how could I tell him that I thought it was his beloved mother who was responsible? It had to be Evelyn. Tamara hadn't been around for a few days, and how would she have got hold of my sandals? Whereas I knew that Evelyn came into our rooms. I couldn't accuse her of it without concrete proof. And it seemed that Evelyn was cleverly covering her tracks.

I messaged Tasha on Monday morning to tell her about my fall and asked if I could work from home tomorrow as well as today. She replied that I should take today off and rest to make sure that I didn't have concussion, then I could work at home until Thursday but they needed me in then. I was lucky to be working for such a supportive boss, I thought.

Lynne had messaged me back last night, worried about my fall, and asking if she could come and see me today, as it was her day off. Sam was pleased, as he had an appointment and was worried about leaving me. 'Mum will let her in and bring her up. I don't want you going down those stairs until you're feeling completely better, please,' he said. I promised that I wouldn't.

The door knocked then opened. It was Lynne. 'Evelyn told me to come straight up,' she said.

I was so pleased to see her that I almost burst into tears.

Lynne sat down on the sofa beside me. 'Well, you seem to be constantly in the wars just lately.' She ran her eyes over me and I could see her taking in the bruises on my arms. Similar bruises covered the right side of my body and legs but my clothes concealed those. 'You would tell me if...'

'If what?' I asked, puzzled.

'If Sam, well...' Lynne hesitated as if wondering how to

phrase her question, and suddenly it clicked with me what she was trying to say.

'If Sam is hitting me? Is that what you're getting at?' I demanded, horrified. 'How can you even think that?'

Lynne fidgeted awkwardly. 'You've been looking a bit tense and anxious. Not your normal self at all,' she pointed out. 'I'm worried about you. I want you to be happy but you seem under such a lot of strain and suddenly you're having these "accidents" and have lots of scratches and bruises. Remember Martin?'

Martin was a former boyfriend of Lynne's and it turned out he'd had a temper and used to lash out at her. Not that Lynne would admit it at first.

'Sam is nothing like Martin. He doesn't hit me.'

'That's what I used to say.' Lynne met my gaze. 'You would tell me, wouldn't you? It there was something wrong? You can tell me anything, you know that, don't you?'

'Of course I would. There is nothing wrong,' I said adamantly.

'Okay, forget I said anything. It's only because you're my friend and I care about you.' Lynne leaned forward and touched my hand. 'There will always be room for you in my flat. If everything gets too much, and you need to get out, just turn up.'

'I promise you everything is fine,' I assured her. I was touched by Lynne's concern, even if it was misplaced. She had always been there for me. The only one who ever had. 'Everything will be good once we're married and we've moved into our own house,' I said.

'I hope so.' She looked so concerned that I found myself blurting out: 'Sam isn't hitting me, Lynne, but I think someone is trying to hurt me. I think they wanted me to fall down the stairs.'

Lynne's eyes opened in alarm. 'What?'

I told her about the broken sandal strap. 'The thing is, I'm wondering if my sandal broke before the fall, or if I fell because the strap had been tampered with.'

Lynne's eyes widened and she leaned forward, her gaze fixed on me. 'Are you saying that you think someone deliberately broke your sandal strap so that you would trip over and fall down the stairs?' she asked, incredulous.

'Yes...'

'But who and why?'

I could tell by the way she was looking at me that she thought I was imagining it, so I related all the things that had happened to me since I moved in with Sam.

She whistled. 'That's a lot of accidents. And you haven't mentioned half this stuff to me,' she added accusingly.

'Because I didn't want to believe it. I kept telling myself that I was imagining it, reading more into things. But I'm certain now that someone is trying to hurt me to stop me marrying Sam.'

'Who?

'Well, neither Evelyn nor Tamara want me to marry Sam. I think they might be working together.'

Lynne didn't look convinced. 'I know they're both night-mares, Dana, and I get that you feel uneasy around them and can believe that they are trying to cause trouble between you, but it's a little far-fetched to think they're actually trying to harm you.'

'There've been far too many "accidents" for it to be a coincidence! Evelyn actually warned me to be careful when she came up to see me yesterday. She said that the way I was going I'd be lucky to make my wedding day.'

'Well, I was about to say the same thing...'

'You didn't see her face though, when she said it. Her eyes were all cold, and she was staring at me, and her voice – it sounded like a threat.'

'She's in her seventies, Dana – she's not a gangster's moll. I think maybe you're getting a bit carried away here.' Lynne looked at me thoughtfully. 'Look, I grant you that Evelyn is an interfering busybody but suggesting she'd cut the straps of your sandals so you would fall down the stairs, or sneak in and fray the kettle cord so you would be electrocuted is going a bit far. I mean, she didn't know you were going to wear those sandals, did she? And Sam could have used the kettle, then he would have been the one electrocuted.'

'I know, I thought the same myself,' I admitted. None of it made sense.

'And as for all the other stuff,' Lynne continued. 'Well, you are a bit stressed, hun, so it's no wonder you're dropping things and falling over.'

Just what Sam had said. I desperately wanted to tell her about Evelyn not being Sam's mum but how could I when Sam didn't know himself? I either had to keep the secret to myself or tell Sam. It wasn't fair to tell anyone else until Sam knew. If it got back to Sam, he would never forgive me.

Then I noticed that Lynne was staring at my wrists. 'Those scratches don't look like they've been caused by falling down the stairs.'

She was right; they hadn't.

'They're nothing.' I dropped my gaze and chewed my lip as I thought things over. 'I know it sounds far-fetched but I'm terri-fied what will happen next,' I confessed. 'Evelyn spooks me out.'

'She'd spook me out, too. She's a dragon in a twinset and pearls,' Lynne said. 'But you have to get it into perspective. She's an old lady who doesn't want to lose her son. A lot of women are like that. That doesn't mean that she's out to harm you.' There was a pause and then she asked, 'Look, are you sure you're not having second thoughts about the wedding? No one would blame you; it's a big step and it's all happened very fast.'

'Definitely not. I love Sam and I know he really loves me.'

'You're not just marrying Sam, though, you're marrying his

family too. And if you don't get on with his mum, then you've got a stormy road ahead.'

'It will be okay once we are married. Evelyn will have to accept that I'm Sam's wife and deal with it.'

I can't believe that I was really stupid enough to believe that.

33

Seeing Lynne really cheered me up, and I was sitting on the balcony in the sunshine when Sam came home, trying not to worry about what would happen to me next.

'You look brighter,' Sam said, giving me a lingering kiss then taking the seat next to me. 'Seeing Lynne has done you good.'

'It definitely has. And Tasha, my boss, wants me to work at home until Thursday, so I have plenty of time to recover.'

Sam wrapped his arms around me. 'Good. I want you to stay at home and keep safe. I am worried about you with those stairs, though. I don't want you falling again. You gave me the fright of my life.'

'I can't avoid stairs all my life!' I told him. 'Besides, I fell because my sandal was broken. Don't worry, I'll be extra careful in future.'

'Good.' He kissed me on the forehead. 'I wish I could work from home too but I've got such a lot to do before I take two weeks off for our honeymoon, so I will have to be out of the house quite a bit, I'm afraid.'

'I will be fine on my own,' I reassured him. I was determined to stay in our rooms as much as possible, out of Evelyn's way.

The next morning, when Sam had left for work, I went into the study to work too, but my mind kept going back to Evelyn's words. *The way you're going, you'll be lucky to make your wedding day.*

Did I really, in the cold light of day, think that the old woman was threatening me?

Maybe it was all a coincidence, as Lynne said. Maybe I was stressed and building things out of proportion.

Again.

I thought back to the incident eight years ago that had caused me to have a complete breakdown. An incident I'd never told Sam about. I didn't want him to think I was fragile, because I'm not. I'm strong now. But for a while I was broken, destroyed. It took me a while to claw back. It was not long after I'd moved into my own flat. My aunt and uncle had put two months' deposit down on it, helped me get some basic furniture and then, obviously feeling that their duty was done, off they moved to Cornwall. It was strange at first, living by myself, but I settled in and started to love the flat. Then, one winter's night, when I left work and was walking to the car park, someone jumped me and went off with my handbag. I was really shaken. I knew I was lucky that I wasn't injured, apart from bruises where my attacker had thrown me to the floor, and I managed to contact the bank and stop my bank card being used, so only actually lost the thirty pounds cash that was in my purse. But my house keys were in my bag and even though my landlord changed the locks for me, I was terrified for months afterwards that someone would sneak into my house in the middle of the night, or would be lying in wait for me. I only went out to go to work, and was so paranoid that someone was out to get me that Lynne became really worried about me. She tried to persuade me to see a doctor, but I wouldn't. I kept telling her I was all right but I wasn't. It got so bad that I started scratching myself again. Then one day Lynne came around and found me shaking and crying in the bedroom. I'd got myself in such a state that I couldn't even go to work. The doctor gave me antidepressants for a while. Slowly, I got better but I knew that Lynne was wondering if the stress of the wedding had brought back my paranoia about people being out to get me again, fearing that I was exaggerating perfectly ordinary incidents and taking them out of proportion.

The broken mirror, upset tummy, frayed kettle flex and my fall down the stairs could all be dismissed as coincidences. And I knew that Evelyn adored Sam, but would she really go to such lengths to prevent our marriage?

And why would Tamara? Yes, she was a snob and didn't think I was good enough for Sam, so was trying to cause a bit of mischief, I could see that. But to try and actually injure me? Maybe even kill me? It was a bit far-fetched, I had to admit.

I pushed my chair back and slowly got up, my leg and side still painful. I needed a break and a coffee. As I flicked on the kettle, the door knocked. 'Come in,' I called.

The door opened and Ruby poked her head around it. 'Mrs Corbett asked me to come and clean around up here. She doesn't want you exerting yourself after your fall. Is that okay with you, Dana?'

I nodded, appreciating her checking with me first. 'Yes, thank you. Would you like a cuppa first? I'm about to make one,' I offered. I wanted a chance to talk to Ruby and find out a bit more about the missing earrings but she shook her head.

'Thank you but I need to get on. I've somewhere else to go after I'm done here.'

'You go ahead, then. I think I'll go onto the balcony and drink mine,' I told her. It was a lovely day and I felt like some fresh air.

Ruby nodded, wiping her hand across her forehead. Her

black hair was swept up in a ponytail and as she walked into the bathroom to start cleaning, I noticed a red birthmark below her hairline, just like Sam's. I hadn't realised they were so common.

As if she felt my eyes on her, Ruby turned around. 'Is something wrong?'

I felt awful staring like that. 'Sorry, I didn't mean to be so rude. It's just that I noticed your birthmark. Sam has one exactly the same.'

I saw her eyes widen in surprise then she asked quietly, 'Exactly the same? And in the same place?'

'Yes. He said that Evelyn used to tell him when he was little that it was where the stork had held him to carry him to her.'

'My mum used to tell me that too,' Ruby said, in a wobbly voice and I saw tears brimming in her eyes.

'I'm sorry. I didn't mean to upset you,' I apologised, feeling awful. Judging by her reaction, her mum must be dead. 'Is your mum—?'

'Dead.' Her eyes met mine as she said the word. 'She died when I was four. My dad never got over it.'

I knew what it was like to lose a parent as a child; I'd lost both of mine. 'I'm sorry,' I whispered. 'That must have been so awful for both of you.'

'It was. And the worst thing was that when my dad discovered that my mum had had an affair and my baby brother wasn't his, he gave him away to his real dad. So I lost my mum and my brother.'

'When was this?' I asked her softly, holding my breath as I waited for her answer.

'Thirty-five years ago.'

Sam was thirty-five! I stifled a gasp as her eyes met mine. Sam's birthmark was identical to hers. Could Sam be her brother?

34

Ruby's words kept going over and over in my mind. She had obviously never got over the loss of her mum and her baby brother. Could Sam be her brother? Surely it was too much of a coincidence? I kept thinking of her poor dad, imagining the grief of losing his wife then discovering that the baby she had just given birth to wasn't his. It would be devastating.

It could be possible. Perhaps Harold had heard that his mistress had died, wanted his son, so contacted Ruby's dad and confessed to being the baby's father. It must have been such a shock to Evelyn, but she had forgiven him and taken the baby in, which actually was really kind-hearted of her. And she genuinely loved Sam, looked on him as her son. Anyone could see that.

Was I reading too much into it all? It could be a coincidence that Sam was adopted and Ruby's little half-brother had been adopted by his father, that they were both the same age, and Ruby and Sam had the same birthmark...

'That's me done, Dana!' Ruby called.

'Okay, thanks!' I shouted as I came back in from the

balcony, my coffee now finished. It was time I got back to work. I returned to the study and dealt with the emails that had come in during my coffee break then did a quick internet search on stork-bite birthmarks and discovered that they were very common and often disappeared as the child got older. Obviously not in Ruby and Sam's cases. Apparently, they could also appear on the baby's face, where they were called 'angel's kisses'. They weren't thought to be genetic, but could be.

I thought back to the conversation I'd overheard between Harold and Evelyn, about Sam's real mum being Harold's mistress and once again wondered if I should tell Sam. But if they denied it, what proof did I have? They could make it sound as if I was causing trouble. And what if Sam actually knew but didn't want it to be common knowledge?

I remembered thinking that Sam's real mother's name would be on his birth certificate. I decided to look at Sam's birth certificate and see what name was on there. Then I could ask Ruby what her mum's name was. It had to be here somewhere; we'd both had to submit them for the marriage certificate. They would probably be in Sam's desk. I got up and went over to it, pulling out the drawers one by one. The first drawer was full of pens, staples and paper clips; the second one contained more stationery and the bottom drawer held various letters. I glanced at them quickly, but saw nothing that looked like a birth certificate. Where would he keep that? I usually kept mine in a tin with various other bits and pieces from my past. I had no idea if Sam had such a tin but I imagined him keeping his important papers somewhere like a briefcase.

Maybe he kept it with his passport. I remembered passing Sam my passport to book our honeymoon and he'd held onto it, saying that he might as well keep it with his. I racked my brain trying to remember where he had put it. Then it came to me; he'd slipped it into a small black leather zipped folder and put it on a shelf in the top of his wardrobe. I went into the bedroom, opened the wardrobe and, mindful of my injuries, carefully climbed onto a chair to look on the shelf. There it was, tucked into the corner. I took out the folder and unzipped it. Both our passports were in it, and Sam's birth certificate. My pulse racing, I unfolded it and looked at the names of the parents. Harold Sam Corbett and Evelyn Mary Corbett. Evelyn was registered as his birth mother. How could that be when I had definitely heard Evelyn say that Sam was the result of Harold's affair? Unless his mother had died before his birth had been registered and Harold, being his birth father, had managed to fudge it that Evelyn was named as his mother so that no one would know the truth, especially Sam. Surely that wasn't legal, though?

'What are you doing, Dana?'

I almost toppled off the chair at the sound of Sam's voice. The leather folder fell out of my hands and onto the floor, the passports and papers spilling out.

Sam raced over, held the back of the chair, and helped me down. 'Well?' he asked.

I looked at his face, trying to gauge whether he was annoyed or not, but he simply looked curious.

'I was looking for my passport. I'll need to change the name on it when we get married and wanted to see how much time was on it.'

'I wish you'd waited for me to come home; you could have slipped and hurt yourself again. After all, there's no rush, you can't change it until we come back from honeymoon,' he said, picking up the passports and papers and slipping them back into the zipped folder.

'I didn't know what time you would be back and it was on my mind,' I said lamely.

Sam put the folder back in the wardrobe, then came over to

me. 'Surely it wasn't that urgent? The fall down the stairs really knocked you about, Dana. We can't risk another accident – especially this near to the wedding.'

'I know. I'm sorry. I wasn't thinking.'

Sam took my hand and gently sat me down on the bed, beside him. 'I'm a bit worried about you, Dana. You seem very anxious. Are you having second thoughts about the wedding?'

I shook my head vehemently. 'Of course not. I love you and can't wait to marry you. It's just that...' I hesitated, wondering whether to tell him my concerns.

'What? What is it? You can tell me anything, surely you know that?'

Could I? Would he believe me if I told him I thought his mum was doing everything she could to ruin our wedding? That she had deliberately tampered with my sandals and caused a fall that could have killed me?

That she wasn't his real mum?

'Dana?'

'It's just that so many things keep going wrong and I'm scared that something will go wrong on our wedding day and prevent us getting married,' I said. At least this was true, if not the whole truth.

Sam wrapped his arms around me. 'Nothing will stop us getting married, I promise you. Now please try to relax and look after yourself. You seem so... edgy at the moment.'

I wondered if he had been about to say 'highly strung' and thought better of it. I had often been called 'highly strung' in my life, because I was nervous and liked to keep busy, not giving myself time to think. Was it any wonder when my parents had died when I was so young and my strict aunt and uncle were so quick to criticise? I'd had a lonely, loveless childhood. I leaned my head against his shoulders and drank in his warmth, his smell, his calm presence. I had Sam's love now and was deter-

mined that nothing was going to stop us getting married. I'd be
on my guard at all times. No more accidents for me. And no, I
wouldn't tell Sam about his birth mother until after we were
married and in our own house. That would be much safer. But
if I could get chance to talk to Ruby again, I would.

35

Tasha was only giving me a light amount of work to do at home, so I'd finished by mid-afternoon on Wednesday and went downstairs to sit out in the garden, only to find Evelyn and Tamara already there, sipping a glass of prosecco. I hadn't seen Tamara for a couple of weeks; Evelyn said had that she was working in London again and wouldn't be back until our wedding day but here she was huddled up to Evelyn, whispering and giggling. I was glad that at least Sam was out at work.

'Oh, hello, Dana. How are you? I heard about your fall,' Tamara said, surveying me over the rim of her glass. 'Sounds like you had a lucky escape.'

'She did. I told her she needs to be more careful instead of running down the stairs,' Evelyn said.

'I wasn't running. The strap of my sandal broke,' I told her. 'That's why I tripped.' I watched her face carefully to see if I could see any sign of guilt, but she was focussed on Tamara.

Tamara looked down at my feet, and I was suddenly conscious of the scuffed trainers I was wearing. Tamara was sporting a pair of what looked like Jimmy Choo's. 'That's the trouble with cheap things; they don't last,' she said.

I felt my cheeks go hot but was determined not to let her drive me away. Sam and I were getting married next week. Evelyn and Harold were going to be my in-laws. And I lived here, for now anyway. This was my home. I pulled out a chair and sat down, replying as coolly as I could, 'Good to see you again, Tamara.' I reached for the bottle of prosecco and poured myself a glass.

'Do be careful, dear, drinking on top of your pain killers,' Evelyn said.

I smiled sweetly at her. 'Thank you for your concern but the pain has eased a lot now.' I took a sip of my drink.

Tamara reached over and picked out a large strawberry from the bowl, popping it into her mouth and chewing it before saying, 'We were talking about the wedding before you came down. You're very lucky; it's forecast to be a bright, sunny day. You'll have some gorgeous photographs.'

I nodded. 'That's why we wanted a summer wedding.' I turned to Evelyn. 'I'm very grateful to you and Harold for letting us have our reception in your beautiful garden.'

'You're welcome, dear.' She reached over and patted my hand. 'Anything for my son – and his bride.'

'You're certainly having a wedding to remember. And a spectacular honeymoon too. Evelyn said that you're going to the Caribbean for two weeks.' Tamara bit into another strawberry.

'Yes, I'm really looking forward to it. I'm going honeymoon clothes shopping with my friend Lynne on Saturday.' We'd arranged it when Lynne came around on Monday. Sam had suggested it, insisting I used the credit card he gave me to buy some new things for our holiday. 'That account is just for you. I'll transfer you an allowance every month to spend as you want,' he'd told me. I'd protested, saying that I was working and my wages were more than enough, especially as he'd told me that he didn't want me to contribute anything to the household expenses apart from the mortgage, saying that he could more than cover them. For the first time in my life, I was going to be financially secure. It was starting to hit me, how much my life was going to change. I hadn't really thought about it at first; all I'd thought of was that I was marrying Sam, who I loved more than anything. I hadn't stopped to think about the changes this would make to my everyday life. Sam was a well-respected accountant. Evelyn and Harold were very highly thought of in the village, and had influential connections. Harold was a magistrate, for goodness' sake. Tamara was a lawyer. And here I was, thinking that one of them was actually plotting to harm me. Lynne was right; I was overreacting.

'Enjoy yourself, dear, but don't overdo it. The wedding is almost upon us. We don't want you to add any more bruises to the ones you've already got,' Evelyn added.

'Thankfully there's another ten days until the wedding; they should be gone by then,' I said ruefully. 'And talking of the wedding, is there anything I still need to do for it?'

'It's all sorted. Evelyn and I have taken care of it. We're used to organising functions and events,' Tamara said. 'All you have to do is turn up and look beautiful.' The way she looked at me after that last statement insinuated that this would be difficult for me. *Okay, so she doesn't like me but that doesn't mean she's being trying to harm me,* I told myself.

'As Tamara said, it's all sorted, but we can run through the details again just to settle your mind. I know how anxious you get,' Evelyn said.

I gave her a sharp look, wondering if they had all been whispering about me, but she was getting out of her seat. 'I'll go and get the folder.'

She set off up the garden into the house, leaving me and Tamara alone. I felt a little awkward, waiting for the inevitable barb but Tamara merely smiled and picked up her glass. 'Congratulations, it looks like you've pulled it off and next week you'll be Mrs Corbett. I hope you and Sam will be very happy together.'

'Thanks,' I said, trying to work out if she meant it, or if it was another dig, but she carried on sipping her drink, and neither of us spoke until Evelyn came back with the wedding folder. I guessed that Tamara was telling me she had resigned herself to our marriage. Evelyn seemed to have done, too. Maybe my fall down the stairs, which could have killed me, had made them both assess things. I knew Sam had been devastated and they both loved Sam. We all loved Sam. None of us want to see him unhappy. Perhaps they had both decided to accept me for Sam's sake. I hoped so. That was what I needed to do too. Accept Sam's family and friends because they were important to him. As for him being adopted, what did that matter? Evelyn had been a good mum to him; there was no need for me to drag it all up. It was Evelyn and Harold's secret and it was up to them when they chose to divulge the truth, if ever. No one knew what I had overheard and I was going to keep it that way. All I had ever wanted was a happy family and it was looking like I was going to get one.

'Here we are, dear.' Evelyn passed me the folder. I looked through it and saw everything ticked off. As she said, it was all in hand. All I had to do was enjoy the day.

Tamara went home after an hour or so, saying she had a date that evening. When Sam came home, he joined us and so did Harold. We sat out chatting until late. It was a very pleasant evening and I finally felt accepted as part of the family. Sam and I hadn't been together long when we announced our marriage, I reminded myself, no wonder it took time for everyone to get used to the idea. Everything was going to be okay now.

36

'You look happy,' Lynne said when we met up on Saturday morning.

'I am,' I told her, linking my arm through hers. 'And I can't wait to hit the shops and buy some new clothes for my honeymoon.'

'I bet. I wouldn't say no to two weeks in Barbados myself. Mind, not on a honeymoon. Me and Spencer are back together but marriage is definitely not on the agenda,' she said. ''All okay at home then? No accidents?' she asked as we walked along together.

'No, all good. We've actually sat out in the garden chatting to Evelyn and Harold a couple of evenings this week. I think that she's finally accepted me.'

'Good. Now where do you want to start first? Sexy lingerie?' Lynne stopped outside Victoria's Secret.

I grinned. 'Why not?'

It was a fun afternoon. I bought a few bikinis and some evening dresses, as well as shorts and tops for the daytime.

'It must be nice not to have to worry about money,' Lynne said as we sat having lunch – my treat. 'I bet once you're married and moving in posh circles, I won't be seeing much of you.'

I glanced at her worriedly. She'd said something like that before. Did she really believe that? 'You'll always be my best friend, Lynne. Nothing will change that.'

She looked thoughtfully at me. 'Circumstances change things, Dana, and I'm not saying that because I'm resentful. I'm happy for you, really I am. I'm saying it because it's inevitable that we will grow apart but I want you to know that I'll always have your back, no matter what. If you ever need an ear to whinge into, a bed for the night, whatever. Ring me.'

I felt tears well in my eyes. Lynne and I had always been there for each other. Was she right and we would drift apart? I'd make sure we didn't, I vowed. I'd make sure that I messaged her at least once a week and that we met up every now and again. I don't know how I'd have got by without Lynne's friendship. She'd kept me sane – literally.

'And me you,' I told her.

'Hello, Dana, isn't it?'

I looked up at the woman hovering over our table. She looked vaguely familiar. 'I know it wasn't our fault, but I've felt so bad about letting you down with the house,' she continued. 'I hope you've found another one. You're getting married soon, aren't you?'

Ping. I realised who it was: Mrs Marsh. 'Next week. And yes, we're moving into a new house when we come back from our honeymoon. I was so sorry to hear about the fire. Thank goodness no one was hurt.'

'It was deliberate, you know. The insurance assessor told us last week. Someone started the fire on purpose. That really shook me up.'

I stared at her in horror. 'That's terrible. Do they know who did it?'

She shook her head. 'We haven't got any enemies as far as

we know, and the fire was started when we were out, so the assessor said he thought it might be kids, doing it for a dare or something. Makes me feel nervous, though. We've got smoke alarms and extinguishers everywhere now. The house will be back on the market as soon as possible. We can't wait to get out.' She nodded. 'Anyway, I'm pleased that you've found something else in time. Good luck with the wedding.' She nodded again then walked off.

I was so shocked I couldn't speak. Someone had deliberately started the fire, and with the intention of causing damage. They had made sure no one was in, so obviously wanted to damage the house not the occupants. Why?

'Are you all right, Dana? You've gone white.' Lynne's voice burst through my thoughts.

I dragged myself out of my thoughts and focussed on her. 'Lynne, that fire. What if whoever started it did it so we couldn't buy the house?'

Lynne looked at me as if I was nuts. 'What? Why would you think it was connected to you?'

'You heard Mrs Marsh; the fire was started to cause damage to the house, not the residents. It wasn't a warning to the family or an act of revenge. It was started so that they would have to take the house off the market to repair it. That meant me and Sam couldn't buy it and I would have to move in with his parents.'

Lynne shook her head. 'Dana, you surely can't believe that...'

But I did. I really did. It was the only thing that made sense. And it scared the hell out of me.

Evelyn had tried everything in her power to stop me marrying her precious son. Was she going to give up now or was she lulling me into a false sense of security?

37

Mrs Marsh's revelation about the fire being arson played on my mind all the way home. I'd just started to feel safe and that my fears were unfounded, but now this. Lynne was adamant that Evelyn couldn't have had anything to do with it, but I wasn't sure. I needed to see her reaction to the news. So I waited until we were all sitting down for dinner that evening and Evelyn asked me how my shopping trip went. 'Really well, I got lots of stuff for our honeymoon,' I told her. Then I turned to Sam. 'Oh, and we bumped into Mrs Marsh, you know, the woman who was selling the first house we were buying?'

He nodded as he sliced a potato and put it into his mouth. 'Have they managed to sort out the fire damage?'

'Almost. But you'll never guess what...' I could sense that Evelyn was hanging onto my every word. I glanced over at her as I finished: 'The insurance assessors have told them that the fire was arson.'

Was that look of shock on Evelyn's face because the fire was arson, or because she thought she had got away with it and now the assessors were on to her?

'Surely not? That's terrible. Have they any idea who it was?' Sam asked.

'Not yet, but the police are working on it. They think it was someone who waited until everyone was out because they wanted to damage the house, not the occupants.'

Harold frowned. 'It sounds as if someone has a grudge against them.'

'Or as if the arsonist didn't want them to sell the house,' I added, still watching Evelyn.

'That sounds a strange reason to start a fire,' she said, neither her face nor voice showing any sign of guilt. She was either a good actress or it was genuinely nothing to do with her.

'It's awful but I'm glad that the sale didn't go ahead now. If someone has got a grudge against the family, they might have started the fire when we were living there, not realising the Marshes had moved out,' Sam pointed out.

He had a point. I hadn't thought of that.

'Besides, I like the new house better, don't you?' Sam said.

'Yes, I do,' I agreed. And it was true, I did.

'This time next week we'll be man and wife,' Sam added, smiling. 'And in Barbados.' He reached out and touched my hand. 'I can't wait.'

'Neither can I.' *If nothing happens to stop the wedding.* I had to stop thinking like this; it would drive me crazy.

The rest of the week passed so quickly. I'd booked the Friday off for last-minute wedding preparations so was really touched on Thursday to discover that my work colleagues had had a collection and given us a one hundred-pound John Lewis voucher, plus a lovely card that they had all signed, and a horse-shoe. It was so kind of them when I'd only been there for six months.

Next time I go into work, I'll be Mrs Corbett, I thought happily as I left the office. I was so excited. A whole new life. If anyone had told me this a year ago, I would never have believed it.

When I arrived at the manor, the marquee was up – I'd forgotten it was arriving today – and Tamara was in the garden chatting with Evelyn, Sam and Howard. I was determined not to let that bother me. Two more days and Sam and I would be married.

'Hi,' I said with a big smile, sitting down to join them. 'Well, that's me finished work for a couple of weeks.' I looked over at the marquee. I hadn't expected it to be so big. 'That's impressive.'

'I'm glad you think so. Pour yourself a drink, dear.' Evelyn indicated the iced jug of orange juice on the table. 'We were just discussing final timings. I've arranged for the hairdresser and make-up artist to come at nine. That should give them plenty of time to do both yours and your friend's hair and make-up in time for the service at eleven.'

Evelyn never referred to Lynne by her name, I noticed. I could tell that she disapproved of her and wished that perfect Tamara was my maid of honour instead. *Or better still, the bride.* I shut the thought down. I had to move on from this; Tamara was a family friend and I would probably often bump into her, but she and Sam weren't interested in each other, and he was adamant they had never been an item. She was annoying but no threat to me; it was Sam I was marrying. *Besides,* I thought, *look at us all pleasantly discussing the wedding arrangements!* Everyone might have been surprised that Sam was marrying me at first, but they all seemed to have accepted it now, and were all doing their best to make the day a happy one. The garden with the marquee was such a lovely place to have the reception. And even Tamara was helping out. She didn't have to do that, did she? And I wasn't going to listen to the thought that crept into my head, that she was only doing it so she could seize any opportunity to ruin the day.

'Thank you so much for everything you've both done for the wedding,' I told Evelyn and Harold. 'And you, too, Tamara. I'm very grateful to you all.'

'We certainly are.' Sam placed his arm around my shoulders and smiled tenderly at me. It's very kind of you all.'

'It's no trouble at all, son. It's a pleasure,' Harold said.

' Your wedding is the most important event of your life and we all want you to have the best day possible,' Evelyn replied.

I wasn't sure if she was referring to both of us or just Sam, but then Tamara raised her glass of orange juice. 'To Sam and Dana,' she said lightly.

Evelyn and Harold raised their glasses too and joined in the toast.

Evelyn had booked extra staff to help with the cleaning so that everything was spick and span, and the gardener and Harold worked on the garden, so by Friday afternoon, the manor and garden were looking immaculate.

'I'm getting married tomorrow,' I told myself as I walked into the kitchen to get a drink. We were all sitting out in the garden, enjoying the sunshine and a final drink before the wedding.

Evelyn had insisted that I sleep in a downstairs room that evening.

'I don't want you even attempting to come down those stairs in your wedding gown. I'm afraid you might trip,' she told me. 'And it's bad luck for the groom to see the bride the night before the wedding. We don't want any more bad luck, do we?'

I didn't believe in superstitions but neither did I want to tempt fate, so I agreed even though I didn't want to spend the night away from Sam. 'I can't wait until tomorrow,' he said as we kissed goodnight in the hallway.

It felt strange not to be in our suite, and not to be with Sam.

I felt a little nervous, half expecting something to happen at the last minute to prevent us getting married, and wished that I could lock the door. I made do by dragging a heavy armchair across the floor and placing it against the door, hoping that would stop anyone coming in.

I needn't have worried, though; it was an uneventful night and I woke the next morning to find the sun blazing through the window. I flung back the sheet and hurried over to the window which looked out at the back garden, where I could see everything was set out for the wedding reception. It was a beautiful day.

I turned back, my eyes gazing around the huge room, with its floor-to-ceiling wardrobes and elegant silver grey sofa. It even had an en suite. Talk about luxury! I opened the far wardrobe door and took out my wedding dress and Lynne's bridesmaid's dress. She would be here soon to help me get ready. Today I was getting married and tomorrow Sam and I were off on glorious a two-week honeymoon in Barbados then returning to our own house. I would never have to live in the manor again, and I could choose when we saw Evelyn and Tamara. It was over. I smiled and let the happiness flow through me. Life couldn't get any better than this.

38

NOW. AFTER THE WEDDING.

'Dana! Dana! Can you hear me?'

Sam's voice sounded faint, distant, as if he was calling me from another dimension. I wanted to open my eyes and talk to him, assure him that I was fine, but I felt too weak, too tired. I craved sleep. I sighed, deep inside, and let the sleep take me over, resting in its calm and oblivion.

Then, I don't know how long afterwards, I heard Sam calling me again and knew he was near because I could feel his hand on mine. This time I felt stronger and I really wanted to see him, so I opened my eyes and there he was, right beside me, holding my hand, his eyes widening as they met mine. 'You're awake!' he exclaimed. He leaned over and kissed my cheek. 'Oh darling, thank goodness. For an awful moment, I thought I'd lost you.'

Lost me? What did he mean? I looked at him, confused.

Then I realised that I was in a hospital room. The door opened and two people came in, a nurse and a doctor. They asked Sam to step outside while they did some checks on me. I watched him go out, desperately trying to recall what had happened. Why was I in hospital?

'You gave us all quite a scare, Dana,' the doctor said gently as he and the nurse busied themselves around me, taking my temperature and other basic checks.

'What happened?' I asked. 'Why am I here?'

'It will come back to you in a bit. It's the shock,' the nurse told me. 'If your bridesmaid hadn't reacted so quickly, you wouldn't be here.'

Bridesmaid? Then my memory came crashing back. It was my wedding day. We'd just got married... Sam and I were cutting the cake. An image of the knife slicing through the white and lemon icing down into the bottom fruit layer flashed across my mind. I remembered Sam smiling, picking up a few crumbs of the cake and putting them in my mouth, then my throat tightening, not being able to breathe. 'The wedding cake! It had nuts in it,' I exclaimed.

The doctor nodded. 'You had a very bad reaction, but fortunately your bridesmaid grabbed your EpiPen and injected you while your husband called the ambulance. Their quick actions saved your life.'

Lynne saved me. Thank God! She had been with me when I'd had that awful first attack and seen the doctor use the EpiPen on me; she must have remembered it all these years. I recalled slipping the two EpiPens in my white sequinned clutch bag that morning, and Lynne holding the bag for me as I walked down the aisle.

'Where's Lynne?' I asked.

'Outside with your new husband. They've been very worried about you. All your family have.'

Husband. Family. They were strange words to me. I was married. Sam and I had finally got married. She hadn't managed to stop us, even though she had tried her damnedest. She'd even tried to kill me! The memories were now flooding back: the broken mirror; the stomach upset, frayed kettle lead; tumbling down the stairs... And now the wedding cake. Evelyn, my mother-in-law, had certainly pulled out all the stops to prevent me marrying her precious son.

She'd tried to kill me on my wedding day. My blood ran cold at the thought of what could have happened if Lynne hadn't been there to save me and Sam hadn't called the ambulance. I shuddered and closed my eyes. I couldn't bear to think of it.

'I think you should stay in hospital a little longer; you're still very weak,' the doctor said. 'I'll call your husband back in. He hasn't left your side since you were brought in this afternoon.'

I imagined Sam sitting beside my bed, holding my hand, willing me to open my eyes and talk to him. It must have been such a shock to see me collapse like that, holding my throat, struggling to breathe.

The doctor and nurse went out, and Sam came in, still dressed in his wedding suit. He was pale and had dark bags under his eyes but he was smiling. 'Dana, darling, the doctors said you're going to be okay. I can't tell you how worried I've been about you.' He sat down beside the bed and reached out to clasp my hand in his.

'How long have I been here? What about our honeymoon?' I asked, remembering that we were meant to fly out to Barbados the day after our wedding.

'You've been here a few hours. I've cancelled the honeymoon for now. We'll go in a few days when you feel stronger. Right now, all I want to do is get you home. I'd barely made you my wife when I almost lost you.' His face clouded over.

Home. I couldn't wait for us to go home, to be in our own house at last, away from Evelyn. I didn't feel safe around her. Then I remembered that the paperwork for the sale hadn't gone through yet. We were supposed to be moving in when we came back from honeymoon. Which meant that now we had to go back and live in the manor for another two weeks.

Panic gripped, tightening my chest. 'No, we can't! I won't go back there!' I screamed.

Sam jerked his head back, shocked, his eyes flying to my face. 'Dana! What's the matter?'

'It's your mum. She tried to kill me! She's been doing everything she can to prevent us getting married ever since I moved in.' The words tumbled out of my mouth and I knew that I sounded crazy but I had to tell him before something else happened. Before his mother actually succeeded in her evil plan.

'Dana!' He sprang to his feet, looking at me as if I was a mad woman. The door opened and the nurse rushed in.

'Is everything all right? I heard shouting.'

'It's his mum. She tried to kill me! She knew that I was allergic to nuts. She was the one who ordered the wedding cake. The bottom layer was supposed to be fruit only.'

Sam's eyes were wide with alarm. 'She's not making sense. Mum would never do anything to harm her.'

'What about all the other things?' I reminded him. 'All the accidents? She's been trying to get rid of me for weeks. And she nearly succeeded. I'm not going back to live with her. I'm not. Please don't make me.' My voice broke.

'Dana!' Sam was horrified. 'Calm down, please, sweetheart. How can you think that Mum would hurt you? She's shown you nothing but kindness—'

'She hates me! She wants you to herself!' I sobbed. Why couldn't he see what she's been doing? All the things that had happened to me...

'I think I'd better get the doctor. He'll give you something to sedate you for a while,' the nurse said, hurrying out of the room, coming back in a couple of minutes later with the doctor.

I fell asleep again. When I woke, Sam had gone and Lynne was sitting by my bed.

'Hello, hun. You've given us all a scare,' she said softly, stroking my forehead. 'How are you feeling?'

'Tired,' I told her. 'And scared. Evelyn tried to kill me. I would have died if it wasn't for you. You saved me. Thank you.' I squeezed her hand.

'Sam told me what you've been saying – he's really upset about it. It wasn't Evelyn's fault, Dana. It was a cock-up by the caterers. They've taken full responsibility and apologised,' Lynne explained .

I shake my head. 'It was Evelyn. You don't know what she's like.'

'Dana, you can't keep making accusations like this, people will think you're crazy,' Lynne warned me. 'I know that Evelyn is a bit possessive with Sam, but accusing her of trying to kill you is going a bit far.'

'It's true! She will do anything to get me out of Sam's life.' I tilted my head to meet Lynne's gaze and clutched her hand tightly, urging her to believe me. 'I'm not going back to the manor to live with her again. I can't. I'm terrified what will happen.'

Lynne's eyes were full of concern, and I relaxed. She did believe me. Thank goodness someone did. Lynne would help me; I knew she would.

'Hun, if you keep saying things like this, you won't be going back to the manor, you'll be going to a psychiatric ward,' she said gently.

I gasped in horror. She was serious. I could see that. So she didn't believe me, after all. Neither did Sam. I was on my own.

'I know you've had a nasty shock, and have been over-wrought and stressed about the wedding, but your mind's working overtime, Dana. I told you, the catering company made a mistake with the cake.'

'How could they? I told them countless times about my allergy.'

'Someone ordered a similar cake to yours and a new member of staff put your cake in the wrong box. They've apologised and offered compensation.'

I didn't believe it. As always, there was a reasonable explanation. Evelyn was an expert at covering her tracks. I wanted to protest, to insist that Lynne call the police so I could give a statement and have Evelyn arrested – or at least cautioned – but I knew it was useless. Defeated, I closed my eyes wearily. 'I guess you're right. I'm still really tired. I could do with some sleep.'

'Good idea. Rest and you'll feel better when you wake,' Lynne replied.

I kept my eyes closed, pretending I had dropped off to sleep, not wanting to talk any more. Not even opening them when Sam came back with coffee. I kept them firmly shut all the while they both whispered about the strain I'd been under and how worried they were about my paranoia.

The doctor came back and said that it was best if I stayed in overnight so they could keep an eye on me. I flicked open my eyes at that; I didn't want to spend our wedding night apart but I was exhausted and terrified about going back to the manor.

Sam bent over and kissed me gently. 'Rest up, sweetheart. I'll come and get you first thing in the morning.'

I wanted to cry, but instead I smiled weakly. 'Not much of a wedding night,' I whispered.

'There will be other nights. We've got all the time in the world,' he said. 'All that matters is that you rest and get better.'

I lay there thinking, once he and Lynne had gone, angry and hurt that neither of them would believe me. I wasn't under strain or paranoid. My mind was as clear as day. Evelyn had tried to kill me. I felt nauseous at the thought of going back to live with her but I knew that I had no choice. I couldn't prove anything. My mind went over all the things she had done, right up to that horrible moment at our wedding reception when I couldn't breathe and had looked around in panic, my eyes finally resting on hers, seeing the triumph there, thinking she'd won.

Only she hadn't won, had she? I'd survived. Just like I'd survived everything else she had tried to do to me. I was stronger than she had thought. Stronger than I had thought. It was as if I flicked on a switch in my mind. I was on to Evelyn now. No one else believed me but I knew that I wasn't imagining it. I had taken everything she'd thrown at me, survived it all and still married Sam. Strength and resolve flooded through my veins. Evelyn wasn't going to get the better of me. I was Sam's wife, despite everything she'd done to prevent it, and I wasn't going to be a doormat any longer. I had to live at the manor until we could move into our house, but from now on it was going to be on my terms.

39

Sam turned to smile at me as the gates opened, allowing us to drive through the next morning. 'Mum and Dad have been so worried about you. Mum blames herself. She said she should have double-checked with the caterers, but she kept the box the cake arrived in and it was clearly marked "nut-free".'

She blamed herself because it was her doing. She wanted me dead. I didn't say the words that were screaming in my mind. I couldn't prove it and I had to face reality; it did seem that it had been a mistake on the caterers' part, but I couldn't help feeling that Evelyn had played some part in it. That was why she'd been so pleasant to me in the days up to my wedding; she'd wanted to lure me into a false sense of security so I would be off my guard and trust her. Besides, even if the caterers were responsible for sending the wrong cake, I was certain Evelyn was behind all the other things that had happened. It was pointless to say this to Sam, though; he was convinced his mum could do no wrong.

'I can't get it out of my head that you could have died, Dana,' Sam said, his voice shaking, as we pulled up outside the front of the manor. 'I'd never have forgiven myself if anything had happened to you. Mum wouldn't have, either. She's been beside herself with worry.'

I bit back the words that rushed to my tongue; that Evelyn would have been very pleased if I had died, so she could have her precious son all to herself. Maybe she had only meant to make me ill so we couldn't go on honeymoon, rather than actually harm me. A lot of people didn't realise how severe a nut allergy can be, how quickly you can die. I shuddered at the memory of my throat closing, of struggling for breath, of how only minutes had separated me from life or death. I hoped that the knowledge that I'd almost died had given Evelyn a shock, and now that we were married, she would accept me as Sam's wife and stop trying to harm me. I needed to keep my wits about me though; she might still try to cause trouble between us. Or do something to delay us moving out into our own house – she was so desperate to keep Sam at home with her. Well, she wasn't going to succeed. Two weeks and we'd be out of here. I'd be counting the days and watching her like a hawk.

I hated to see Sam distressed, so forced a smile on my lips. 'Let's forget about it now. It's over. It's such a shame we had to miss our honeymoon, though. Can't we jump on a plane and go anyway? The hotel's booked.'

'We could. We're covered by travel insurance, luckily, so we'll get the original flight money back, but I wanted to run something by you first,' Sam said. 'I telephoned the estate agent earlier to tell him what's happened and ask him if we could possibly complete the house sale earlier, seeing as we weren't on our honeymoon.' He took my hand in his. 'He said it could all be finalised by the end of this week, if we wanted. How do you feel about that? It means we could move in and get it all straight before we go on honeymoon. Or would you prefer to wait until we get back?'

My spirits lifted at that news and I nodded eagerly. 'Yes, definitely. I'd love to move into our house first.' I didn't want to spend a day longer in the manor than I had to, and didn't want to risk anything happening to stop the sale – as had happened before. I started to relax now I knew that we could move out earlier than expected. I could manage a few more days with Sam's parents.

We both got out of the car and Sam clasped my hand as we walked towards the front door, as if he sensed how anxious I was. *Be strong*, I told myself, remembering my resolution last night when I was in hospital. *No more doormat, stand up for yourself. You're Sam's wife now.*

The door opened and Evelyn came out. She must have been waiting for us. 'Welcome back, dear. It's so good to see you. We've all been so worried,' she said as she held out her arms to greet me. I stiffened as she hugged me. I would never trust this woman, no matter how friendly she acted.

'Thank you,' I said, stepping back a little. 'I'm relieved to be out of hospital. An anaphylactic attack is terrifying. I really thought I was going to die.' I watched her reaction carefully. She seemed very distressed.

'I am so sorry.' She wrung her hands. 'I feel terrible, as you trusted me to order the cake. The caterers are very apologetic, but it's not good enough. It could have been a devastating tragedy.' She looked and sounded so genuine. Had I imagined the look of triumph in her eyes when my throat was swelling up and I was struggling for breath?

'Thank goodness it wasn't.' Sam had released my hand when his mum hugged me but now reached for it again and squeezed it tight, gazing at me, his eyes full of love. 'I don't know what I'd do if anything had happened to you.'

Evelyn turned to Sam now, almost as if to assess if he was serious. *Doesn't she see that by harming me she's hurting Sam too?* I thought. *Doesn't she realise how much he loves me, or does her obsession for him block out everything else?*

'Well, I'm sure we'll all be extra careful to make sure that nothing like that ever happens again,' she said. 'Now, let's sit out in the garden, it's such a lovely day. I've made a fruit punch and fresh salmon sandwiches, followed by fruit flan, if you both fancy some.'

'That sounds delicious, doesn't it, Dana?'

We'd only be here a few more days and, despite everything that had happened, I wanted us to be on good terms with Sam's parents, so I nodded. 'Thank you, that would be lovely.'

Evelyn and Harold were both very pleasant, but as we sat out in the garden chatting, I found it difficult to relax, wondering whether Evelyn would give up on her attempts to harm me now we were married, or would she still try to prevent us from moving out.

'Dana. Are you okay, darling? You were miles away.' Sam tenderly placed his hand over mine. 'Are you tired? Would you like us to go up now and you can have a rest?'

I did feel really weary. 'Yes, please.' I turned to Evelyn and Harold. 'Thank you for the lunch.'

Sam got to his feet and held out his hand for me to take. 'Excuse us both,' he said.

I slipped my hand in his as we walked back inside and up the stairs, all the while thinking that we should be on honeymoon now, but instead we were back living with his parents.

Sam pushed open the door of the suite and led me in then, to my surprise, he slid a bolt across the top of the door. He must have noticed my eyes widen because he shrugged ruefully. 'It is our honeymoon, after all, and Mum does have a habit of walking in unannounced.'

So he had taken notice of some of the things I'd said and was trying to make me feel more comfortable here. A surge of love for him coursed through me. He loved me and was trying to make things better. Maybe everything would be all right now. I wrapped my arms around his waist. 'Talking of honeymoon...'

He lowered his head so this his nose was touching mine, his eyes holding my gaze. 'Are you sure you aren't too tired?'

'Absolutely not!' I assured him.

Then his lips were on mine and we were kissing and caressing and I was lost in the pleasure of his touch.

I'm so happy, I thought much later, as we sat up in bed, drinking champagne. Sam and I were actually married. And soon we would be moving into our very own home. Okay, so Evelyn was possessive but maybe she'd learned her lesson, and wouldn't risk doing anything else. If she did... well, I would be on my guard, prepared to fight back. And Sam has realised now that his mother can be a bit over the top so would surely support me.

The next morning, the solicitor phoned to confirm that we could exchange contracts and complete on the house on Friday. I was ecstatic. It was worth postponing our honeymoon to be able to move into our new home so soon. Sam and I talked about it and decided to spend a week getting the house straight, then go on honeymoon in early August instead.

'I know it's officially our honeymoon, but if we want to go away next month I'll have to go back to work tomorrow, then I'll take Friday off for the house move,' Sam promised. 'Do you think that you'll be able to swap your annual leave?'

I hoped so. I hadn't been working at the company for six months yet and was aware that I'd already had a bit of time off but, luckily, Tasha, my boss, was very approachable. 'I'll phone Tasha tomorrow, let her know what's happened, and see if we can sort something out. Perhaps I can go back into work on Wednesday and Thursday, take Friday off to move into our house and work again all next week. If she agrees, we can book the new honeymoon dates when you get home tonight,' I told

Sam. 'I'm sure we can work out something.' I was so happy, eager to start the next part of our lives as a married couple. No Evelyn, no Tamara. Just me and Sam. And our very own home where, at last, I'd feel safe.

'Let's go and tell Mum and Dad the news,' Sam suggested.

His parents were out in the garden, sitting at the table, drinking Pimm's with Tamara.

'Well, you gave us all a scare,' Tamara said as we walked over to join them. 'What a shame your wedding day ended like that! And that you couldn't go on honeymoon, either.'

I smiled pleasantly. 'It was awful, but it seems that it's all worked out for the best, doesn't it, Sam?' I turned to him, waiting for him to explain.

'What do you mean?' Evelyn put her glass down and sat bolt upright.

'The solicitor has just phoned. It's all sorted. We're finalising the house sale on Friday. Which means we can move in and settle into our new home, then reschedule our honeymoon.'

Evelyn looked really put out. 'That quickly?' she said, her eyes darting to me. 'Why not stay here for a while until you get your new house straight? It'll be much easier to do if you don't have to live in the mess.'

'We don't mind. We're excited and can't wait to move in, can we, Sam?'

Evelyn's eyebrows shot up in surprise at my reply. I usually held back and left Sam to do the talking but not any more. I was Sam's wife now and no one was walking over me. I felt a new strength flood through me.

'Well, I think it's delightful news,' Tamara said, beaming. 'I must come and visit you.'

'We'll be taking a little time to settle in so won't be accepting guests for a while, but then I'm sure we'll have some sort of get-together, won't we, Sam?' I asked, reaching for his hand.

'Whenever you're ready, darling,' he replied.

I noticed the look of astonishment pass between Evelyn and Tamara and couldn't resist throwing them a triumphant look. The meek mouse they thought they were dealing with had grown sharp teeth. And she would use them if she had to.

40

I locked the door as soon as Sam went to work the next morning so that Evelyn and Ruby couldn't disturb me, then made myself a cup of tea and some toast. I was eager to build up my strength now, I had so many plans for our new home. I opened the curtains to let in the sun and got back into bed with my breakfast, taking my laptop with me too, so that I could browse for soft furnishings. I selected some curtains and a few sofas and suites, bookmarking them for Sam's approval. We'd agreed to take a look at some furnishings tonight and to go shopping on Saturday for other items.

It was such lovely weather that I was tempted to sit out on the balcony for the day but decided that it was too nice to stay inside. Sam had mentioned that his parents were out today, which meant that I could spend an hour or so in the garden by myself. That would be heavenly.

I waited until the busy morning period at work was over then phoned my boss to explain what had happened. Tasha was really sympathetic and agreed to rearrange my holiday so we could go on our honeymoon in August. 'We've got cover for you this week and next, as we thought you'd be away, so no need to rush back in. We can manage. Take the rest of this week off, give yourself time to recover and settle into your new home. Come back on Monday,' she said. 'Then you can take two weeks next month – you're entitled to three weeks' holiday leave.'

I thanked her, pleased with how well it was all working out, then went for a shower. Pulling on shorts and a vest, I slipped my feet into some trainers, picked up a book to read and went downstairs. It was so quiet and peaceful. I headed to the kitchen for a cold drink from the fridge then took it outside with the book and sat on one of the reclining sunbeds already laid out on the lawn. It was nice to have a bit of quiet time to myself.

After a pleasant couple of hours out in the sunshine, I started to feel hungry so headed back inside to get a snack. As I opened the back door, I heard the sound of shouting coming from the hall. Were Harold and Evelyn back and having another row? I paused, not sure whether to go inside or not.

'Tell me why I shouldn't fire you on the spot! I've caught you snooping red-handed.' That was Evelyn's voice. So it was Ruby she was arguing with, not Harold, I realised.

'I was cleaning, that's what you pay me to do!' This was from Ruby. She sounded angry too.

'And what part of cleaning requires you to go through the drawers of my dressing table?' Evelyn's voice was icy cold.

'I've already explained that I was putting your creams away so that I could clean the surface of the dressing table.'

'I know what I saw; you were searching through my personal items, which is absolutely unacceptable. I want you to leave immediately. And I shall complain to the agency and make sure that they take you off their books. You aren't trust-worthy enough to be employed as a cleaner.'

Wow, it sounded like Evelyn's caught Ruby snooping and was really furious with her.

'Please don't do that, I need to work – I've got a little girl.

And I've done nothing wrong!' Ruby pleaded, her voice breaking.

'Now that's a bit harsh, dear,' I heard Harold protest in his mild way. 'I'm sure that Ruby didn't mean any harm. I don't think we need to sack her. I always ask her to put anything away she finds on my bedroom floor. I expect she was simply doing the same for you.'

'I was...'

'You were not! I caught you mooching through my drawer, so please don't insult my intelligence by denying it,' Evelyn insisted.

'I think we can give her another chance; she has always been trustworthy,' Harold replied.

Had she? I thought back to the earrings that Ruby said she had found on the floor and slipped into my jacket pocket. I'd seen her coming out of Evelyn's room earlier that day. Had she been mooching then and stolen the earrings, and when Evelyn realised they were missing, had panicked and slipped them in my jacket pocket? I'd always felt that excuse was suspicious. Surely Ruby knew that floral jacket was mine? Evelyn would never wear a jacket like that.

'No. I'm not satisfied with her performance at all,' Evelyn retorted. 'I don't want you working here any longer, Ruby. In view of you having a young child to support I won't sack you myself. I will leave you to tell the agency that the job isn't suitable for you. Tomorrow, I'll ask the agency to send us a replacement cleaner.'

'Now, dear...' Harold protested but Ruby remained silent.

'My mind is made up. I'm giving a talk at the WI this afternoon, I only came back to get my notes,' I heard Evelyn say. 'Leave your keys with Harold, Ruby.' A few seconds later, I heard the front door open and close.

I couldn't help feeling sorry for Ruby; she'd put up with so much from Evelyn and it seemed like she really needed this job. And I didn't want to lose contact with her. What if Sam was her step-brother? I recalled the similar birthmarks on their necks, and her story about her dad giving her baby brother to his birth father and wife, who couldn't have children. It might all be a coincidence – lots of people have affairs and lots of babies are adopted – but what if it wasn't and Sam was her missing brother? If she left, I would never know the truth.

I hurried around to the front of the house and pretended to be searching in my car for something while I waited for Ruby to come out. She emerged a few minutes later.

I waved and shouted. 'Hi there!'

She looked at me, a little puzzled. 'Hello, Dana. Are you feeling better now? It must have been a very scary experience for you.'

I walked over to her as I replied casually, 'It was. I literally thought that I was going to die.' I stopped just in front of her. 'I'm so sorry that you've lost your job.'

She looked surprised so I explained, 'I overheard Evelyn shouting at you when I went in for a drink. Will you be okay? If Evelyn doesn't make a complaint, the agency will give you more work, surely?'

Her gaze held mine. 'I'm not a cleaner. I'm actually a pharmacist.'

'A pharmacist!' I repeated, surprised. What was she doing working here as a cleaner then?

As if she'd read my mind, Ruby delved into her handbag and pulled out a photo. 'This is why I'm here.'

I took the photo from her and studied it curiously. A woman with chestnut hair and brown eyes stared back at me. Hair and eyes just like Sam's. I could feel Ruby's eyes boring into me, and when I looked back up at her, I noticed for the first time that her eyes were exactly the colour of Sam's, and of this woman's. She had the same nose too, although Ruby's face was narrower. I turned the photo over and saw one word written on the back. *Alma*. Who was she?

'She's my mum. I think she's Sam's mum, too,' Ruby explained quietly. 'Harold had an affair with my mum.'

So I was right. 'Were you searching through Evelyn's things because you wanted to find something that would prove Sam is your brother?' I asked.

She tilted her head to one side. 'You're not surprised to hear this,' she replied without answering my question.' Did you already know?'

'I know Evelyn isn't Sam's birth mother. I heard her and Harold having a row about it.'

Ruby's eyes widened and she looked furtively over her shoulder. 'We can't talk here. Can you meet me in an hour? In the big Costa on the high street in Worcester?'

I guess that she'd suggested a café away from Malvern so that we wouldn't get seen together. What would she do if she discovered that Sam was her half-brother? I wondered. Was she intending to blackmail Harold and Evelyn, to threaten to tell Sam if they didn't pay up? I wanted answers, so I agreed to meet her, deciding that once I knew the full story – and we were safely in our own home – I was going to tell Sam. He had a right to know. We were married now, so as his wife my first loyalty was to Sam, not his parents.

'I'll be there,' I promised.

I waited until Ruby had left, then went back into the house, hoping that Harold hadn't seen us talking. There was no sign of him. I walked down to the kitchen and looked out of the window, relieved to see him out in the garden, digging. I opened the back door and shouted, 'Do you fancy a cuppa?'

He beamed. 'That would be nice. I could do with a break.'

He said that as if he'd been out in the garden for hours when I knew that it could only have been ten minutes or so. 'I'll bring it out,' I offered.

I made two mugs of tea and got the biscuit tin out of the cupboard, putting a selection on a plate, then took them all outside. 'Ready?' I called.

Harold put down his spade, took off his gloves and came over to join me. He squirted his hands with the anti-bacterial gel Evelyn always kept on the table, rubbed them together then sat down. 'This is very nice of you. Sam's lucky to have met someone like you.' He picked up a ginger biscuit and nibbled it. 'I was always worried he would end up with someone really unsuitable.'

Why, had his tastes been unsuitable before he met me? I wanted to ask but instead I said, 'I get the impression that Evelyn disapproves of me, though. I think she was hoping Sam would marry Tamara.' I watched his reaction.

'Tamara has always been like a daughter to Evelyn, to both of us, but a marriage between her and Sam would never have worked out. Not that Sam or Tamara have ever been interested in each other in that way. Despite the combined efforts of Julia and Evelyn,' he added with a rueful smile.

So Sam had been telling me the truth; they had never dated.

Harold picked up a rich tea biscuit next and dipped it into his mug of tea. 'I know that Evelyn can be a bit... difficult... but I'm sure that she will start to look on you as a daughter too, once you both get to know each other a little more,' he assured me.

'I hope so.' I took a swig of my tea. 'I understand that Sam is Evelyn's only child and she only wants the best for him.' I studied Harold's face over the rim of my mug for any sign of unease, guilt, anxiety. Nothing. He clearly thought of Evelyn as Sam's mother even though she hadn't given birth to him.

'Evelyn waited a long time to have a child. She – we – thought that we would never be blessed with one, so when Sam came along, he was doubly precious.' His eyes were full of compassion behind his silver-rimmed glasses. 'It is very hard for her to let go, but she is working on it. Be patient with her.'

He was a good actor. But then I guessed he'd been spouting this story for years. Maybe he even half believed it himself now.

I didn't trust myself to speak. I was scared that I would call him out, tell him that I knew the truth and I didn't want to do that just yet. I needed to know what Ruby had to tell me first. So I sipped my drink and said nothing. We both sat there in silence for a while, a silence that didn't seem to perturb Harold at all, but was full of unspoken questions for me. Finally, drink finished, I stood up. 'Well, I'd better go and meet my friend.'

Harold gave me a smile. 'Have a lovely afternoon.'

41

The café was packed when I arrived. I glanced around, looking for a spare table, wondering if Ruby would think to look upstairs if I went up there. Then I spotted her in the queue. I went up and tapped her on the shoulder. 'Let me get the drinks, you grab a table.'

'Okay, thanks.'

I took her place in the queue and she went off to check if there were any tables at the back. She came back a few minutes later. 'We'll have to go upstairs.'

'That's fine. Do you want a cake?' I asked her.

She shook her head. 'No thanks, just a white coffee will be fine.'

I followed her upstairs a few minutes later with the two coffees, where I found her sitting at a table overlooking the street. 'Do you live in Worcester?' I asked as I put the tray down and sat down opposite her.

'No, but I'm renting a house in the town for a couple of months,' she told me. 'I live in Exeter. That's where my mum met Harold. The Corbetts moved away as soon as Dad gave them Sam. They went to another area so no one would know he was adopted.'

'Did Evelyn and Harold pressure your dad to give up Sam because Evelyn couldn't have children?' I asked.

'Leo. My mum called the baby Leo,' Ruby snapped abruptly. She tugged at a lock of her dark hair. 'I think Dad was probably glad to hand Leo over. He already had me to look after – I was only four. He didn't want a newborn too, especially one that wasn't even his child.'

'I'm so sorry, that must have been awful for you. But how did your dad know for certain that Sam wasn't his son?' I had to ask. 'I wouldn't think DNA tests were widely used back then.'

Ruby took a sip of her coffee before replying. 'Apparently the timing wasn't right; my parents hadn't been "close" for a while. But Mum denied she'd had an affair. They split up for a while, my aunt said, and Harold used to come and visit Mum. She said that he was planning to leave Evelyn and move away with my mum but my parents got back together just before Leo was born.' Her eyes glistened. 'Then Mum died, and Harold wanted Leo. He was Harold's son, so Dad agreed. He was heartbroken over Mum and didn't want to bring up another man's child.'

'It must have been a difficult time.' My heart went out to her, to the little girl that she had been, growing up without a mum. I wondered how her dad had been; grief-stricken and angry, I should imagine. I hoped he'd been good to Ruby.

'It was. Dad was a good father. Kind, loving. Never said a bad word about Mum. I never knew about the terrible secret he was keeping from me until after he died six months ago.' Her face clouded over. 'It was a sudden heart attack.'

'I'm so sorry.'

She swallowed. 'Then my aunt gave me a letter Dad had written years ago for me to have if anything happened to him. It explained everything.'

'That must have been awful for you,' I said softly. She looked so distraught that I wanted to hug her. 'How did your mum die?'

She stared down into her mug for a while and I didn't think she was going to answer. Then she looked up, her face anguished. The pain was obviously still raw.

'She fell down the stairs and broke her neck when Leo was only a couple of weeks old. Dad was devastated; he couldn't cope with the grief and guilt. There was a loose tread on the stairs... he'd been meaning to fix it but hadn't got round to it.' She bit her lip. 'My aunt took care of me until Dad managed to pull himself together. He never spoke about Leo, and over the years, I forgot all about my little half-brother. I was only four. I might never have remembered if it wasn't for Dad's letter,' she admitted. 'My aunt filled me in with the rest of the details. I was determined to find Leo, so took a few months' compassionate leave from my job and started searching for them. It was easy enough to track Harold down – my aunt knew his name and that he used to be an accountant; an internet search provided the rest of the details.'

'So you decided to apply for the cleaning job? How did you find out about it? Did you sign on to the agency and see it advertised?'

'I was trying to think of a way of getting to know Harold and Evelyn, so I rented a room in a local B&B at first, for me and my little daughter Isla – she's at nursery at the moment – and the woman told me her cousin, Helen, was their housekeeper but had to go away for a bit and they were looking for another cleaner. I said I'd be interested as I needed a job, so she gave me the name of the agency and said to tell them she'd sent me. I signed up and they gave me the job.' She grimaced. 'I can't stand the job, to be honest – Evelyn is a nightmare to work for and wants me to come in on Saturdays, which means that I have to send Isla to a local childminder – but I decided to use the opportunity to try and get to know Sam, and to get some evidence that he was my brother. When you told me about his birthmark, I was certain he was. I was looking for paperwork in Evelyn's room today but she caught me and accused me of snooping.'

My mind was reeling at the tragedy of it all. Poor Ruby, growing up without a mum, and Sam, never having the opportunity to get to know his sister or real mother. How would he feel when he learnt the truth? He'd had such a charmed life, doting parents, never having to worry about money, everything he wanted, whilst Ruby had lost her mother and baby brother when she was so young – although she seemed to have had a fairly happy life. It would surely be mind-blowing for Sam to discover that his father had an affair, that his birth mother had died and he had a half-sister.

'All I want to do is find my brother and make sure he's okay. I know that Dad did the right thing giving him away. The baby would have been a constant reminder of Mum's unfaithfulness and Dad would have struggled to cope. Besides, Harold was Leo's natural father; he had parental rights and Dad didn't. It would have been nice to have a little brother, though. It was so lonely sometimes.' Her eyes misted over. 'It all adds up with Sam's age, and the birthmark. I'm sure he must be my brother.'

'I agree but the thing is...' I paused, not wanting to put a damper on it but feeling I had to warn her that we might be wrong. 'I've seen Sam's birth certificate, and it names Evelyn as his natural mother.' That was what had puzzled me most.

Ruby shrugged dismissively. 'It's easy enough for someone in Harold's position to get a forged birth certificate.' She leaned forward earnestly. 'We need to have a DNA test to prove it. I got one of Evelyn's hairs from her hairbrush today. Can you get one of Sam's? That will prove if Evelyn is his birth mother or not. And I can send one of my hairs to be tested to see if we're related.'

My heart thudded. 'We need to be careful. Evelyn is

dangerous,' I warned her. 'If she discovers what we're doing, she'll do anything to stop us.'

42

Ruby frowned. 'What do you mean? What's she done?'

I hesitated. No one had believed me when I'd said that Evelyn was behind all the 'accidents' I was having; everyone was taken in by her kind, friendly act. Would Ruby?

'She tried to stop me marrying Sam. She kept causing trouble between us to drive me away. She's so obsessed with him that she doesn't want him to move out even now. She'll have probably given all his previous girlfriends a hard time, no doubt.'

'I can believe it. I thought it was terrible how you were accused of stealing the earrings. I'm surprised you stuck it out,' she added admiringly. 'You must really love Sam.'

'I do.' I took a deep breath. 'My parents died when I was young too and I was taken in by an aunt and uncle who never wanted children and only looked after me out of duty. I know I should be grateful for that, but I always felt in the way. I always wanted to be loved, to be part of a loving family. When I met Sam, I thought my dream had come true – but it's turned out to be more of a nightmare.' I cupped my hands around my mug and stared into the frothy liquid for a moment before looking back at Ruby. 'You know that she tried to kill me? The wire on the kettle – I was electrocuted, and if I hadn't been wearing my sneakers with rubber soles, it would have been fatal. The fall down the stairs; that was caused by a broken strap on my sandals. I'm sure it was deliberately broken. And there's more.' I related all the incidents to her. 'I thought she was just trying to make me feel awkward and drive me away at first. I'm not convinced that the nuts in the wedding cake were accidental.' I shivered as I remembered the look of triumph in Evelyn's eyes when she'd seen me choking. She had played some part in that, I was convinced of that.

We both sat in silence for a while, finishing our coffees, deep in thought. Then I remembered Ruby mentioning the incident with the earrings. 'Why did you really put those earrings in my pocket? Did you take them?' I asked.

Ruby shook her head. 'No. Evelyn did. I saw her slip them in the pocket of your jacket, which was hanging on the back of the chair in the drawing room. She was trying to frame you. So when I heard about it, and how you'd called the wedding off, I decided to say that it was me. I knew she wouldn't contradict me because then she'd have to admit what she'd done. She was fuming, though, always looking for a chance to fire me after that.'

'Thank you for that but I still don't understand why you did it?' I said.

'Because I like you and anyone can see Sam adores you. I didn't want everyone to think you were a thief. It wasn't fair. And if I'd told anyone that it was Evelyn, no one would have believed me and I would have been sacked. I couldn't risk that, not before I found out the truth.'

So I'd been right all along; Evelyn had been trying to get rid of me. Now we were married, would she stop?

We arranged for me to give Ruby a hair from Sam's hairbrush tomorrow so that she could send it off for a DNA test. 'We'll get the results within forty-eight hours,' she told me.

We swapped phone numbers, then Ruby stood up and pushed her chair back. 'I have to go. Be careful,' she warned me. She waved and walked out of the café.

I ordered another coffee and sat there for a while, thinking. I knew that Ruby was right and I had to watch my back. I was sure that Evelyn would do anything to prevent me finding out and telling Sam their secret.

I wished that Lynne wasn't at work; I would have loved to have talked it over with her, but then it would be wrong of me to tell anyone else before Sam knew. It was his life, his secret. He might not want to tell anyone else when he found out the truth, and I would respect that.

I finished my coffee, did a bit of shopping and headed back to the manor. I'd just pulled up when I got a call from Sam. 'Sorry, sweetheart, I've got to work late. We've been invited to tender for a high-profile business and I need to do costings for tomorrow. Will you be okay?'

'That's marvellous news, and yes, I'll be fine. See you later,' I said, trying not to be disappointed. Sam was a successful accountant; it was good that he was in demand.

As I walked in, I could sense a bit of an atmosphere between Evelyn and Harold and wondered if they had rowed again, perhaps over her sacking Ruby.

'Sam's working late tonight and I'm a little tired,' I said. 'I think I'll go upstairs and relax for a while.'

'I'll call you when dinner's ready,' Evelyn told me.

'Thank you.'

I mulled over the afternoon's events once I was upstairs in our suite. I hoped that Sam would be home for dinner; I didn't fancy sitting around the table with Harold and Evelyn. Not after what I'd found out. I couldn't help feeling sorry for Evelyn; how terrible it must have been to have had several miscarriages and been told that you could never have the baby you desperately yearned for, only to discover that your husband had fathered a child with his mistress. She must have loved Harold so much to forgive him and take on his baby as her own. She idolised Sam, anyone could see that, but what if the truth destroyed their relationship?

But I couldn't sit on this. Once we had definite proof, Sam had a right to know.

I got up and paced around. Evelyn and Harold should have told Sam years ago, not left it for him to find out like this.

I turned as I heard a knock on the door. 'May I come in for a moment, Dana?'

Harold?

'Yes,' I called, trying not to show surprise when the door opened and he walked in.

He coughed and looked a little awkward. When he finally did speak, his words floored me. 'I wanted to talk to you, dear. I went shopping in Worcester today and saw you with Ruby in the coffee shop this afternoon.'

I felt my chest tighten. *He knows I know.* I could see it in his eyes.

'Can we sit down and talk?' Harold walked over to the sofa and sat down, indicating for me to join him. Speechless and feeling rather uncomfortable, I complied, perching a little away from him, my hands on my knees as I half turned towards him. Thank goodness it was Harold who had guessed I knew his secret, not Evelyn! I dreaded to think what that woman would do.

'I've recently become aware of who Ruby really is,' Harold said slowly. 'And I presume that you are now aware of this?'

I licked my lips before replying. 'Sam's half-sister?'

He nodded, then reached out and placed his hand over mine. 'I'm begging you to let me break this to Evelyn, and for us both to tell Sam together. I know we should have told him years ago – we kept meaning to, but time passed and we could never find the right opportunity. And then it was too late. Sam has grown up thinking Evelyn was his mother, and to all intents and purposes, she is.' His grasp on my hand tightened. 'I can't tell you how much it hurt her to discover that I had been unfaithful, but she was big-hearted enough to realise that it wasn't Sam's fault, and to offer the poor motherless child a home. She has loved him and brought him up as her own. Not a day has gone by when I haven't regretted my actions, but I don't regret Sam. Neither of us could regret his birth; he has brought us nothing but joy. Please, Dana, allow us the opportunity to tell our son the tragedy of his beginning ourselves.'

I could see the pain and suffering in his eyes. How could I refuse? Besides, it was a relief; I didn't want to be the one that ignited the bomb that destroyed Sam's life. 'Of course I will. When will you tell him?'

His face broke into a smile of relief. 'Thank you, dear. I am very grateful. First, I must tell Evelyn about Ruby, then we will tell Sam together. I think it best that I don't mention to Evelyn that you know, don't you?'

I agreed. 'I won't say anything to her or Sam,' I promised.

'I really do appreciate your discretion. Sam is very precious to us both and we have to consider how we are going to break this devastating news to him.' He got up. 'Thank you, my dear.'

I watched him walk out, his head bowed. He must be dreading telling Evelyn. She would be furious that she would have to confess to Sam she wasn't his real mum. It would be hard for Harold too, having to own up to his son that he cheated. I felt sorry for them both. I almost wished that I hadn't discovered their secret. I couldn't even gauge what Sam's reaction would be. *How can you tell how someone will react when they discover that they've been told a lie all their life and their mum isn't their real mum? That the dad he idolises is a cheat and a liar? That the cleaner is his half-sister?* I was glad that

Evelyn and Harold were going to tell him themselves, that it was they who would have to find the words, because I didn't know how I would be able to. And at least now I could be the one who supported Sam rather than the one who broke the news that destroyed his world.

Sam had returned home by the time dinner was served and was in a good mood. We all sat at the table chatting as if the past few months hadn't happened. As I watched Sam and his parents, I hoped that that the truth didn't shatter the wonderful relationship they all had. Sam was bound to feel anger towards his dad. And while I hoped it didn't cause a big wedge between him and Evelyn, I had to admit that I did hope that it would make him cut the apron strings a bit so that we could live our own lives. At least, I think, the fact that Harold asked for the chance to tell Evelyn, then Sam himself, showed that he was willing to take responsibility for his actions.

How wrong I was. I should never have trusted him.

43

Sam had to go to work early the next morning and I was tempted to miss breakfast, not wanting to be alone with Evelyn and Harold, but Evelyn called me to join them, so I went down. There was no tension between them, which made me wonder if Harold had told Evelyn about Ruby yet. They were both making a big effort to be friendly to me though, so maybe Evelyn did know and wanted to keep me on side. Thank goodness we'd be out of there the next day. I couldn't wait to move into our new house.

'What are you up to today, Dana?' Harold asked pleasantly as he buttered his toast.

'I'm meeting Lynne for lunch then doing a bit of shopping,' I told him. I was supposed to be meeting Ruby too, to give her one of Sam's hairs for a DNA test, but there was no need now that Harold had confessed. I was still going to meet her though, and tell her about Harold's confession.

'That sounds fun,' Evelyn cut in. 'I'm sure it will be good to catch up and have a gossip.'

Harold shot me a look and I wondered if he was worrying that I might tell Lynne about Sam's real mum, so I smiled reassuringly at him, trying to let him know that he needn't worry; I'd given him my word. I was looking forward to meeting Lynne and shopping for some things for the new house. Sam and I had chosen a sofa online and paid extra for it to be delivered on Friday afternoon and I wanted to get some scatter cushions for it, and a rug. 'Choose whatever you want to make you feel at home,' Sam had told me.

I was a bit nervous; my flat had been cheap and cheerful, whereas our new house had to be classy but comfy. I'd browsed a bit online and would be glad to have Lynne's opinion too. I could always take the items back if Sam didn't like them, I reminded myself. It was a new experience for me to have a blank cheque to buy what I wanted. I appreciated Sam's trust in me and was determined to make the new home look good enough for him to invite his colleagues and friends back to.

'Well, don't overdo it, dear. You still look a little pale,' Harold told me.

'I won't,' I promised, touched by his concern.

As soon as I'd finished breakfast, I went up to our rooms to get ready to go out. I felt as if a load had been taken off my shoulders. For the first time since I'd moved into the manor, I felt safe. Evelyn was no longer a threat to me. I had the upper hand. I knew their secret.

I did a bit of research on the laptop, trying to find out more about Ruby and Sam's mother. There was a newspaper article about her falling down the stairs, with the suggestion that she might have thrown herself down them, as her sister said she'd been struggling with postnatal depression. That must be the aunt Ruby had talked about. Was that depression triggered by her guilt over her affair with Harold? I wondered. The article mentioned her having a little girl of four and a newborn baby. It was such a tragedy.

Noticing the time, I shut my laptop down, grabbed my bag and went downstairs and outside. As I walked past the double garage, I heard someone shout my name. I spun around and was surprised to see Harold up on the roof, trying to adjust the satellite dish. We'd had a poor signal last night and I guessed he was trying to fix it so he could watch the cricket match that afternoon. I waved to him, pleased to see that he was using the scaffolding tower instead of the ladders. Evelyn was always berating him for using ladders, saying that they weren't stable enough.

I took the car keys out of my bag as I headed for my car, glancing over my shoulder at Harold then gasped in horror as I saw the scaffolding tower falling towards me. It was going to crash onto me! Sheer panic fuelled me as I leapt out of the way but I wasn't quick enough. The tower crashed down on my ankle and I fell to the floor, screaming. Through a haze of pain and disbelief, I looked up at Harold, who was standing on the edge of the roof, watching me, a strange expression on his face. Why hadn't he shouted to warn me?

'Dana! Are you all right?' he called. 'I'm so sorry! I accidentally knocked it over.'

That tower was too heavy to be accidentally knocked over. It would need a hard push to topple it, I realised. That was why he hadn't warned me. He had pushed it over deliberately. He had tried to kill me.

Oh my God! It wasn't Evelyn who was trying to hurt me. It was Harold.

44

'Dana! Dana! Are you okay!' Sam jumped out of a taxi and sprinted towards me, his face white. I didn't know why he'd come back, or what he was doing in a taxi, but he'd returned just in time to see the platform fall on me.

Pushed over onto me.

I bit back the tears. My ankle was throbbing; I was sure that it was broken. If I hadn't moved out of the way, the platform would have fallen on my head.

I would have been killed.

'I accidentally knocked the platform over. I'm so sorry!' Harold shouted from the garage roof. 'Is Dana okay?'

Sam hauled the platform off my leg, dropping it back down on the ground beside us. Then he bent down and examined my ankle. 'I think you've broken it.' He raised his head, his eyes wide, frightened. 'Oh God, Dana. You could have been killed!'

That was what Harold had wanted. He wanted to kill me. Why? Was it to stop me telling Sam about his sordid affair? Tears stung my eyes. I was tired of it all. And so scared. For weeks now I'd had to live with the fear that someone was trying to harm me. I'd thought all along that it was Evelyn, but I'd never dreamed it could be Harold. He'd always been so kind, so supportive. I see now that it had all been an act, part of his plan to reel me in so I wouldn't suspect him. Or was it both of them? Were they working together to make sure no one found out about their secret?

Sam embraced me lovingly. 'Don't cry, we'll get a doctor to look at it.'

Evelyn must have heard the commotion because she dashed outside, her eyes darting from the scaffold on the ground to me, then up to Harold on the roof before running over to me. 'Sam, help your dad down off the roof before he tries to climb down. I'll take care of Dana,' she said.

Sam jumped to his feet. 'I'll just help Dad, then I'll take you to the hospital,' he told me.

'I'll go and get some ice to put on your ankle, Dana.' Evelyn hurried back into the house.

Through a haze of pain, I watched Sam grab a ladder from the shed and take it over to the garage, holding it steady while his father climbed down. Then Harold rushed over to me, his face stricken with guilt.

'I am so sorry, Dana. I caught the scaffolding with my leg. I feel terrible.'

He really did look sorry. I was so confused. Surely that platform couldn't be knocked over by his leg catching it? It was far too heavy. Sam had struggled to lift it off me. It would have to be pushed to topple like that. Had Harold really tried to kill me, or was it an accident?

My ankle was throbbing. I was sure it was broken, as Sam had said. I stared at Harold, unable to find the words that I wanted to say, knowing that, once again, no one would believe me.

'Here we are, this will soothe the pain.' Evelyn returned with a bag of ice wrapped in a towel and a small bottle of water.

'Let me do it.' Sam took the towel-wrapped bag of ice from

Evelyn and gently applied it to my foot. I gritted my teeth. It hurt like hell.

Evelyn passed me the water and a packet of paracetamol. 'Take these, they'll ease the pain.'

I checked the packet – to make sure they were paracetamol – and the bottle, which was still sealed, then took two with a gulp of water. Evelyn observed my actions with her sharp button eyes. Did she know that I didn't trust her?

'I think it's definitely broken. Let's get you to hospital to get it checked out,' Sam said, taking the ice pack off my ankle and giving it back to Evelyn. 'We'll take your car, Dana. I've had to drop mine off at the garage. The power-steering has gone,' he said.

So that's why he was in a taxi.

Sam picked me up and carried me over to my car, opening the door to carefully place me onto the passenger seat.

'No! Stop!' Harold shouted, running over to us. He stood by my car, gasping for breath, all the colour drained from his face. 'You're in shock, you shouldn't drive, Sam. I'll take you both to the hospital in my car.'

'I'm fine, Dad. And you've had a shock, too,' Sam replied as he closed the passenger door and went around to the driver's side.

'Stop!' Harold dashed to the front of the car as Sam got into the driver's seat and stood with his arms outstretched. 'No! You can't drive this car!' He looked frantic, his face bright red, his breath coming out in shallow gasps.

Goodness, he really was overreacting! Sam looked calm and composed enough that I felt quite safe for him to drive.

Sam wound the window down. 'Dad, you're being a bit over the top. I'm good to drive, honestly.'

Harold shook his head, and seemed unable to speak for a moment. Then he stammered. 'It's not that. The car... isn't safe.'

'What? Of course it is!' I protested. What on earth did he mean?

Harold turned his head and shot an accusing glance at Evelyn then turned back to us. 'It isn't.' He paused. 'Your mother's messed with the brakes. I saw her do it,' he blurted out. 'I was trying to stop Dana getting into the car when I knocked over the platform. I was trying to save her life.'

Evelyn gasped. 'Liar!' she yelled, running over to Harold, her eyes bulging. 'Why are you saying this? I haven't touched the car. You know that I haven't!'

'I'm sorry, Evelyn, but I can't cover for you any longer. You're unhinged. All the things you've done to this poor woman, to try and stop Sam from marrying her. I should never have turned a blind eye to them. But this, this is a step too far. You could have killed her.'

My jaw dropped at Harold's words. He knew what Evelyn had been up to!

Evelyn stared at him, speechless. I guessed she was shocked that Harold had finally stood up to her.

I could hardly believe it. My suspicions about Evelyn were true. And Harold had known about it. I felt weak with relief. At last someone was confirming what I'd been saying. Sam looked stunned.

'Mum, tell me this isn't true?' Sam stammered.

The colour had drained from Evelyn's face. She was shaking her head, stuttering. 'Of course it isn't! He's lying! It was him. I was covering for him. Like I always do.' Trembling, she pointed a quivering finger at Harold. 'How can you stand there and say this? After everything you've done?'

'I have to. You need help. It's time we told everyone the truth about what you did.'

'Liar!' Evelyn flew at him, her hands clawing at his face. 'It's you. You did this. It's been you all along!'

'Mum! Stop it!' Sam grabbed her around the waist and pulled her off his father .

Blood trickled down Harold's face where Evelyn's nails had caught him. He took his handkerchief out of his pocket and wiped his face. 'I'm sorry, Evelyn, but you've done this before, and I can't stand by and let you do it again.' He grabbed his phone and dialled. 'Police.'

Evelyn sank onto the ground and broke down, sobbing. Sam stared at her, shell-shocked. I wrapped my arms around him, relieved that my nightmare was over but sad that he had to discover how evil his mother was.

It wasn't until the police arrived to question Evelyn that I remembered that Harold had said Evelyn had done this before. What did he mean?

45

Everything happened so quickly. The police arrived shortly, immediately arresting and handcuffing a weeping Evelyn when Harold informed them what she had done, and taking the car off for a forensic report. Harold had to go with them too, to make a statement.

'We'll need to take statements from you both as well,' the police officer told Sam and me. 'But you should go to the hospital and have that ankle seen to first. We'll talk to you both later.'

Sam was too shaken up to drive, so he called a taxi to take us to the hospital. As we'd feared, my ankle was broken. Luckily, it wasn't a severe break. The doctor put on a cast, then a special boot and gave me some crutches. I was more worried about Sam than my broken ankle. Apart from apologising profusely for Evelyn's actions, and the accident with the scaffolding, he had barely spoken all the while we'd been at the hospital. I could see that his mother's arrest had hit him hard.

What would happen now? I wondered. We were supposed to be moving into our new house tomorrow but would Sam want to, or would he want to stay and support his father? And how would I be able to get up and down the stairs now, let alone help with the unpacking and sorting everything out? And what about our honeymoon? I couldn't go with a broken ankle, could I?

Harold had returned from the police station when we got back. 'I think you should stay here until Dana's ankle is healed,' he said when I hobbled in on crutches. 'She's not going to be able to manage by herself while you're at work. You could both use the bedroom downstairs until her ankle heals. We don't want to risk Dana falling down those stairs again.'

I wanted to protest, I was desperate to go to our own house, but Harold and Sam both looked so distraught. They needed time to talk things over, process everything and work out their grief together. I was stunned myself at how things had turned out. Although I'd long suspected that Evelyn was trying to harm me, it was still a massive shock to realise that she had actually planned to kill me.

Evelyn's been arrested. It's over with now, I told myself. It was only right that Sam would want to support his father. We could stay for a while, at least until I felt a little stronger.

Sam's reply surprised me. 'Thanks, Dad, but I think it's better for Dana if we move to our new house tomorrow, as planned. She needs to get away from here. It's got too many bad memories for her. I want to get away too. I can't believe that my wife has been in such danger and I didn't see it. What kind of person does that make me?'

'One who loves his mother dearly,' Harold said softly. 'Don't blame yourself, Sam. Evelyn had us all fooled. I didn't want to believe it either.'

'You said she'd done this before, so you should have known it was her,' Sam retorted. 'Who did she do it to?'

Harold took off his glasses and wearily wiped his forehead before replacing them. 'I can't talk about it now, son. I'll tell you tomorrow, I promise. I need time to collect myself, to come to terms with things. And I'm sure you do too.'

Sam sighed. 'Okay, but I want answers. I don't want you keeping anything from me. Dana, my *wife*, could have been killed.'

Harold swallowed. 'I know, son.' He got to his feet. 'I'm sorry for everything, Dana. Truly, I am. I just didn't think Evelyn...' He dabbed his eyes with his handkerchief. 'I'm sorry. I need to lie down for a while, to be on my own. I hope you understand.' He looked at me, as if begging for my understanding.

'Of course.' I felt so sorry for him; he looked broken. Whatever Evelyn had done, he'd obviously forgiven her for it, and maybe he would again, but I didn't think Sam would. Neither would I. I was trembling at the knowledge that I had been in so much danger, although relieved in a strange way to know that my instincts had been right, and that I hadn't been paranoid.

Maybe Sam would be relieved to discover that Evelyn wasn't his birth mother after this, I thought, but now wasn't the time to give him another shock. As I hadn't met up with Ruby as we'd planned, she'd messaged asking me where I was, but so much had happened I hadn't picked up the message until a few minutes ago, along with two missed calls and a message from Lynne wondering where I was too. I quickly messaged Lynne back apologising that I'd been held up and would explain tomorrow. I'd reply to Ruby tomorrow and explain, I decided.

Sam brought me breakfast in bed the next morning. 'I've got a few things to sort out so I'll come back for you when it's time to go to sign the papers for the house sale,' he said. 'Will you be able to manage with your ankle?'

'I'll leave that leg out of the shower and use the movable shower head,' I told him. 'Don't worry about me. You get off.'

Sam kissed me then left. I ate my breakfast, then exhaustion washed over me. I lay down, closed my eyes and drifted back off to sleep, a sleep disturbed with dreams. Someone was chasing me, trying to kill me. I was running, my breath coming out in ragged gasps, my chest hurting with the effort, but when I glanced over my shoulder I saw that they were catching up with me. They were almost upon me. Suddenly, something was thrown over my head and I couldn't breathe. I was gasping, trying to push it off, but it was pushing down so hard I couldn't move it. Wake up! Wake up! I told myself.

Then I realised that there really was something over my face. It was pressing down on me. Suffocating me. Covering my nose, my mouth, squashing the breath out of me. What was happening? I felt a feather tickle my nose and realisation gasped through me. Oh my God, someone was holding a pillow over my face. They were trying to suffocate me! It had to be Evelyn, she must have been released and was now trying to finish the job. The police only had Harold's word it was her after all, so probably couldn't keep her for long.

I wasn't going to let her win; I had to fight back. I gathered up all my strength and raised my arms, trying to push her away, but she was pressing down so hard and I was so weak...

'Don't fight it, dear. It will be easier if you relax and let it happen.'

Harold!

Were they both in it together? It was so hard to breathe. I couldn't get any air in my lungs. I could feel my strength fading. I closed my eyes and stopped struggling. I couldn't fight it any more. They had won.

46

'For God's sake, Harold. What are you doing? Are you trying to kill the girl? What on earth's got into you?' Evelyn was shouting.

The pressure of the pillow eased, and with a huge thrust, I manage to push it off. I blinked, gasping for breath; my throat sore, my chest tight. I struggled up onto my elbows, gaping at the scene before my eyes. Harold was lying on the floor, the pillow beside him. It was as if he'd been thrown there. Evelyn was standing over him, furious.

'What are you doing out?' he gasped.

'Did you really think your lies were enough to get me arrested? The police need evidence and there is none! It's your word – your lies – against mine!' she shouted. 'You messed with the brakes of that car, not me!'

'If that was so, why would I knock over the tower to try and stop Dana driving off in the car?' Harold struggled to his feet. 'You've been trying to drive the girl away for months! You can't stand the thought of Sam moving out. You're obsessed with him.'

I looked from one to the other, trying to figure out which one was telling the truth. Or were they both guilty?

'Maybe you thought killing her by knocking the tower over onto her would look more like an accident. Who knows what goes on in your twisted mind? You're insane! You messed with the brakes on the car and would have suffocated Dana if I hadn't come along!'

'That's rubbish. It was you. You've killed before. You've got form. I'll tell the police what you did.'

I gasped. Evelyn had murdered someone? And now Harold had tried to kill me. They were both mad. And dangerous. I was terrified. I wanted to jump out of bed and run, but how could I with a broken ankle? It was probably best if I kept still and didn't remind them that I was there. They were so busy arguing with each other that they seemed to have forgotten about me. I eyed my phone on the bedside table. If I could just reach it, I could call for help.

'I feel awful about that, and you know it. You've held it over me for years. But it was your fault as much as mine. We both made her do it, but it was an accident. This, Harold, this is attempted murder. Why?'

I eased myself up a little more so that I could grab my phone. I had no idea what they were talking about but it sounded important and I wanted to record it. I swiped the screen and pressed the record button.

Harold uttered a strangled cry. 'What else can I do? She knows that you aren't Sam's mother. She's going to tell Sam and then we'll lose him. I can't bear to lose him. I had to stop her.'

Evelyn gasped, her hand flying to her mouth. Were they both going to turn on me now? I almost burst into tears. My nerves were shot. I didn't know how much more I could take. The last few months had been such a strain for me, but I knew that I had to be strong, or I'd never get out of there alive. I kept my phone recording, wanting evidence of everything.

'Are you serious? You'd rather kill Dana than have Sam find out the truth?' Evelyn sounded incredulous.

The fury on Harold's face scared me. 'I don't *want* to kill her. But what else can I do now that she knows the truth?'

'So it was you?' I croaked, unable to keep quiet any longer. 'You did all those things? The broken mirror, the fan, the kettle lead, my shoe strap, the wedding cake...'

Evelyn spun around in surprise, as if just remembering I was there. She looked at me apologetically. 'Some of it was me. I'm sorry.'

'You!' So, I had been right. I felt sick, faint, terrified. Both of them were mad. 'And the house fire at the Marshes'... Was that you?'

Evelyn shook her head vehemently. 'No. That was nothing to do with me, I swear. Anyway, I read in the paper that they've arrested someone for that. But the other little things – adding more liquid to the dishwasher so you would look stupid; the fan, to cause an argument between you and Sam...'

'The mirror? You broke the mirror too?'

She looked ashamed. 'Yes. I didn't mean you to hurt yourself so badly. I was just trying to stop you going to look at houses. I put some laxatives in the biscuits too – I'm so sorry, but I was desperate.' Tears sprung to her eyes. 'Harold is a bully. He always has been, but once Sam got older, he couldn't get away with it because Sam stuck up for me. I was scared he'd start abusing me again if Sam left, so I thought if I could cause a bit of trouble between you both, you might have a row and split up.' She swallowed. 'The truth is, I really am scared to be alone with Harold.'

'What about the kettle flex? My sandals?' I was still desperate for answers.

'That was nothing to do with me. I promise.' She glared at Harold 'Was that you? Were you trying to kill her then? Had she already found out the truth about Sam?'

'Of course not! You're a liar!'

But I knew it was Harold. It all made sense now. I recalled how Harold had looked at me when he came out in the hall after the big argument they'd had in the kitchen. He'd guessed that I'd overheard about Evelyn not being Sam's real mother and had been trying to kill me ever since. Nausea swept over me. I felt sick as I realised the terrible danger I had been in. *Still was in.*

'Please forgive me, Dana. I've been terrified of Harold for years.'

'You could have left him. But you won't, will you? Because he gave you the baby you always wanted – my brother – and you're scared of him telling Sam that you aren't his real mother.' Ruby was standing in the doorway.

'Ruby! You're Alma's daughter?' Evelyn spluttered, looking from Ruby to Harold. 'Did you know who she was?'

Harold didn't reply, his eyes fixed on Ruby in disbelief.

'I have proof that Evelyn isn't Sam's mother, and that he is my brother. I've got a letter from my dad telling me all about it. And a DNA test will prove it.' Ruby looked over at me. 'I was worried when you didn't turn up yesterday, Dana, so came to see if you were okay. Good job that I did.'

'What do you want? Have you come to blackmail us?' Harold demanded.

'I'm not like you!' Ruby retorted. 'I wanted to find my brother. The precious son you would do anything, even murder, to keep.'

I eased myself out of bed while Evelyn and Harold were distracted by Ruby, swinging my legs over the side and reaching for my crutch. I felt safer now that Ruby was there, but if Harold or Evelyn came for me, I'd use it to defend myself.

'You destroyed my dad's life!' Ruby yelled at Harold. 'And my mother's, too. The guilt ate away at her. My aunt said that she hated herself for what she'd done to my dad. She thinks that

Mum didn't fall but threw herself down the stairs because she couldn't live with the guilt.'

'Alma threw herself down the stairs because of *her*. She drove her to it!' Harold jabbed a finger at Evelyn. 'She went to see her. Begged her to *sell* Sam to her. She was obsessed with having a baby and couldn't have one of her own. And your mother was a mess. She could barely look after you.' He almost spat the words out.

I had never seen Harold like this. It was a whole personality change. He had been acting all along and was now finally showing his true colours.

'I did offer her money, Ruby, that's true,' Evelyn admitted. 'I know it was wrong but Sam was Harold's baby and your father was struggling to accept him, whilst Harold was desperate to be part of his son's life, and I knew we could offer him a good, loving home. Alma refused, though. She was determined to keep her child and fight for her marriage.' Tears sprang to her eyes and she wiped them away with the back of her hands. 'Yes, we did argue, but your mother was alive when I left. I swear she was.' The tears spilled out and flowed unstemmed down her cheeks as she glared accusingly at Harold. 'You've held this over me for years, telling me I was responsible for Alma killing herself. I never wanted that to happen. I never hurt her.'

'I remember it.' Ruby's voice was deadly quiet. 'I was so young, so scared, I must have blocked it all out, but the memories have been coming back to me in flashes the last few days. I remember a lady coming to see Mum. They argued and the lady was crying as she left. That was you?'

Evelyn nodded. 'I was crying because I thought I was going to lose my husband, and he was going to bring up his baby with your mum. Your mum might have said that she was going to fight for her marriage, but Harold always got his own way. I knew he would win her around in the end.'

'They did split up once, Dad told me in his letter, but Mum

came back.' Ruby frowned. 'I remember a man coming too, not long after you left. I'd seen the man a few times – he came to visit my mum sometimes. I heard him and Mum arguing upstairs. I hid in my bedroom and peered around the door to watch them.'

Evelyn's eyes widened with shock. ' Harold went to see Alma, too?'

'Of course I didn't.' Harold glared at Ruby. 'You were barely four, you can't remember anything.'

'I remember seeing my mum and this man standing at the top of the stairs, then she was falling down the stairs. I thought I knew the man. It must have been you. My aunt said that when my parents temporarily split up, you used to visit us.' She moistened her lips, her eyes glazing as she continued. 'Mum hit the bottom of the stairs and the man ran down after her, bent down beside her then left. I came down when he'd gone and held my mum's hand.' Rivers of tears poured down her cheeks. She pointed at Harold. 'That man was you, wasn't it? You killed my mum. You pushed her.'

The colour drained from Harold's face. 'You can't possibly remember! You were too young,' he protested feebly. 'Besides, you were playing in your room all the time...' He blanched as he realised what he'd said.

'It was you! All these years you've blamed me for causing Alma's death and it was you!' Evelyn blazed.

'You killed my mum and you took away my little brother. You killed her so that you could have Leo, her baby. My brother.' Ruby was shaking now.

'I didn't push her – she fell. I didn't mean it to happen,' Harold protested weakly.

'You murderer!' Ruby cried. 'I'm calling the police. They're going to lock you away for a very long time.' She reached in her pocket for her phone.

'I can't let you do that.' Harold picked up a vase and raised it above his head. I knew that he was going to hurl it at Ruby. I raised my crutch, ready to hit him but Evelyn got there first and knocked the vase out of his hand. Furious, he wrapped his arms around her waist, pulled her back and hurtled her across the room. She fell back against the corner of the table and slid to the floor, leaving a smear of blood down the wall. I screamed, my hand flying to my face as I saw the gash in Evelyn's temple where a steady stream of blood flowed out. Had Harold killed her? Was he going to kill us next?

Then suddenly, there was an angry yell, and Harold was thrown backwards, landing sprawled out on the floor by my bed. Sam was standing over him, fists clenched. 'That's the last time you ever lay a finger on my mum,' he said through gritted teeth.

47

'Now, son, you've got this wrong...' Harold attempted to get back up, but Sam held him down.

'Ruby, check on Mum, will you?' he asked. He looked anxiously at me. 'You okay, Dana?'

I nodded. I was shocked to the core by everything that had just happened, but Sam was here now, so I knew that I was finally safe.

'Can you call the police and an ambulance please?' His voice was thick, raw, his eyes full of anger and pain.

'I've got it all recorded,' I told him as I dialled 999 and asked for the police and an ambulance.

Ruby was bending down by the still-unconscious Evelyn. 'She's breathing and her pulse feels strong,' she said.

Thank goodness she's alive! I was relieved to hear this and could see the relief on Sam's face, too. 'If you'd killed her...' he growled at his father.

What? Would Sam have killed Harold? Did he have a temper like Harold? I could see the fury in Sam's eyes, but he was controlling it, only using enough force to stop his father from escaping, even though he must have wanted to really punch him. Like I did. I wanted to punish him for what he'd done to me, and to Alma, and to Evelyn.

The police and ambulance arrived shortly, and the room was swarming with officers and medics. Evelyn had recovered consciousness and assured everyone that she was all right but was taken to hospital for observation, with Sam promising to come and visit her later. Harold was taken away into custody, and Sam, Ruby and I were all asked to go down to the station to make a statement. It was a good hour later before the three of us were left alone to talk. It turned out that Sam had arrived just in time to hear about Harold pushing Alma down the stairs, so Ruby and I had to fill him in on the rest. It was a lot for him to take in: that it was his dad who had been trying to kill me, not Evelyn; that Evelyn wasn't his birth mother; that his dad had had an affair and was the cause of his birth mother's death. And that Ruby, their cleaner, was his half-sister. I felt for him. He had no choice but to believe it, though, as I had recorded it on my phone, right from the moment Evelyn pulled Harold off me when he was trying to smother me. I played it all to Sam, who listened attentively, his eyes wide, his face ashen.

'I can't believe it.' He shook his head, hugging me close to him. 'I'm so sorry, sweetheart. I should have protected you more. I knew that Dad could be violent but since his heart attack a few years ago, he's been different. That's why I thought it would be okay to move out and leave Mum now. I thought she was safe.'

'You knew that your dad used to abuse your mum?' I asked in surprise. Then I remembered Sam's comment on our first date, how women should always be treated with respect, and how upset he got with himself if he got angry when we argued – not that he had ever raised a finger to me.

'He never did it in front of me, but I saw the bruises. She made excuses for him, and when I was a kid I believed her. As I grew older, I realised that Dad was a bully; he was controlling, he dominated her. That's why I agreed to live at home whilst I repaid my loan. It gave me chance to keep an eye on them, to make sure Mum was okay. She felt safer when I was around; she knew that he wouldn't dare hurt her in front of me. I guess that's why she was upset that we were getting married so quickly, and was desperate for us to live here. She was worried about being left alone with Dad, but things had been so much better since his heart attack that I thought she'd be all right.' He ran his hands through this hair. 'And now, he's tried to kill you. And to kill Mum... Evelyn.' I could see that he was struggling with the knowledge that Evelyn wasn't his biological mum.

'I should have been here. I should never have left you alone.'

'You weren't to know; you went to deal with the house sale. Evelyn came back, she saved my life, and Ruby's. I'm so glad she's going to be okay.' We'd phoned the hospital to check and they were keeping Evelyn in overnight for observation but didn't think that there was any cause for concern.

'You kept telling me someone was trying to hurt you, and I kept saying you were imagining it.' Sam looked distressed as he held me close.

'I don't blame you for that. I had no proof and it's hard to accept that anyone could do such a thing,' I told him, comforted by his embrace. 'Besides, I thought it was Evelyn. I didn't suspect Harold.'

'I should have. I know what he's like, but I thought it ...' He turned his head to Ruby. 'I'm sorry. He left you without a mum. That must have been so hard for you.'

'It was but it isn't your fault,' Ruby said softly. She rubbed her nose. 'I'm so glad that I found you again. That means so much to me, and I know that Mum would be pleased too.' She looked as if she was trying to control her emotion. 'I'm going now; I think you both need time alone, to talk. Dana has my phone number. Call me if you want to see me. If you don't ...' She shrugged. 'Well, I understand.'

FIVE MONTHS LATER

'What do you think?' I asked, standing back from the Christmas tree so I could see the full effect of the gold baubles against the white branches, the shimmering lights flashing on and off, the gold star shining brightly on the top of the tree. Underneath the tree was a pile of beautifully wrapped presents, tied with ribbon and bows. I had taken so much time over wrapping them. I wanted this, our first Christmas as a married couple, to be really special. I'd come to love this house, pleased that I'd gone along with Sam's choice. It was bright, airy, modern, comfy and best of all, it felt like home. I felt safe here.

Sam draped his arm around my shoulder. 'It looks wonderful. Thank you for doing this.'

'I've enjoyed it,' I told him. And I really had.

The last few months had taken their toll on Sam. Evelyn had recovered from the head injury, and Harold had been charged with my attempted murder, assaulting Evelyn and the manslaughter of Alma. There was no forensic evidence to link him to messing with the brakes of my car, but my recording of his confession to Evelyn, although wouldn't stand up in court, had been used to get a proper confession out of him.

All charges had been dropped against Evelyn, but she was a changed woman, a shell of her former self. The knowledge that Harold had killed Alma and had tried to kill me had shaken her to the core. She'd started divorce proceedings against Harold and retreated into herself, locking up the manor and going to live with her sister in Somerset. Sam visited her in hospital and assured her that she would always be his mother, thanking her for taking him in, bringing him up and showing him so much love. I thanked her too, for saving my life, and apologised for blaming her for Harold's terrible actions. She hadn't been completely blameless, but she hadn't wanted to harm me, just protect herself.

Sam refused to see Harold and had not said a word about Ruby. I didn't push it, wanting to give him space to come to terms with things.

When my ankle had healed, we rebooked our honeymoon, both desperate for a break. The two weeks in Barbados had done us good; Sam had colour in his cheeks again and some of the anguish had gone from his eyes. I felt more relaxed, too. I'd spent the last few months looking over my shoulder, living in fear, and was relieved that it was now over. While we were away, we finally talked about it all and Sam said he'd like to get to know Ruby. He'd grown up an only child and now he had a half-sister and a little niece. So I'd messaged Ruby and invited her over when we came back. It had been awkward at first, but since then she and Sam had grown close and she was coming for Christmas. Evelyn was coming too. She was a good woman, I realised. She'd taken in her husband's child and brought him up as her own. It was a tough time for her, at her age, and I wanted to support her. She had reached out to Ruby, apologising for any part she'd had Alma's death, and for what Harold did. Ruby had finally forgiven her and had even allowed her to visit her and Isla sometimes.

Harold was sentenced to fifteen years in prison, his guilty plea being taken into account. He'd probably die in prison.

Sam kissed me tenderly on the cheek. 'To think that this time last year we hadn't even met each other.'

So much had happened that it was hard to remember that we hadn't even been together a year yet.

'Do you regret meeting me?' he asked, his eyes searching my face. 'After everything Harold and my mum put you through? I wouldn't blame you if you did.' He had never called Harold 'Dad' from the day he'd found out the truth about him but said that Evelyn would always be his mum because she had loved him like a mother.

'I would never regret meeting you,' I said, wrapping my arms around his neck and pulling him towards me so I could kiss him. 'And you are not responsible for Harold's actions.'

The doorbell rang. 'That must be Evelyn or Ruby. Shall I answer it, or will you?' I asked, a smile on my lips.

Sam took a deep breath and stood up straight as if to compose himself. 'I will,' he said.

It was Ruby. She and Isla were laden with presents. Isla jumped into Sam's arms as soon as she saw him. 'Uncle Sam! We've got you a present!'

'Have you? Is it something to eat?' he asked, picking her up and carrying her into the house.

'I can't tell you – it's a surprise,' she said. Then she gasped, her brown eyes wide and round when she spotted the Christmas tree. 'So pretty!'

'I think there might be a present there for you. Shall we take a look?' Sam asked.

'Oh, yes!' Isla clapped her hands. 'Please!' she added.

Ruby and I exchanged smiles as Sam and Isla walked over to the tree. 'Thank you for this,' Ruby said softly.

'It's a pleasure. You're family,' I told her.

Then Evelyn arrived, also carrying a bag of presents. She

looked a little better, I thought. Living with her sister by the sea was doing her good.

We exchanged our presents – Ruby and Isla's present to Sam was a framed photo of his mother, Alma. I could see by his expression as he placed it on the sideboard that it meant a lot to him.

It was a quiet day, apart from Isla's squeals of laughter, but peaceful. As I watched Isla play, I couldn't help remembering that Ruby had been that age when her mother had been killed. By Harold. Sam was watching her too, and I wondered if he was thinking the same thing.

'Are you okay?' I asked softly.

He put his arm around my shoulders and kissed my cheek. 'Not yet, but I will be,' he said.

We both will be, I thought as we stood on the doorstep, our arms wound around each other, waving goodbye to Evelyn, Ruby and Isla a little later. It had been tough, but it was over. We had to look to the future and make it a happy one.

A LETTER FROM KAREN

I want to say a huge thank you for choosing to read *The Mother-in-Law*. If you enjoyed it, and want to keep up to date with all my latest releases, just sign up at the following link. Your email address will never be shared and you can unsubscribe at any time.

www.bookouture.com/karen-king

I love to explore relationships in my books, especially family relationships, and the ones with our in-laws can be very complicated. Particularly with our mothers-in-law. Mothers-in-law are often the butt of comedians' jokes, especially women's mothers, whereas the men's mothers seem to get off lightly. Which is rather unfair, as they can often be the most difficult. My own mother-in-law was a lovely, kind lady who treated me like a daughter, but I know that this isn't always the case. I've heard many stories from friends of how their mothers-in-law have constantly caused trouble between their sons and wives and made it clear that they didn't consider the wife/partner good enough for their precious child. That was the springboard for the plot of this book. I wanted to explore the theme a little deeper, though; for there to be a reason for Evelyn's behaviour, why she doesn't want her son Sam to get married, and will do anything to stop him moving out with his wife, Dana. As we read the story, we discover that this isn't just because Evelyn is obsessive; she is fearful of being left alone with her abusive husband, and her love for Sam is even deeper than we realised.

I hope you loved *The Mother-in-Law*, and if you did, I would be very grateful if you could write a review. I'd love to hear what you think, and it makes such a difference helping new readers to discover one of my books for the first time.

I love hearing from my readers – you can get in touch on my Facebook page, through Twitter, Goodreads or my website.

Thanks,

Karen

www.karenking.net

facebook.com/KarenKingAuthor

twitter.com/karen_king

ACKNOWLEDGEMENTS

There's a lot of things that goes on in the background when writing a book, and a lot of people who help with the process. First and foremost, I'd like to thank my fantastic editor Isobel Akenhead, and the Bookouture team of Jennie Ayres, Alexandra Holmes, Rebecca Millar, Aimee Walsh and Sarah Gunton for all their hard work and constructive advice. A special thanks to Aaron Munday for creating me such a stunning cover. And to the fabulous social media team of Kim Nash, Noelle Holten and Sarah Hardy who go above and beyond in supporting and promoting our work, and making the Bookouture Author Lounge such a lovely place to be. You guys are amazing! Also to the other Bookouture authors, who are always so willing to offer support, encouragement and advice. I'm so grateful to be part of such a lovely, supportive team.

Thanks also to all the bloggers and authors who support me, review my books and give me space on their blog tours. I am lucky to know so many incredible people in the book world and appreciate you all. Special thanks to the authors in the Savvy Writers Snug who shared with me their experience of anaphylaxis.

Massive thanks to my husband, Dave, for all the love and laughter you bring to my life, for being a sounding board for my ideas and for supplying the much needed logic to some of them. Thanks also to my family and friends who all support me so much. I love you all.

Finally, a heartfelt thanks to you, my readers, for buying and reviewing my books, and for your lovely messages telling me how much you've enjoyed reading them. Without your support there would be no more books.

Thank you xx

Made in the USA
Las Vegas, NV
25 August 2022

53994558R00156